"Sal McGrane's fantastic debut ... is, in its observations and arginalia, a whole-hearted declaration of love for the mad ess of Russia in general – and Moscow in particular."
Die Welt (book of the week)

"A v thy successor to John le Carré ... A fast-paced, well-writ spy thriller, full of unexpected twists and turns."
Buchbord

"Gr ! Tense right up to the final page ... A multi-layered, thri g novel that is difficult to resist and hard to put dov from beginning to end." *Süddeutsche Zeitung*

"Yc on't need to compare this book to Le Carré or For – it stands very comfortably on its own two feet."
Frankfurter Allgemeine Zeitung

"T ok is perfect anyone who loves exciting detective a stories." *Sankt Michaelsbund*

MOSCOW AT MIDNIGHT

SALLY McGRANE

CONTRABAND

Contraband is an imprint of Saraband
Published by Saraband
Digital World Centre
1 Lowry Plaza, The Quays
Salford, M50 3UB

www.saraband.net

ISBN: 9781910192818
ebook: 9781910192825

10 9 8 7 6 5 4 3 2 1

Editors for this edition: Jenny Hamrick and Angela Harms
Typeset by Iolaire Typography Ltd.
Printed and bound in Great Britain by Clays Ltd, St Ives plc.

For Helge

PART I

1

Max glanced around the bright hall. The six orderly queues. The new booths, shiny and cheap. Like witness stands. He groaned. He could be anywhere: Frankfurt, Bangkok. Not at home, he thought. Dulles, with its grimy carpeting, the stale smell of fast food shops and broken people movers, was unmistakable.

Max toyed with the navy blue passport. An old trick. He flashed the golden eagle imprint so his neighbors could see it, if they wanted to—it was the best way to satisfy, and thus dispel, their curiosity. He shifted the weight of the leather briefcase in his left hand. Nonchalant. His suit was a passport of its own. Max had had it made in Berlin, in a dark little shop off Ku'Damm with a bent German tailor and old-fashioned fixtures. Halfway through the fitting, the little brass bell over the door announced a new arrival, and from the dressing room, Max caught a glimpse of the man. Heavyset. Max pegged him as American, the way he carried himself. Shoulders forward, head down, ready at any moment for the salesman's duck-and-weave. Belly out: a man unashamed of his appetites. The stranger picked up three suits, sheathed in plastic, and walked out into the summer rain before the tailor called Max back out for his fitting. Something about the fat man struck Max as familiar, but he hadn't been able to place it.

When it was his turn, Max presented his passport to the girl behind the counter. She was young and, under the stark lines of her blue cap, very pretty. A lock of dark hair had escaped the blue cap, and fell to her temple. Her navy uniform was belted, military.

3

An etched nametag, brown and beige, was clipped to her breast. She didn't so much as glance at Max.

"Passport," she said, curtly.

"Yelena Victorovna!" said Max. When she showed no sign of response, he leaned in, and whispered, "Why are you always breaking my heart?"

"Reason for travel?" she said, eyes fixed on the passport in her hands.

"Business," sighed Max.

"Last date of entry into the Russian Federation?"

"It's been thirteen months, Lenochka. If I could have come sooner, I would have."

"Proposed length of stay?"

"If you were mine, I'd never leave." The girl coughed, a frown appearing on her brow. Max added, quickly, "But it looks like three weeks. Depending on how business goes."

The girl flipped through the pages of the passport, stopping at the business visa glued to a page in the middle. She nodded once and grasped the stamp on her desk. It came down heavily, a click and a thud, one-two. Only then did Yelena Victorovna Krasnobaeva, Moscow's prettiest immigration official, glance up at him. Her eyes were like a cat's, large and arresting, light brown. She handed Max back his passport and said with an enchanting smile, "We've missed you, Mr. Rushmore."

And that was done. Max was in. He noticed he was sweating. Get it together, Maxyboy, he told himself. You're back in the game, so you better play. Squaring his shoulders, Max breached the gauntlet of men in undertakers' suits clutching handwritten signs and gained the lobby. Pyramids of luggage, checkers and leopard stripes, taped shut and tied together, teetered precariously in the lobby. A row of cash machines, lined up like casino slots.

Through the glass doors, past the sulky men in gray leather jackets and the skinny drivers lurking by their shiny Korean cars and *marshrutka* buses, Max saw that it was still summer. The sky overhead was gray, but the air was warm and heavy, with a mild, sulfurous smell. Just a note of diesel, pleasingly organic. Max hailed a beat-up Lada and told the driver to take him to the city.

They drove fast. An unexpected feeling of freedom came over Max, washing through his body. As if he could feel it too, the driver—a hulk of a man—started talking. He was from Georgia. Out in the countryside. Had come to Moscow because there was no work. "Here there's not always work," he said. "But there, there's none." He reached his big hand between Max's knees. Max jumped. "Don't worry young man," said the Georgian as he pulled open the glove compartment. "Ha ha, what did you think?"

He extracted a photograph of a woman with dark hair pulled back in a red handkerchief. Her face was deeply lined; she didn't smile. On her lap was a little boy. The Georgian held the glossy paper in his thick, brutal fingers for a long moment, studying it, his other hand on the steering wheel. They rushed past a freight truck that lay beside the road, wheels in the air still spinning. The Georgian didn't slow.

"My family," he said, handing the photo to Max. Wife, son.

"Lovely," said Max. "Beautiful."

The fields on either side of the highway were green and lush. Ragged at the edges, weedy, but full of life. Here and there a grove of birches reared up, their spindly white trunks like God's chalk marks. Max started to relax. He could feel it in his throat where, just half an hour before, a lump had spontaneously appeared, blocking his intake of air no matter how many times he tried to swallow it away. Now his breath came easily. He had stopped sweating. The muscles at the back of his neck relaxed.

He handed the driver back the photo, which the man stuck up under the visor, and then Max sat back and watched the fields until they ended. A billboard standing in the middle of one of the last empty spaces read, 'Coming Soon Elite Mansions'. Max shrugged. Past that came the first outskirts: blocks of housing, concrete high rises, abandoned-looking supermarkets. Sputnik Palace, a defunct movie theater. The city began. Concrete block after concrete block. Max's heart lifted, a little. He was in. He was back. He was ok.

"Europe?" said the Georgian. "America?"

Max nodded. "American."

"You like Russia?"

"Sure," said Max. Without knowing why, he tightened his grip on the leather case.

"I can tell," said the Georgian, with a smile that showed his missing teeth. Then he frowned. "Maybe it's nice for a rich guy like you. The girls must go crazy-crazy for such a handsome one! But for us … it's not such a good place. Dangerous." He laughed. "But if you get too rich it's dangerous for you, too. Real dangerous."

Max nodded. "I'm not that rich," he said.

The driver glanced at him out of the corner of his eye. Sizing him up. Rich beyond the Georgian's dreams, yes. Rich enough to get in trouble, no. At a stoplight the Georgian nodded at three women standing on the corner.

"The girls are at work," he said with a chuckle—of approval or camaraderie, Max couldn't tell. Max grunted: not interested.

The light changed and the Georgian sped on. They crossed the river, and the Lada's cracked windshield framed a sudden, glittering borealis of church domes. Beyond, the red stars of the Kremlin came into view. The sky had cleared, and the golden domes caught the light, gleaming against the pale blue sky. Early evening—Max's heart leapt, in spite of himself, again.

As if he had just made a decision, Max said, "Drop me at Red Square."

The Georgian shrugged. It was all the same to him.

2

What was to happen next was to go according to a plan known, unofficially, as the Purloined Letter play, as expounded upon by Jim Dunkirk before his audience of one (Max) in a deserted bar on Pennsylvania Avenue in DC, some twenty years earlier. It was one of those moments that had been, for whatever reason, etched in Max's memory in sharp detail.

The place was a dump: A deer's head mounted over the bar and the smell of flea powder. Max was a rookie, and Dunkirk was supposed to be briefing him before his first tour in the newly-former Soviet Union. Instead, tall, graying Jim Dunkirk—he of the Mayflower ancestors and the impressive limp, acquired in the '80s passing Russian secrets to Afghan rebels—had taken Max drinking. They were both 'three sheets to the wind,' as Dunkirk later put it, when the older man, adopting a new and friendlier tone that made Max nervous, patted Max on the back, and laid out his theory.

"Covert is passé," Dunkirk growled. He leaned in close. "As soon as you start hiding, you give off a smell. Any hunter will tell you this. How do you tip off your prey? Your scent. Takes a good nose, but we've got 'em. They've got 'em. The solution? Don't give off that smell. Don't hide. Right under their noses—that's where they won't look." The next day Max had a raging headache.

Max stepped out of the car and onto Red Square. Banished Dunkirk from his thoughts. After all, Max reminded himself, he was back. That was what counted. He was back—even if it was only part-time. Even if he was only a private contractor. Even if the Agency he had given his adult life to had downsized him—him! Max Rushmore, whose Russian network was voted 'Most Eclectic' three years running. Him! Maxyboy Rushmore, who had learned Chinese in nine months, at 38, when the cells of the brain no longer accept new grammatical forms! Downsized! Him! Affable, larcenous, Max-a-million Rushmore, whose non-transferable skills included never having met a Russian he couldn't drink under the table.

Max closed his eyes and took a deep breath. Inhale, one-two-three-four, exhale, one-two. The news had hit him hard, that was true. Not least because he hadn't seen it coming. The morning was like any other, except that he had spent the night before in his little beige Bethesda pied-a-terre, to give Rose, his wife, some space. Well, or to get away from her endless kitchen renovations, her apparently fruitless search for the perfect center island (three had been delivered, installed, rejected, and returned, leaving a gaping blank space in the heart of the kitchen).

Rose had encouraged him to rent that little dump, she said they could both use a break. And anyway it would shorten his commute during the week. Then she had turned away from him with the look of distraction that had settled over her round, pink Danish features ever since they had decided to stop trying to have children. It wasn't his fault, or hers: the doctors had determined that, in an unusually unfair sleight of fate, they were both infertile. Rose had smiled when they got the news—a smile Max had never seen before, brittle and heartrending—and patted his hand with her own little dimpled one and said, in the slightly foreign way she had sometimes, from spending so many formative years in her mother's country, "Ah." Then the renovations had started.

The mortgage alone was an albatross—sometimes Max felt like he carried it around his neck, like a weight—but he couldn't shake the feeling that he owed it to her to redo the kitchen, if she couldn't redo her life. Later, once the news sunk in, they could talk about alternatives. Adoption, babysitting, who knew. But each time Max thought Rose was finished, she found something else that wasn't quite right: the cabinets, the cutting boards, and began again. He adopted a new tactic: when he came home and saw a bill on the kitchen table, he slipped it, unopened, into the top desk drawer. Rose lost weight. For months they ate only from the microwave. The dust and the noise and the plastic wrap grated on him. The backsplash—a word he learned from Rose— in particular hurt him almost physically to look at. The little blue mosaic tiles were exactly the color of Rose's eyes, scattered in bright, broken pieces on the wall.

Increasingly, even before he rented the place in Bethesda— that had required a loan of its own, discretely staked against the house—Max had begun to take refuge in his little office at the Agency. He worked in the old building, affectionately known as the Flying Saucer, with its permanently dusty windows, 1950's linoleum and worn-out optimism. This was where the Russia hands were kept, with the Africa people, while the important departments (Middle East, etc.) moved to the state-of-the-art, glassed-in Greenhouse. One fine morning, a month shy of his forty-fifth birthday, Max was fired.

Max accepted the end of his career with a sangfroid that was surprising even to him. "This has nothing to do with your, uh, performance," said the Agency's HR Prick, a man singularly un-endowed with 'people skills' (hence his nickname, which he had earned during a series of non-optional sexual harassment seminars). "We wish you—I personally wish you—a successful future." Max nodded, shook hands, thanked him. Then he saun- tered over to the beige rental in Bethesda, where he proceeded to drink vodka and milk—a particularly deadly combination he had picked up in Kharkiv, one long, dry summer—uninterrupted for three days.

At the end of this tenure came a call from an outfit called Nightshade. At first, as he stood with the receiver pressed to his ear, Max wondered if he was imagining things. A strangely familiar voice assured him this was no hallucination: Nightshade was the private contracting firm the Agency had shifted a third of their workload over to, while Max had been drinking.

The voice was indeed familiar: the HR Prick's position had also been made redundant, and he'd been picked up by Nightshade as well. Max felt a strange solidarity, a weird emotional oneness, well up in him as the HR Prick explained, in his same, squeaky voice that, if Max accepted the new job, he would still be working with all his old Agency contacts—for a fraction of the pay, zero job security, and no benefits. "We're pioneering the shift to a multi-tier flex model," the voice squeaked. "It will give you a chance to explore your options on the commercial market. For a higher rate of income fluidity."

Max took the job, of course. Relieved that, for the present at least, he didn't need to tell Rose a thing. She could finish her renovations and he would pay off the bills a little more slowly than he had planned. Fine.

The next morning, when he opened his laptop, his history menu showed that, in the depths of his vodka and milk binge, Max had been researching graduate schools. He had even checked a few boxes. In the sober light of day, Max saw that in a state of advanced inebriation he apparently considered himself a 'relatively strong' candidate for the study of Romantic Poetry. It was that discovery, more than anything else, that made Max worry about his psychological health.

Now, getting out of the cab, Max took another deep breath. Then he stood for a moment, eyes closed. He tried to feel his body, like he had learned in the Israeli body-awareness classes Rose had dragged him to. The broad flat soles of his feet, his toes, his strong legs, spreading stomach, middle-aged lungs.

He opened his eyes. He took a step, then another. Red Square spread out ahead of him. Beckoning. Shimmering. The evening sun cast a warm light on the smooth, uneven cobblestones, red-hued shadows undulating all along the great distance of the square. The Kremlin walls rose up, regal, visceral, ancient. St. Basil's thorny domes, gaudy and glorious. They'd pleased the Czar so much that he'd had the architect's eyes put out. Max wondered if there was a lesson about job security in there for him.

By the time he reached Lenin's tomb Max was already feeling better. He made his way through the clusters of tourists hailing from Omsk, Tomsk, Yekaterinburg—the far-flung outposts of a far-flung empire. Bright colors, the loud patterns of the provinces. A trio of giggling girls waylaid him. They stopped laughing as soon as he raised the camera, stuck out their hips and sucked in their cheeks. They giggled again when he said he was a famous fashion photographer and the catwalks of Milano had nothing on them. Then he turned right and headed straight for the glassed-in shopping arcades of the GUM.

At a brand new café with outdoor tables facing the Kremlin, Max sat and ordered espresso. When it came, brought by a boy with acne in a pristine white waiter's uniform, Max was surprised at how good it was.

The terrace café was deserted. Max sat back, watching as the sun slid back out from its black cloud, its rays reflecting off the tomb. The black marble's dull sheen. Lenin's face rose up in his mind's eye, waxy, embalmed. Eyes closed, not quite peaceful. There was another story, also something about keeping a job under difficult circumstances. Oh yes—when Lenin died his body was cut up for the autopsy. But if you want to embalm somebody, it's much better to leave the circulation systems intact. So the embalmers had to make it up as they went along, patching up the corpse with plastic and alcohol. It was such a hard job that the head embalmer kept his job even when Stalin wanted him killed. In the end he died just before Stalin, in one of the last purges.

At the sound of his name, Max looked up. "Rush-MORE!" Striding towards him, his short legs propelling a padded, Hobbit-like body, was Toby 'Bad Boy' Smithers, the worst-dressed and possibly least-respected on-again, off-again (but mostly off-again, particularly since the Episode of the Wig) member of Moscow's American Intelligence Community.

Max had been less than thrilled to hear that Dunkirk was his point man. That he had sent an emissary—well, it wasn't a good sign. That it was Toby 'Bad Boy' Smithers, whose nickname referred not to his exploits but to an almost total lack of competence—well. Better not to dwell on that. After 'the reassignment,' as the Agency's in-house psychologist (aka 'The Feeling Eater') had so delicately referred to it during his exit interview, Max was in no position to complain.

Max grinned.

"Rush-MORE!" Toby repeated, waving his short arms in greeting.

"Toby," said Max.

"Couldn't stay away, huh?" said Smithers, sitting down and immediately destroying one of the cloth-napkin swans. "Missed me?"

"You and a pay check," said Max. His voice caught, a little.

"Yeah," Smithers said. "Heard about the 'reorganization.' Tough break, buddy. But you'll land on your feet. You're Maxyboy Rushmore!" Then he hesitated, like he didn't know what to say. The flash of concern in his eyes made Max feel naked. "Guess the job market's a bitch?"

"Put it this way," said Max, refusing Toby's empathy. "Never in my life have I been so glad to hear that a lumber contract wouldn't go through without the immediate delivery of a hot pink iPhone encrusted in pink cubic zirconia."

Toby laughed. The vodka tonic he must have ordered the moment he set foot in the place arrived, brought by the boy with acne. Toby was the kind of man, thought Max, who would have ended up in Russia no matter what. If not law then business. If not business then translations, press, helping out on movie sets and living with an actress from a family of acrobats—which, if

Max wasn't mistaken, was Mrs. Smithers' actual background.

From somewhere in the corners of his memory, a story came back to him, one Toby had told him in earlier, easier days, when they were both younger and, each in his own way, more carefree. As Toby droned on about joint ventures and the falling ruble, it came back to Max: once, Toby locked himself out of his fifth-floor apartment. But—as Toby had gamely explained it—when your fiancée is from a family of acrobats, you don't call a locksmith. He simply rang up his future brother-in-law, who scaled the wall and let him in. This attracted the attention of some neighbors. The police, in turn, were delighted to find the door opened by a foreigner not in possession of papers proving he owned the apartment. In the end, bribing the police not to arrest him cost three times what he saved on the locksmith.

"Lumber," Toby was saying. "We had a client at the firm who started trading lumber. Coupla years ago. A good bet—he was really raking it in! Then the government wanted to buy him out and he said no. Next thing you know, his wife finds him at the bottom of the dacha swimming pool. Hog-tied, hands and feet behind his back. Coupla burns, nasty, electric, I won't tell you where. Court ruled suicide, and all the lumber went to the government." Toby guffawed unnervingly. "Of course, those were the good old days."

"I caught this Canadian deal at just the right time," Max agreed. "Joint venture, out in the Taiga. The Canadians have been looking the other way for fifteen years. Now they're getting lower returns, all of a sudden Russian 'cost of doing business' expenses start to look a lot like embezzlement. Bingo, I'm back."

"Good for you, buddy," said Toby. "Couldn't happen to a nicer guy."

Max winced. He tried to make it look like he was shading his eyes from the last of the sun. Toby 'Bad Boy' Smithers feeling sorry for him! Toby 'Bad Boy' Smithers, who had once thought it would be a good idea to transport some semi-secret documents wearing a fake blonde wig which was so bizarre-looking that it attracted the attention of Moscow airport security (a feat in itself), at which point Toby decided to run, which led to his tackling, arrest, and a photo that circulated in the international press.

"When the ruble really tanks, they'll cut and run," said Max, to say something. "Then I'm out of a job."

"Well, it's all going to hell here," said Smithers cheerfully. "You'll find something. Where're you staying?"

"Metropol," said Max, nodding towards the far end of the square. "The Canadians are paying."

"That's a silver lining," said Smithers, ordering Max another vodka, and it came along with Smithers' double. "They still got that harp player at breakfast?"

Max shrugged, said he would let him know in the morning. Max half listened as Toby regaled him with details of well-heeled Moscow expatriate life: Toby's kids' teacher, who sent the boys home thrilled that the Motherland had annexed part of Ukraine ("You shoulda seen them," said Bad Boy, "'Crimea's ours, Dad! Isn't it great?' The thing is we were going to a party at the American Embassy that night, and bringing the kids. I told them to pipe down. But whaddaya gonna say? Half our adult friends feel the same way."); Bad Boy's new mistress, a twenty-year-old student of media communications ("'Media communications!' What is that? That's what I wanna know.") for whom he had recently bought a Jeep and to whom he continually referred as his 'friend'.

Max took the shot glass that the kid with acne had placed in front of him. It was icy. The burning in his throat brought Max back to life, got his senses working again.

"You gonna be here awhile?" Toby was saying. "You should come by for dinner. Marina and the kids would love to see you ..." Somehow, Bad Boy had managed to order two more vodkas, which he and Max promptly drank as Toby returned to memories of their days in Washington.

When Max said he should get going, a flash of disappointment crossed Toby's face. He's lonely, thought Max, with surprise. Toby paid the bill and, on the cobblestones, in full view of the squat black tomb, they shook hands and parted ways. Only a very astute observer would have noticed that the leather briefcase Max Rushmore had brought was now in Toby 'Bad Boy' Smithers' right hand, and that Max himself carried Toby's briefcase out and away, across the square, into the deepening shadow cast by the high, strong walls of the Kremlin.

3

Gerard Dupres put on the hardhat that the pale Estonian foreman handed him. It smelled of old sweat, and Gerard's thin lips curled, involuntarily, in moment of undisguised disgust. If the Estonian, a thin, wiry man with unhealthy, sallow features, saw the look, he made no indication of it.

Gerard was a good-looking man, lithe, petite but well-built, with steel gray hair and a hand-made linen suit that gave him the look, even here in these forlorn Baltic badlands, of someone who had just come back from a round of tennis. Gerard's lip curled again. He had reached a decision recently. Namely, that the only place he really felt comfortable was Paris. In the last years he had spent plenty of time in civilization's backwaters: Sao Paulo, Washington DC.

The last time Gerard was here, it was winter, and the construction was covered in ice. The entire region was plunged in blackness, but the nuclear plant's construction site was ablaze with lights—the harsh sodium glare reflected in the soft, falling snow. The plant should have been done by now. But here he was again, in high summer, no need for safety lights.

The site itself, however, looked eerily the same. Red cranes against concrete. The foundation partially laid. The circular base from which the Supér—really, it was called the SAEPR, the Super Atomic Energy Pressurized Reactor, but internally no one called it anything but 'the Supér'—would grow. But not yet. The Supér was Dynacorp's poster child prototype. The first of the next generation of nuclear power generators, bigger and better than anything else on the market.

Of course, reflected Gerard, if the PLUTO project's reprocessing worked, the Supér would be small fry, obsolete. If PLUTO worked, everything would change. The name fit, too, because if PLUTO worked, it would be, quite simply, out of this world. Even the previously unthinkable levels of plutonium waste PLUTO generated wouldn't stop it: it was too powerful. Too good. If—that was the question. If.

Delicately, Gerard nudged a clod of dirt with his handmade shoes, lost for a moment in his thoughts. The engineers had laid out the plans for PLUTO nearly seven years ago. Paris. A gorgeous spring morning, when everything seemed possible—no, not just possible. Probable. The birds and the fresh green buds and Baron Haussmann's cool pale streets had conspired to make everything seem utterly likely, full of hope. Even PLUTO's Achilles' heel, the one that made testing so tricky—the super-toxic waste it generated—seemed manageable.

Of course, once they could show that PLUTO worked, no one would mind the collateral damage. Everyone loves a winner. But convincing politicians to take a risk? That was another thing altogether. So Dynacorp determined to prove PLUTO worked first. "It's better to apologize than ask permission"—one of the few interesting things he had learned at Harvard Business School, from a drunken American at one of the program's deadly boring beer-soaked parties.

That still left the question of what to do with the waste while they were still in the testing phases. Disposing of it through the regular channels was out of the question. Normally, Dynacorp would have sent the PLUTO experiment's waste to the national processing plant in Normandy. But the waste's levels of toxicity would be sure to raise an alarm, sooner or later, if they tried to clean it. After the environmentalists had made their ruckus, corporate espionage would be sure to follow. Wouldn't Siemens love to get their hands on this!

Even Gerard thought that the plan Dynacorp struck on for hiding the waste during the testing phase was ingenious. It was a rival's idea, but a good one. Brilliant, even. And when his rival died, unexpectedly—what reasonable person has a heart attack at forty-seven?—Gerard had taken over supervision of the waste disposal gladly. Lately, though, he had had his doubts. Nightmares, even. Twice, Gerard dreamt he was flying over frozen tundra, league after league, using his arms to stay aloft. It was pleasant, at first. Then came the pit. As he approached, he saw a giant black hole appear below him. As he drew closer, it seemed to pull him in. Gerard flapped his arms, faster and faster, trying to stay aloft, but in vain, the enormous cone-shaped pit pulled him down, into the darkness, faster and faster, until ... both times, Gerard woke in a sweat. Nerves, he thought.

The PLUTO project was already over budget by a factor of 1,000. A lot was riding on it—too much, he thought. Now, as Gerard looked around at the half-finished Supér site, he wondered if they had been too optimistic, all those years ago. If it wouldn't have been better if the PLUTO presentation had fallen in late autumn, when the light was failing and the very sound of the wind in the streets outside chilled you to the bone.

But what was done was done. The Old Man had decided: the Supér would hold them over while they tested PLUTO. "*Avec tout discrétion*," he had said, when the engineers left. His voice trembled in the silence of the wood-paneled office, his hands resting, white as death, on the desk that had belonged to Louis XIV. Negotiations with the Russians—who still understood secrecy best, it was in their blood, though it had to be paid for—had begun almost immediately.

The Estonian shouted something at one of the workers, slouched over a welding torch, rousing Gerard from his reveries. PLUTO could wait. Dynacorp needed the Supér, now. After

Chernobyl, the trend was away from nuclear. Now, there looked to be a renaissance in the works, and Dynacorp was ahead of the pack. They had to consolidate their gains. There was another Supér in the works in France, on the condition that this one delivered in the Baltics. And three more were on order for China. Of course, if PLUTO worked, even the tree-hugging Teuton would be eating out of Dynacorp's hand one day. Still, for now he had to concentrate on the Supér. The Supér was a sure thing. More energy, cheaper, faster, better. And French.

Gerard followed the Estonian, whose heavy work clothes were too big. The site looked more like a ruin than a work in progress. Metal rods sticking up to nowhere. Plastic sheets over concrete slabs, piles of heavy metal tubing. The Estonian was talking, pointing. "Here and here the concrete would have cracked, in fifteen, twenty years," he said as they descended a wooden walkway to the floor of the site. "Waterlogged. Then there," he gestured up, to where the reactor vessel would be, "there we had a problem with the welding. Here," they came to the site: blackened, charred. "Here was the fire."

"You have to move faster," said Gerard. "The fire put us another nine months behind. We're 70% over on costs. This has to move."

The foreman nodded. "We are doing what we can. But the last shipment of concrete was sub-par and we've already cut the welders' training time to two weeks."

"Cut it to one," said Gerard, in French, to the chief engineer. "And next time, use the concrete."

4

"Hit me," said Max as he entered the unprepossessing Moscow branch offices of McGovern International Consulting, Inc. 'Offices' was something of an overstatement. In matter of fact they were two adjoining, closet-sized rooms, one of which had a window, one of which did not. Though to be fair, most of the year it didn't matter; During the long winter, the only light to be had was provided by the fluorescent bulbs overhead.

And, reflected Max, you couldn't say the place was totally lacking in glamour: downstairs, in the lobby's drafty glass atrium, a wilted Mediterranean salad cost as much as a school teacher's official monthly salary.

Marie looked up with a start. She had been sitting at the desk nearest the door, her straight brown hair falling over her practical jacket's square shoulders, staring absently into her laptop monitor, her face perfectly round and pale, like the moon. Before she had a chance to stand, Max crossed the tiny room and positioned himself behind her. On the screen, he could read: "the tempter was at hand: for a little black bird, commonly called a merle or an ouzel, began to fly about his face, and forthwith the holy man was assaulted with such a terrible temptation of the flesh ..."

"As I suspected! Who is it this morning? Ah—I see. St. Benedict."

Marie blushed and closed the screen. Then a smile spread across her broad, pleasant face. "Max!" she said. "You're such a bully."

"No," he said, bending to kiss her on the cheek. "You're a freak."

Before he knew what was happening, she jumped up and put her arms around him. Then she stepped back, looking at him quizzically. "Welcome back, Max," she said, softly. They were both embarrassed. Marie took her seat again, quickly, crossed her legs and scratched her nose awkwardly with the tip of a very long, very red fingernail.

"Nice nails," he said, doing his best to recover his jocularity.

"Don't start," she said, rolling her eyes. "I can't even open the filing cabinet."

Max laughed. "What's the story?"

Marie turned red and looked at the ground. She was a nice girl, thought Max, feeling calmer. And smart—the Agency was lucky with her. In Max's day, they had given agents intensive language training: he himself had spent two years in Monterey at the institute to make sure his intonation was just so. Now, they mostly played native speakers back in the field—the children of émigré families who left in kindergarten or first grade ("I couldn't sit cross-legged at circle time," Marie told him once, "It was a big problem for me. The teachers in America couldn't understand it. I was like, 'In Russia we had chairs!'").

Max's generation watched it all fall apart. There were still dinosaurs like Dunkirk, with their pensions and their paid-for housing, a world that had in effect disappeared, even if you could still go to dinner there. Marie's generation, on the other hand, was used to uncertainty: unpaid internships to prepare for jobs in industries that would have ceased to exist by the time they were ready to enter them. They didn't know anything different, didn't expect better.

Still, Marie was a good egg. Sure, she complained about being a glorified secretary, that her generation wanted more. Not money, not security. But action, excitement, meaning. Moscow, she said, was just one great big Brighton Beach. If she'd known,

21

she would have stayed at home, closer to her grandmother. She was constantly threatening to go to graduate school. A PhD in theology, maybe? How about a PhD in homelessness, Max would retort. Marie just shrugged.

Now her voice, usually clear and strong, dropped to a murmur. "The old guy at the 24-hour place by my apartment told me I'd better find a man. Before it's too late."

"Old coot," said Max. "What makes him so sure you don't have a man?"

"That's what I said!" said Marie, a hint of outrage creeping into her voice.

"So?" said Max.

Marie lowered her eyes again. "He pointed to my fingernails. I chew them, ok? He was like, 'With hands like that? Ha!'" By now, Marie was almost laughing herself. She caught herself and frowned. "Now I have to make another appointment just to take these things off."

"Don't worry, Marie," said Max. "Some men prefer women without claws."

"Shut up," she said. "So, when did you get in?"

"Last night. Now, Marie, what've we got?"

She sighed and with some difficulty typed. "Everybody's freaking out about the price of oil—for every dollar a barrel drops, Russia loses, like, I don't know, a hundred billion dollars or something. And in the last week already it's dropped three dollars."

Max whistled. She continued: "A new crackdown on 'Foreign Agents,' they just put the head of Moscow's Ukrainian Library in jail for anti-patriotic activities ... the last of the telecom companies have installed state-of-the-art listening devices ... hey, did you know that before 1991, the KGB only had the capacity to listen in on 300 lines in Moscow?"

"Are you serious?"

She smiled her strawberries-and-cream smile and nodded.

"All those 'not for the telephone' conversations my parents were always going on about. I was like, 'you guys, this is Brighton Beach, you're talking about, like, ancient history, nobody cares!' Anyway guess I was right. It's just like, like—a Panopticon! You know, like Foucault?"

"Yes, Marie, I also went to college."

She blushed. "Anyway. Oh, and here's a nice one—the FSB ordered, like, sixty leather coats, cut exactly like the old NKVD ones. I mean, O-M-G."

Max shook his head. "Anything for me?"

A pained look crossed Marie's face. It didn't go with her freckles. "Dunkirk wants to see you."

Max groaned. "Now?"

"Yes," she said. "He said to send you over if—when you showed up."

Max nodded. "Can't be helped, I guess."

Marie shook her head. As Max stood to leave, Marie stood too. "Max," she said, as he reached for the door. "I'm really sorry about—about the job."

Max felt a burning sensation in his throat, around his eyes. Nameless, though if he had to label the pain (like he had learned with Rose at that stupid awareness seminar), he might say 'anger.' 'Fury.' 'Shame.' Hurt? He jerked his head, once, and before she could say anything else, was out the door.

5

Outside, under a heavy gray sky, he walked. One foot in front of the other. The low roar of the traffic. The sound of blood in his ears. Rasp of breath. Then, like a revelation: the river. Max looked up. Five lanes of traffic hurtled westward, under a thick blanket of exhaust. Beyond that ran the Moskva's deep, muddy current. He stood, bouncing on the balls of his feet, Bad Boy's leather briefcase chafing his fingers, and waited for a break in the traffic. When it came, he sprinted across the artery.

Max was only halfway across when he saw the black Corolla accelerating towards him. Out of nowhere, crossing three lanes in as many seconds. Max's heart raced as he propelled himself forward. The blast of dirty air. The gasp of the car's metal body passing. Inches. From the safety of the walkway, Max saluted the back of the Corolla. Such sportsmanlike attempts to hit the capital's pedestrians used to be commonplace, but no one had tried it on him in a long time. It almost made Max feel young again.

The city seemed sleepy, emptier than he had ever seen it. On a bridge near the Kremlin, a small crowd milled around a wilted shrine: bouquets of carnations in sawed-off one-liter water bottles, red wax melted into immobile little pools on the sidewalk. A handful of people walked, singly or in pairs, slowly past the photos in cellophane sheaths taped to the stone bridge. They read the paper messages alongside them. Their faces, downturned, were blank. Max joined them. Filing past.

Even with this makeshift memorial, it was hard to believe that a man once in the running to rule the country had been shot here. In full view of the Kremlin. Under the bridge, rush hour had paralyzed the wide street. Every last car, down to a boxy little Golf sedan, was fitted with black-tinted windows. Max watched them crawl along, inch by inch, like a parade of the blind.

*

The Annex came into existence in the '80s, after it came to light that the nearly complete new state-of-the-art American embassy had been bugged from top to bottom during construction and would have to be abandoned. The diplomats went back to the old building, a creaky mansion in the center, and the spies decamped to the unspectacular but relatively secure Annex—a former residential building whose previous occupants had been forced to quickly relocate when the Soviet foreign minister decided to turn it over to the Americans as a kind of mea culpa for the fact that his own intelligence agency's assault on the expensive new American headquarters had come to light.

Shortly thereafter, the Soviet regime had fallen, and with it vanished the impetus to find new quarters quickly. As with so many temporary measures, nearly a quarter century later the Annex was still in permanent use.

When the answering buzz came, Max pushed the metal door open. Inside, in the cracked linoleum entryway, a pair of security guards rifled through his things. Whatever they were looking for, they didn't find. He passed through the Czech-made metal detector's battered arch. Abandon hope all ye ... thought Max, then remonstrated with himself: cut the pathos, Maxyboy. The elevator protested as Max stepped in, but consented to carry him to the third floor where it deposited him in a brightly lit hallway. The floor was carpeted, honey-colored. A pair of glass doors, one of which had a single crack running through it, opened onto a small lobby. An American receptionist sat behind the desk. Friendly, competent, Mid-western.

"Mr. Rushmore?" she said, looking up with a smile. Max nodded. "Mr. Dunkirk is expecting you."

Max nodded and took a seat, barely suppressing his groan. He had started to sweat again. Nerves, this time, not the heat. An unexpected development. He made a note of it. The sweats: part of the new condition of his life. Max wiped his brow.

"Max!" Dunkirk had appeared in the doorway, his greeting ringing false, a note too hearty, for all his breeding. Dunkirk looked sleeker, leaner, more expensive: success suited him. His broad stride into the reception area still marked by that impressive limp. Max wondered if he cultivated it, just a little, after all these years.

Dunkirk wasn't much older than him, maybe fifteen years, but it had been an important decade and a half, and where Max's career had floundered, Dunkirk's had taken hold in the fertile ground of the super-paranoid final years of the Cold War, then grown up, strong and tall and solid.

"You're looking better than expected," said Dunkirk, putting an arm around Max's shoulder to usher him into his office. Max thought he detected a flinch as Dunkirk's hand came into contact with the dampness of Max's shirt.

Inside, the room was barren, institutional. A desk. A framed, faded color poster advertising the state of Montana. A dragon plant, dying. A single window. Through the drawn vertical blinds, the Moscow suburbs crouched outside like a great, gray beast. The blinds were dirty. For no reason at all Max thought of a sinking ship.

Dunkirk sat back and placed a manila folder on the desk. Max took the seat across from him, near the door. "So," said Dunkirk. "They sent you back to us."

Max nodded. "That's how it looks."

"Who are these jokers who gave you the contract?" said Dunkirk. "Why do I want to say, 'Aubergine'...?"

"Nightshade."

"Right," said Dunkirk. "I can never quite keep track. After we started making cuts there have been so many sub-sub-sub contractors I can't get them straight. Do you even have health insurance?"

Max winced. "Obamacare."

Dunkirk raised his eyebrows. "How's Rose taking that?"

Max was taken off guard. He saw Dunkirk understood his secret—that he hadn't told Rose—and was ashamed. Dunkirk shrugged, glanced down at the paper in front of him. "And the Canadian consultancy? That's bona fide?"

Max nodded. "Nightshade put us in touch. I've got the experience they need—rotten joint ventures aren't exactly rocket science."

"So they're paying your freight," said Dunkirk, approvingly.

"Yep," said Max. "Putting me up at the Metropol."

Dunkirk raised his eyebrows and let out a long whistle. "Well, I guess that's the idea. Get PI to pay for it."

"PI?"

"Private Industry. Our funds have been slashed. No plane tickets, you gotta buy your own water. That's got the Gaza people up in arms." He shrugged: that wasn't his problem.

"There's still a company credit card," said Max.

Dunkirk shook his head, no. "We can allocate you five hundred bucks up front. After that, legitimate expenses will be considered on a case-by-case basis. With receipts, of course."

"Five hundred bucks?" said Max. "I spent a hundred meeting Toby. And I got a new suit in Berlin."

"For Chrissakes, Max. Send the bill to Costumes—this once." Dunkirk turned back to the papers in front of him. Picked one up.

"Got the brief from Smithers," he said. "So you managed not to fuck that up. You still got his briefcase?"

Max nodded and tapped the bag on the floor.

"Keep it. A memento. Look, I'm not supposed to tell you this," said Dunkirk. "But I think you're a big enough boy to hear it."

"Shoot," said Max, coolly.

"There was nothing in it," said Dunkirk.

An uncontrolled sensation boiled up in Max. The nerves. The lump in the throat. The bullshit banter. All for nothing? For an open exchange of equally worthless leather bags?

"It was a test. Pure and simple. Just a test. Wanted to see where you're at."

Max's anger flared. Grew. Brighter, clearer. He was going to stand up, lean over, and punch Dunkirk in the face. Smash his jaw and be done with it. Once and for all. Retire. Join a commune. Like his mom, before she died. Raise bees. The soft, wet, warm impact of knuckles on skin. The feel of teeth cracking. The ... Dunkirk was still talking, oblivious to the violence the man sitting across from him felt himself capable of.

"Don't mention it to Bad Boy if you see him," the older man was saying. "You shouldn't see him, of course, if you're playing by the book. Which you oughtta be." Dunkirk shrugged. "I wouldn't want to hurt his feelings."

'Which you oughtta be'—Max heard the dig. Felt it, too. Somehow it took the wind out of his sails. The moment of violence passed. In its place he felt—what? Emptiness, a hopeless, passive acquiescence. Sorrow. He made an effort to direct his attention back to Dunkirk, who was still talking in that Washington monotone that Max had never quite mastered. His mind wandered.

As part of his 'rehab' following the 'reorganization,' the Feeling Eater, acting in conjunction with Nightshade, had sent him to a series of lectures at the State Department. Caucuses on 'Internet Technology' and 'Third World Economies' whose trilling descriptions implied the United States government had only very recently discovered these exciting phenomena.

Max trundled along dutifully. Passed through the shiny, old-fashioned marble hallway, under the eagle seal which was suspended, larger than life, overhead. Through the warm, windowless lecture halls where everything was beige—the carpets, the seats, the stage, the women. Cushy. Dull. He'd felt safe there, listening to the drone, expert after expert fumbling with the microphone. Bulbous men in gray suits—portents of what Max himself could have become in five, ten, fifteen years, if he had been luckier—nodding off in the audience.

Only at the end of the day, when it was time to go home, back to the little rented apartment in Bethesda, did the anxiety set in. What would he tell Rose? When would he tell her? How much more money was she going to spend on that kitchen? He still hadn't come up with a satisfactory answer when Nightshade packed him off to Berlin, where he kicked around, couldn't get in to see anyone, then was detailed to 'keep an eye on' the new Embassy's grand opening, which was held entirely outside the newly constructed building, which had all the charm of a low-cost ocean liner crossed with a bunker, and catered by Burger King.

Then they posted him, suddenly and without any kind of warning, back to Moscow. So here he was. Not just part-time with limited access, but still on probation, from the looks of it.

Max noticed Dunkirk's mouth moving, the thin lips contracting violently enough now and then to expose the small, perfect incisors. Max caught the words 'procedural' and 'prescriptive' but couldn't quite grasp the thread.

"Anyway, we've got something for you." Dunkirk tossed the file across the desk. Max let it sit, unopened, on the table in front of him before he reached over, slowly, to take it. It was marked, in black felt tip pen, 'Sonja Ostranova'.

"Ostranova's a Cleaning Lady," said Dunkirk. "NNSA."

For a moment, Max's spirits lifted. This was a case. Some of the most interesting work in Russia went through the 'Cleaning Ladies'—as the National Nuclear Security Administration was known, to the dismay of its mostly male staff. Launched in the '90s by the Department of Energy, the NNSA amounted to a bureaucratic acknowledgement that the Cold War was over—that the building of nuclear weapons was now less important than the securing of them.

The Russians, as it turned out, were broke, and the NNSA, among other things, went in to nuclear reactors and weapons plants across the former USSR, documenting, buying, and securing nuclear materials. More recently, it was the NNSA who tracked the Russian side of bilateral disarmament. Counting missiles. Making sure they were dismantled correctly.

"Or I should say, was," said Dunkirk, handing Max a photo-copy of a Russian death certificate. "American national, born in Russia, immigrated in '91. Based in DC, but started making regular trips here in '05. Part of the missile inspection team. The Moscow stops were one, two days. All routine."

Max said nothing, glancing down at the papers. Born in Moscow. A degree in physics from Moscow State University. No family members in Russia. "She had some bad luck," said Dunkirk. The next words made everything clear: "Heart attack."

Max didn't even bother to respond.

"Look, Rushmore," he said. "We just need somebody to sign off on it."

"Why doesn't NNSA handle this?"

"Budget cuts, politics," said Dunkirk, with a wave of the hand. "Once the Russians got rich they didn't want our help locking up the nukes anymore. Now they want us out—officially. Was pretty embarrassing for our Red brothers when we came in to play prison guard. Anyway, the NNSA's been cutting down on intelligence. Asked if we could take it over. I said sure. You can handle it, am I right?"

Max nodded. He saw Rose in his mind's eye. That first date, she was going to art school in Baltimore, and he had driven up from DC. She met him in her apartment building's tumble-down lobby. She lit the whole place up, with her upturned face, pink cheeks, flaxen hair, skin you just wanted to touch—somehow in his memory he always pictured her, in this moment, naked, like a short, curvy Venus rising from the sea. Regardless, as soon as Rose appeared (clothed, of course), that dead-end linoleum room with the sleepy doorman was the only place in the world Max wanted to be. She took him to a dive bar on Mt. Vernon and told him about following her ex-boyfriend all over Asia, until the love ran out, and skydiving for the first time, her porcelain blue eyes shining all the while; he had never met someone with such an unabashed lust for life, it was like she glowed from the inside … Dunkirk's voice pierced his reverie. Max realized he had lost track of the conversation entirely.

"Hey! Hey! Hey, Max, you still with me?" Max nodded. "Jesus Christ," said Dunkirk, and a look of disgust crossed his gray features.

"Didn't the other inspectors see it?" said Max.

"See what?"

"The accident. They usually stick together, right?"

"Well," said Dunkirk, hesitating. "That is one oddity. She wasn't here for work this time. Death in the family."

"I thought she didn't have any more family here," said Max.

"Apparently it was a stepmother, there had been a falling out. Ostranova was the only one left to organize the funeral. Her bosses were more than happy to let her go. January's a slow month, and they were pretty crazy about her, so—"

"January?" said Max, suddenly alert. "She's been dead for eight months?"

Dunkirk was silent.

"What's the delay?"

"Paperwork," Dunkirk said, with a wave of the hand.

"Give me a break," said Max.

"You got a break," said Dunkirk, and his piercing look said it all: if Max wanted to talk about it, Dunkirk would be happy to, and, unlike the Feeling Eater, he wouldn't refer to it as 'the reassignment.' Max lowered his gaze. He had gotten the message. Dunkirk was already standing; the debriefing was over.

Max stood, too. At the door to the cramped office, Dunkirk paused. He knocked on the wall, absentmindedly. "Full of diodes," he said. "Soviets spiked the walls before we moved in. So we wouldn't find their bugs." He paused, thoughtfully, the shadows gathering in the folds of his neck. "Lot of good it did them."

∗

Max was alone in the stuffy room. He crossed to sit in the chair Dunkirk had occupied, facing the door. An instinct. Never sit with your back to the door. The Chinese said your enemies would enter unseen and cut off your head. Max glanced around. Visit Montana! The dying dragon plant. The smell of diesel, Moscow in high summer, musty and organic. The shades were drawn. The overhead light flickered.

Sonja Ostranova. Max slid the file across the desk. Three photos fell out. An ID snapshot: long brown hair framing her face, green eyes, delicate brow. Wonderful cheekbones. The next, taken at a distance, surveillance: Ostranova leaving a meeting at Brookhaven. Long legs, high heels. Green raincoat, cinched like a promise. The third was social, taken at a cocktail party from the looks of it. She held a champagne flute. Her dress was sleeveless, black, with a deep V at the neck; she was tanned and smiled straight at the camera. A handsome man, gray haired, athletic, well dressed like a European, had his arm around her. She looked very happy. The pictures were imperfect, but even from them Max could see that she was beautiful.

The files were paltry. Max rifled through them, the pages making a whispering sound in the silence. Just as Dunkirk had said: left Russia in '91, SUNY, graduate work at Cornell, top of her class. Area of expertise: waste disposal. No husband, no children, parents deceased. Started at DOE, moved to NNSA. Promoted shortly before her untimely death on January 11th due to a heart attack at or around 1am in central Moscow. No witnesses were forthcoming.

Max shrugged, studied the photos again. That smile! Like she was letting you in on a secret you had never realized you needed to know. What was it about a woman's beauty? That desire loveliness evokes, thought Max: to hold it, take it in your hands. To stop time. His glance fell back on the certificate. Something irritated him. He remembered the last time he had seen one of these—ten, twelve years ago. A trainee, a traffic accident. A sad story. Max had had to deliver the news back in the States, and he had taken the death certificate along. The family laid it out on their glassed rattan living room table, and it was the boy's brother—not his mother—who wept. When Max reached out to pat the boy's arm, the child threw himself on Max's shoulder, sobbing.

Now, he read through it again and saw: under eye color, it read 'brown'. He double checked. Her NNSA file read, 'Eye color: blue.' He studied the picture again. It was hard to tell. He would have said green. Anyway, it was probably just a mistake. The European in the gray suit would know, thought Max, what color her eyes really were.

6

Leningradskaya was empty. The street stretched, long and gray and concrete under the hazy afternoon sun. A busy six-lane highway separated one side of the street from their neighbors on the other with a kind of super-human finality. The building itself was identical to all the others. Flat, crumbling façade. Metal fire doors. Push button locks. Propped open, here and there, by a cinder block.

At number 59, Max waited. He had spent the better part of the afternoon in the archives. The petite blonde secretary had led him down there and handed him over to an American who kept guard of the room full of dusty and, for the most part, useless files. It was a motley collection: old Party newspapers, lists of Communist party members going back to the 1930s. Following a hunch, he checked the MGU listings. Piotr Ostranov headed the philology faculty, starting in 1978. There was an address, too: Mayakovskaya Ullitsa.

Max recognized the area—the neighborhood had been bull-dozed three years back. Real estate developers put up a recreation of the Czar's summer palace, adding a certain Mediterranean flair to appeal to the modern taste, then carved the place up and sold it as condos. So the path ran cold.

But Max had another idea. He checked the department list again and, sure enough, starting in 1985, an 'Ostranova, Agata' was the University's teacher of French, no address listed. He returned to the '82 and '84 lists. Indeed, a 'Grotowski, Agata' taught in the

French department. In the parched pages of the KGB's notorious yellow 'phonebook,' which a disgruntled secretarial employee had handed over to the Agency, Max found the address registered in Madame Ostranova's maiden name.

Finally, the door opened. An old man came out onto the sidewalk dragging a small, resistant white dog on a leash. Apartments didn't leave families in Moscow. A hundred to one, the dead woman's relatives would have moved in before a plot was found for the body, graveyard space being even harder to find than rooms for the living. "Come, Snowball, come," urged the man. Finally Snowball acquiesced, stepping gingerly out.

Max hung back, then caught the door before it swung closed. He took the stairs. Smell of urine and garbage. Something sweet—graffiti ink. "Boris loves Sveta." "Fuck You." Charming, thought Max. Charming. On the fifth floor, Max stopped and caught his breath. Below, the sounds of the cars wafted up, distant. Almost comforting.

The hallway was bare. He rang the bell at the last apartment on the landing. The harsh buzz echoed on the other side of the thin door. He heard shuffling footsteps as clearly as if he was in the room with her. Not even the sound of a television, of a radio. The footsteps stopped, inches away. Someone was looking at him, unsure whether or not to answer.

Max had always been sensitive to what his half-sister Evangelina called 'energies'. When the Agency introduced an 'Intuition Test', he scored 98%—they even wanted to study him. Old Rex said no, it might ruin his gift.

Now, standing on the other side of this thin front door with the fish-eyed peephole, Max had one of his hunches.

"Hello?" Max said, softly. Then, deliberately, he switched to French. "It's about Sonja."

There was no answer. But Max felt—in the back of his neck, between his shoulder blades—he was right. Maybe it was the quality of the silence: not the quiet of an apartment whose new

35

inhabitants are out. No. What Max heard was a long-established stillness. One that might have always existed. He tapped, lightly, with his knuckles. "Please," he said, finally. His voice caught. He exaggerated his American accent. "I'm her fiancé."

Max heard the click of one lock, then another. Then a third slid open, a chain was undone, and the door opened.

For a moment, they were both silent, studying one another. She wore a faded, flowered house dress. A knit sweater, in spite of the heat. Her hair was loose and gray. Men's slippers, brown, woolen. In her left hand, she held a cigarette, the gray ash long and dangling dangerously. The old woman standing in front of him was not in the bloom of health, to be sure. But she was very much alive, for all that.

"You don't speak Russian?" she said, finally.

Max shook his head, no. She nodded, absently, a faint up and down of the chin. "*Entrez*," she said, and stood aside.

The entryway was small, plunged in dusk. A single coat hung by the door, and a pair of sturdy leather shoes, battered but polished, stood neatly below it. Madame Ostranova flattened herself against the wall to make room for Max to pass. He walked by the bare kitchen—a gas stove, Soviet, a sink, a single cabinet and a fold-out table—into the apartment's single room. It was as desolate as the kitchen: worn parquet floor, a desk, a rickety wooden chair. Like a monk's cell, thought Max. The only luxury was a wall of books. The shelves reached the ceiling, overflowing. Gilded lettering shone from the spines. He had the impression he was in a fossil, trapped in time, unchanged except for a layer of dust, a slow disintegration. Nothing had changed here in thirty years. Light poured in from the window at the far end of the room, which opened out onto a tiny balcony.

Max heard a toilet flush somewhere in the building. He walked over to the desk. A book lay open: Jean Genet, *The Thief's Journal*. Next to it lay several sheets of paper, covered in careful Cyrillic script. *I felt the need to become what I had been accused of being.*

Painstaking work, translation. The old woman's rendering of the line in Russian, Max noticed, was particularly elegant.

Max heard shuffling steps and took a seat on the hard, flat sofa against the wall. It was low and Max's knees jutted up and out. Max heard the locks click back into place, the jingle of the chain. Then Madame Ostranova shuffled into the kitchen. He heard a match strike, the whoosh of the gas flame taking. Then the tinkle of porcelain. A few minutes later the woman emerged, carrying a tray. Two teacups. A white teapot with a stenciled blue cornflower pattern. Sugar. She set it down on the low table in front of Max, next to a large sea-green ashtray, and slowly poured the tea. Then she took a seat next to Max, on the sofa.

"You are the fiancé," she said, and from the dull monotone of her voice Max did not know if this was a statement or a challenge. She took a cigarette from the pack in the pocket of her housedress, and Max hurried to light it for her. She inhaled, deeply. Then she turned to Max, took him in. In his large, solid frame women saw safety and stability. She narrowed her eyes as she exhaled. Then she laughed, a hard, joyless sound. "We spend our whole lives running after love," she said. "And when we find it, we throw it away." She observed him again, and her wide, intelligent brown eyes asked a question.

"I need to find her," Max said. An emotion surged, unexpectedly, through him. An emotion that had nothing to do with Sonja Ostranova, nuclear expert. The emotion fit, so Max let it be. Madame Ostranova saw it, and he saw her see it. The woman looked at the ground. Suddenly he knew: she had seen Sonja. Max trusted this intuition and waited for her to tell him whatever else there was to say.

"I'm not her mother," said the woman, slowly. Her gaze worked its way to the table where *The Thief's Journal* lay open. "I was Professor Ostranov's second wife. Sonja and I ... were never close."

"Was she here?" Max said.

37

"Yes," said the woman, looking up at him with the full force of her gaze. "Like a ghost at my door."

"When?" said Max.

"January," she said. "She had no luggage, nothing. Just a plastic bag. She changed her clothes. When she left she had on a black dress. Short like this," the old woman made an absentminded gesture, slicing at her lap with the edge of her hand. "Like for a nightclub. Beautiful. Like her mother."

"Did she say anything?" he said.

She was silent for a while, and then said, "She was worried. She had a look. Sometimes I have seen that look—in my students. The girls. When something has gone very wrong. I—" She looked up at Max. "It broke Petya's heart when she left." The cigarette was burning, the ash lengthening. She held it between her thumb and forefinger, and the tips of her fingers were in danger. She glanced around, angrily. "I have my own problems," she said, avoiding Max's eye. "You see how I live! At the university I made $50 a month. And—" Her anger subsided, as suddenly as it had come. She shrugged. "Now I am sick."

"Did she say anything?" Max asked, leaning forward, pleading with his eyes. The bereaved lover. "Anything?"

"It is a long story . . . I never understood what Petya saw in me. But he came to me and I took him. I wanted him. And I took him. I don't know if Sonja told you."

Max shook his head, no.

"Sonja's mother . . . was a woman spoiled by her beauty. She had always got what she wanted, you see. And when Petya couldn't take it anymore . . . when he . . . came to me . . . that woman tried to come between us in the only way left to her. By destroying herself. It worked, too. Petya was broken, afterwards. He lived with me, yes. But he was broken. He loved me, in his broken way. And that was all I ever wanted."

"Sonja spoke . . . warmly of her father," said Max, guessing.

She didn't seem to have heard. "Sonja was not like her mother.

38

Still I could never expect her to forgive me for what happened. And I was always afraid … that she would take Petya away. Instead she went away herself, and it broke what was left of his heart. I think I must have hated her for that."

"What about the bag?" asked Max. Too eager, he thought. He lowered his voice. Filled it with sadness. "The shopping bag. Did she leave it? Maybe it will help…"

The old woman stood. She went to the kitchen and returned with a white sack. She handed it to Max. He looked inside, saw the tissue paper had been carefully smoothed, folded. "Was there a receipt?" he said. Slowly, she reached into her pocket and took out a small white piece of paper. Max glanced at it. GUM. A dress—20,000 rubles. More than Madame Ostranova made in a year. No wonder she had saved it.

But there was something else, something that would have made Max gasp if he hadn't stifled the urge. The machine must have been running out of ink, because towards the bottom of the slip, the numbers were pale, with gaps. Still, it was possible to make out the date of purchase. January 15th. Four days after Sonja Ostranova was supposed to have died of a heart attack on a bench in central Moscow.

Max put the receipt in his pocket, handed Madame Ostranova the bag. She took it as a sleepwalker might.

"I have been telling myself that it was the shock," she said as she set the bag on the couch and folded her hands on her lap. "That that was why I didn't ask what was wrong. A mistake, I know that now. Every night in my dreams her father has come to me…" She looked up at him again. As if she was seeing him for the first time.

Suddenly Madame Ostranova reached out. Her movement was desperate, like a woman drowning. She clutched his hand in her own, which Max saw was bent with arthritis. He smelt stale cigarettes and something else. It took a moment for Max to place it. Then he knew. He knew it from his own mother, when the sickness took over. It was the smell of decay. A body undoing itself, slowly, from the inside. "She is in some kind of trouble," said Madame Ostranova. "Find her. Find her and take her back home with you."

Max disengaged his hand and stood. He slipped an envelope from his breast pocket and placed it on the table. "From Sonja and me," he said. Madame Ostranova paused before placing it in her pocket. She nodded. Max walked towards the door.

"Volkov," said Madame Ostranova, still seated, staring off into the distance—or, it occurred to Max, the past. "She had a boyfriend. Before she emigrated. 'Darling Wolfchik,' that's what we called him, because of his name." She laughed. "Best student of Petya, very brilliant." She paused. "Maybe she saw him, too."

Max paused. "Why do you say that?" he asked.

She looked up at him from the hard flat sofa with the thread-bare blanket, the worn brown pattern of blossoms. Slowly, as if she was fighting some painful internal battle, she took something out of her pocket. It caught the light and flashed, a single intense moment. Madame Ostranova held up her palm to Max, defeated. Max approached, curious. "Because," said the dying woman, "she left me this."

And Max saw, then, that it was an enormous bright solitaire ring that the old hand held. The stone gave off a peculiar blue light, along with all the colors of the rainbow. A promise of love, broken. And, for this old woman, an unexpected windfall. An escape from what would, without it, be her fate: the lonely, painful, protracted death of the destitute.

"Take it," whispered the woman, her voice hoarse. "It does not belong to me."

Max hesitated. Then he slipped the ring into his pocket.

40

PART II

7

"What kind of person!" Olga, the ex-wife of Dmitry, the ex-code breaker, had retreated to her small kitchen to search for the keys. Max waited in the cramped entryway, which she had remodeled in the modern style: purple walls, pink shelves, bright vinyl rug. In the room next door, the TV was on, playing at full volume. He glanced in, at the glowing screen. A noisy blonde was being held up by a thug with a machine gun. "This is my villa!" she shouted. "Shut up!" said the thug. In the kitchen, something dropped with a thud. Olga swore.

Max turned back to the television. The blonde had begun to wail. The villa looked fake. The gun looked real. During a stint a few years back as a Moscow media consultant, Max learned it was cheaper, with weapons, for TV people to get their hands on an original than come up with a fake. He looked more closely: the gun was a Pecheneg PKP. Developed in Afghanistan in the '80s. That long, useless war. Named, with the Russian sense of historicity, for the Pechenegs—violent Turkic nomads, the terror of the ninth century. The TV cut to a French yogurt commercial.

Olga's voice floated in from the kitchen, a frustrated, grating singsong: "What kind of person? Eleven o'clock in the night, he wants the keys!" The kitchen was, apparently, larger than it appeared, or at least contained a multitude of hiding places for the extra set of keys to the apartment on the twentieth floor—the place Dmitry had left her, when he left her, all alone in the cozy little nest on the second floor he had moved into when they married.

43

Max's gaze wandered the living room. A bottle of Georgian red wine, half empty. A solitary wine glass, deep like an onion bulb, with a blurred, dark pink mark at the rim.

"Oh!" Finally, Olga emerged, her outrage barely quelled by the fact that she had, in fact, located the extra key. She was slim and still made-up, though wearing lavender satin pajamas. Now, in the light of the entryway, Max saw that her lipstick was smudged and her eyes were puffy, as if she had fallen asleep in front of the television.

"Money?" she said. Max handed her a week's rent, trying not to wince at the dent this small luxury made in his dwindling expenses. "Come," she said, slipping on a pair of matching purple heels. "As if he thinks this is some sort of hotel, open twenty-four hours ..." she muttered, as she led him through the series of locked metal doors out to the utilitarian concrete lobby. In the elevator, whose plastic floor had a large, ancient burn mark, they stood together, awkwardly.

The mechanism bumped and shook its way upwards. Max stole a glance at Olga's downturned mouth, her eyes fixed on the door. He caught a whiff of her perfume, mixed with the elevator's smell of urine. What did the Russians say? Only a fool smiles without a reason.

This was a private deal, one Max had set up with Dmitry years ago, before Dmitry moved to Dusseldorf to work in IT for a German bank. The apartment was usually empty and as a rule Olga could use the money.

Max hadn't planned to come tonight. But the Hotel Metropol had simply been too much for him last night. Ghosts lurked in the dull green light, in the dark halls, the shadowed marble lobby. Well, of course they did: built by a railway man who went bust pursuing his opera career, the massive art nouveau hotel had become the 'Second House of the Soviets' after the revolution; Lenin and Trotsky delivered their speeches in the dining room, Bukharin and other high-ranking Bolsheviks moved into the hotel's best suites. All the china disappeared.

Now it was a posh spot once again. The renovation was really first-rate, marble and velvet, mahogany. They had switched the clocks over the long brass reception desk from Havana and Hanoi to New York and Sydney. But they hadn't succeeded in scouring away an echo of terror, a whiff of authoritarianism. He hadn't been able to sleep all night.

Now, on the twentieth floor, the elevator stopped with a thud. Expelled them onto the landing. This was a nice building, solidly middle class. Under the harsh electric light, the concrete walls were painted an institutional blue.

Olga brandished her keys and opened first a metal door set into a metal wall, then a plywood door in a plywood wall, then the apartment's front door, which was puffy and plastic, upholstered, like a library's reading chair. She handed Max the rattling bundle, flipped on the entryway lights—Max noted with something like relief that nothing had changed—and strode into the one room. "Sofa's new," she said, like a warning. She reached out and stroked the blood-red sofa, like a favorite child. "New," she repeated, "but old-style."

Max nodded. Then, before he realized what he was doing, he had reached down and placed his hand on hers. Force of habit, he thought. After that afternoon at the doctor's with Rose, he had firmly resolved to follow a path of unerring continence. Now it was too late. Between her fingers, Max felt the rough synthetic plush of the sofa. She looked up at him and he remembered the opaque color of her eyes from a less continent moment, several years ago, during a job Max was working on with Dmitry. Cornflower blue. Opaque.

For a moment, Olga's desire was palpable, almost painful, radiating from her as if she was starving. Max froze. Olga stood, looking up at him, those flat blue eyes performing some kind of silent calculation. Then she withdrew her hand. "Next time, don't come so late," she said, softly. Leaving Max standing alone, hand still on the sofa, she left, locking the door behind her.

Max heard the click-click of the lock turning. He walked to the kitchen and, finding first the bottle, then a cloudy water glass, poured himself a healthy dose of vodka. He drank it in one cool gulp, poured himself another, considered the plastic tablecloth, the bright red flowers, the dusty hanging lamp, the refrigerator that kicked, periodically, in the silence. The gas stove, with little red letters: CCCP. A broken fax machine sat on the low-slung red sofa against the wall. A pile of papers, a slew of paper clips. Max made his way to the free spot next to the fax and sat, twisting his body so that his legs could stretch at an angle under the kitchen table. There was just room.

He reached over and turned off the light with a loud click. The moon was full. Max sat in the moonlight in the tiny kitchen, vodka in hand, and slowly, carefully, breathed deeply. He closed his eyes.

After what could have been hours but was probably minutes, he stood. Another vodka. Glass in hand, Max felt a welling up of comfort, of the known, as he took in the narrow hallway, lined with bookshelves, lacquered wood and glass. Old-fashioned. Cheap Soviet elegance.

The wallpaper, where it peeked through at the top, showed tiny blue and pink flowers interspersed with tiny gilded sparks. Raindrops. The entryway light was rough cut glass, shaped like a star: a promise to reach skies, settle the moon. Max sighed. He took off his shoes. Even Dmitry's suit jackets, smelling of old sweat—no, of old man—still hung on the coat rack. On a whim, Max switched off all the lights in the apartment.

The moon was spectacular. In the pearly stillness, Max walked to the apartment's single room. The desk. He glanced at the new couch, a deep, coagulated red in the shadows. Remembering with his body rather than his mind how to just barely lift the rickety paned door in its hinges, Max turned the knob and let himself quietly out onto the glassed-in balcony. He felt, for a moment, like an astronaut, like an explorer of the cosmos. He ducked under the rotting laundry line and teased open one of the clumsy wooden frames.

The cool night air wafted in. Just ahead of him, almost at eye level, the moon hung, white and round. On all sides, the neighborhood's concrete towers stepped down to the lunar barrenness of the street so far below. Up here, everything was simpler, clearer, reduced to its elements. Building, building, moon, sky. A warren that repeated itself, with minor variation, a million times over across the city, the country, in high rises scattered across the former satellites. The shape of Communism, the architecture of togetherness.

Finally, full of that strange, alert energy that the moon in summer can produce, Max took the diamond solitaire out and turned it over, slowly, in his hands. The light caught, transformed into something fiery and unreal.

Max stepped inside and fumbled his way in the dark to the bathroom. He shut the door and turned on the light. It was tiled in black, roomy, windowless. In the winter it was a kind of miniature paradise, a place to run the bath and retreat, shut out the gray skies, the wet feet, the freezing walk from the metro. Soaps and gloves and disinfectants, brushes, were piled against the back wall, under a metal heating pipe. Max fished around and found two half-used cakes of soap. He ran hot water in the sink, dropped the cakes in. He pulled the seat down, sat on the toilet and waited. When they were soft, he took out the ring. He pressed it into the thicker, less used cake. Then he took the other and lay it on top of the first, covering the ring's imprint. He massaged the edges firmly, until the two pieces looked like one, with no sign of the mysterious jewel that lay sandwiched between them.

8

Sometime in the sleepless early hours of the morning Max drew the winter curtains shut. Afterwards, he dreamt about them. He was running through a landscape whose rolling hills were heavy, beige, dusty. He looked down and saw the curtains' pattern, a flat flower print that reversed itself in checkerboard squares, beige on brown, brown on beige. He was running, and when he looked over to his right, he saw the Red Queen running next to him. "Oh yes," she said, "That's exactly right! You have to keep running just to stand still."

When he woke, his heart was racing and his belly hurt. His single mother used to come home at night after a late shift at the diner and read *Alice's Adventures in Wonderland* to him. In deference to his masculinity, she changed it to Alex's Adventures in Wonderland—it was years before Max found out the protagonist was a girl. The running to stay on your square was from *Through the Looking Glass*: he had never understood it as a child. Now, though, it made perfect sense. Stand still and you slip off, you're yesterday's news.

The sun had reached its mid-morning height as Max dressed for his meeting with Tippney. Of course, Dunkirk would be furious if he got wind of it; he'd made it clear, in so many words, that NNSA was not to be bothered.

Max noticed, with irritation, that he was nervous. A fluttering in his belly tipped him off. Before his hair had dried, he had nearly sweat through his no longer freshly-pressed shirt. He considered changing, deemed it worthless, and put on his dress shoes, the leather ones from Milan, which, he saw for the first time, had a tiny crack, like a fault line, running across the top of the left foot where the shoe creased. It filled him with sadness.

Taking the cluster of metal keys in his hand, Max unlocked the apartment's front door. The keys shook, making a high-pitched tinkling sound, as Max unlocked and relocked the three sets of doors. In the concrete lobby, Max pushed the button for the elevator. He walked over to the window, past the pale-blue metal garbage chute. He looked down. The building seemed to cant a little, so that he was looking directly over the concrete below. The drop was vertiginous. Garbage lay on the roof of the entryway, which jutted out below. Someone had painted, on the sidewalk, 'You are better.' Max wondered: better than what? A man, small as an ant, worked below.

The elevator's stench of urine had not changed. A red-headed matron boarded the elevator one floor down, and they stood so close to one another in the small elevator he could feel the warmth from her skin. Finally the redhead smiled at him, as if she couldn't contain her thoughts any longer. Plucking at the diaphanous sea-green pantsuit that clung to her voluminous body, she said it was so hot! Max agreed: unusually hot! He followed her out the front door, into the heat. She stopped, for a moment, on the threshold. She glanced up, at the dirty blue sky, and crossed herself.

Tippney's office was central and unspectacular. Max was early for his appointment and waited in the lobby until Tippney arrived, pink-faced and freshly shaven, to usher him in to the small, neat cube squeezed into a sheer wall of glass next to Price-waterhouseCoopers. The window overlooked, precipitously, a small, golden-domed church that threatened to be swallowed by the new western-standard high rises that had sprung up around it. Morgan Stanley. Deloitte and Touche. A Belgian bakery chain with outdoor seating. Like Palo Alto. "What can I do you for, Max?" said Tippney, who was some years his junior but exuded the confidence of a person who knew that, of the two people in the room, he was the one holding the cards. The two men knew each other, but not well. By the time Tippney was on the way up, Max was a poorly aging wunderkind who'd been 'extracted' for office work in Virginia twice.

"Ostranova," said Max. "Dunkirk handed it over to me and I had a few questions for you."

"Like what?" said Tippney amiably.

Max shrugged. "Why me?"

Tippney sighed. "Why anybody?" he said, his glance falling pointedly on his watch. "Look, I told Dunkirk. We don't have the capacity. A couple of years ago we had 130 people here full time, plus about that many coming in and out of Washington. Then the Russians got rich and said, 'Quit snooping in my backyard.' So Washington started pulling out. Doesn't mean there's any less work to do when it comes to making sure they're playing by the rules. I'm breaking my neck trying to get things worked out with the Russians before START runs out. No real point in making a deal to check up on nuclear security if you don't actually go down there to check. And you can't trust a Russian any further than you can throw him. Have you heard the one about the Russian astronauts?"

Max shook his head, no. Tippney checked his watch again. He couldn't afford it but bought it anyway, on the wholly correct assumption that it would improve his love life. "They're part of the European team, now," he said. "So all these guys are supposed to spend, like, a month in simulated space conditions—training or what have you. The Germans and the Dutch and even the Italians hole up in pseudo-spaceships, in the dunes on some Dutch beach. They go through the whole routine, pee into a cup for ninety days, pretty unpleasant. Anyway, turns out, the Russians are going out for cigarette breaks! And the Germans and the Dutch and the Italians are understandably furious. They're simulating space conditions! And the Russians say, 'Yeah, but we're not in space. We're on the beach.' And the Euros are just quaking. They're like, 'What happens when we go to space?' And the Russians say, 'Then we won't smoke.'"

Tippney shook his head, pink cheeks like twin beacons waving in the night. He shrugged. "That's what we're dealing with! But it's not space and cigarettes, it's megatons of death and destruction." He shrugged again. "Now they're talking rearmament. NNSA has been taking hit after hit in personnel, and as you can imagine I'm a pretty busy guy these days."

"Sure," said Max. Tippney glanced at his watch, rosily. Max went on: "Look, Grant, I'm not a nuclear man. I'm in the trenches: dirty money, crooked bankers. The odd media consultancy. I'm out of my element here. Break it down for me—what did she do, why, how?"

Tippney sighed again, his cheeks turning a darker shade of pink that could have indicated anger or embarrassment. "I have a meeting in fifteen minutes," he said.

Max shrugged. "I don't want to go snooping around until I have the basics."

"Fine," said Tippney, allowing a slight exasperation to color his tone. "Ostranova was a good girl—hard worker, knew her stuff. Since the Soviet Union collapsed, the Russians have kept running weapons grade uranium plants—not because they want the weapons, but because that's all they've got to do the job of heating the damn place. We've been mostly concerned with shifting those plants to civil use. They refine the uranium to a much less concentrated level, one that can't be used in bombs, thus isn't nearly as dangerous if the head man is getting his palms greased by the wrong folks. You've got a bull, you've got a china shop. So let's try to keep the china shop shut. Anyhow, that's where we're coming from. Ostranova's main job was checking in on the comrades as long as the floodgates hadn't been shut: what were they doing with the leftovers, who was getting their hands on it, where was it getting put."

"Dangerous work?"

"Not really," said Tippney. "All the plants she was active at were well-documented and well on the way to being on the up-and-up, at least by Russian standards." He paused. "Look, Max, we called you people in because we don't think it's a nuclear

51

case. There's just nothing in her work or biography that points to intrigue. It's a sad thing. But there's no story. And we don't have the manpower to file the papers. Don't want to disappoint you, but you don't need this background."

"That's my call," said Max.

"Fine," said Tippney. "I admire your dedication. Look, I know you're looking for a break. If you want to take a look at the docs again, be my guest."

Max nodded. He took a photo from his breast pocket, slid it over the desk to Tippney. "You know who this guy is?"

Tippney picked up the picture, let his eyes wander over Ostranova, in her cinched dress, then focused on the lithe European with his arm around her. "Sure," said Tippney. "That's Gerard Dupres, a high-up mucky-muck at Dynacorp—French nuclear giant. Didn't know they were friends..."

"Make anything of it?"

Tippney shook his head. "Dynacorp's very respected. And it makes sense their paths would cross in DC. Where'd you get this, anyway?" Max—who had, against all possible regulations, pinched it from Dunkirk's file—ignored the question.

"A shame," said Tippney, his eyes lingering again on Ostranova. He shook his head as he handed Max back the purloined photo. "A damned shame." Then he sprung up from his comfortable leather chair. He strode out to his secretary's desk and came back with a file. Checking his watch again with visible pleasure, he said, "I'll check back in with you after my meeting. Thirty minutes, say."

His pink face lit up for a moment, and, out of the blue, he punched Max on the shoulder. "Remember that night at the Red Eye?" He chuckled. "Hell, what was that, fifteen years ago? One of my first nights here, you took us out ..." He rubbed his eyes. "What a night. Don't think I've ever topped it, as a matter of fact."

Max smiled, politely. All he came up with was a dark, sudsy composite memory of the Red Eye, an insalubrious combination of strip club, bar and brothel they had all frequented in the '90s. A girl with stringy brown hair. Whose degree in international relations had been rendered useless by the economic crash. "American," she had said, wistfully, before naming her prices. "You are American." But Tippney? Was Tippney there? Max couldn't remember. Could well have happened. In those days, Max was a kind of welcome wagon, a man about town. Before Rose, of course.

Tippney's smile faded. "Don't steal the silverware, Max," he said, and left.

Max scanned the remaining papers, reviewed the list of sites she had inspected over the past five years. The list was a strange kind of Baedeker, a tour through a world that had, officially at least, not existed until Yeltsin decreed that yes, in fact, it did. Scores of 'closed towns' that had sprung up in Russia after the Second World War to work on weaponry in secret. Out in the tundra, on the banks of Siberian rivers, near mines, places where the land was rich enough to power Soviet ambitions. Right outside Moscow, too. These cities—home to some two million people whose relatives couldn't come to visit, who, if they traveled to the outside world, were not allowed to say where they came from— were called 'post box' cities. To help keep them secret, each of these cities received, instead of a name, a PO box number.

PO Box 45, a place now named 'Red City,' appeared most regularly. A nuclear city, built to refine uranium. Then Max noticed something strange.

"Atom Town," said Max, when Tippney came back to collect the files. "PO Box 46. Isn't that still off limits?"

Tippney frowned and looked at the list. Just before her death, Ostranova had put in an application to visit PO Box 46. "Must be a typo," said Tippney, frowning. "Look, here—the Russian names are almost identical." He shook his head. "90% of the home office's Fact Checkers took buyouts last quarter. 'Cutting the fat.' So we get a lot of mistakes like this these days." He shook his head again and shrugged. "Atom Town is still a no-go."

9

In the heat, the metro bloomed. Like a hothouse, all at once. The vertiginous descent into the Communist-colored earth—plastic panels of reddish brown—was relieved, now, by the girls' abbreviated summer outfits. Skin-tight flower patterns. Snake skins. Fire-engine reds, laces and leopard skins. The wands of light that rose between the escalators, like a funeral march, cast their greenish glow on beautiful legs and lips, bare arms, long necks and plunging necklines.

"Stalin built these so deep so that the Soviet people could take refuge here in case of nuclear war with your country," said one his first trainers, a bristly, white-haired man whose wife refused to cook so he lived on chicken soup. "Ha, ha. What they never figured out was, how are all the Soviet people supposed to get down here?"

At the bottom, Max joined the crowd shuffling through the station under the three-ton chandeliers. Iron lilies, always in bloom, night or day, summer or winter. Something Hades might have forged to try to make Persephone at home in his kingdom.

Above ground, Max made his way through an abandoned asphalt wasteland towards a billowing, rounded structure—once, it had been an airplane hangar. Inside, the pirate media warehouse was still doing a brisk business. The old hangar had long ago been converted to a rabbit warren of shops, selling contraband video, music, ring tones, cigarettes and more—much more, if you knew where to look. Max took a set of makeshift steps to the improvised second floor, built precariously on what had once been an engineer's walkway for tuning up the engines.

Max nodded at the Chinese girl behind one of the counters and she motioned him in. Her father was crouched in the back 'room'—a tiny, insufferably hot place constructed from four sheets of plastic.

"John, my friend!" Max said, in Mandarin.

"Moscow, too hot!"

"Russia is a hot place for a cold country," agreed Max. "And for this reason, I am looking for something."

The man nodded: they understood each other. Max pulled out his phone and took the back off. He removed the battery and pointed to the slot where the SIM card would slip into the phone.

"How many?"

Max made the sign for 'three' in Chinese with his hands. "From different stocks. Not the same place."

John let out a low whistle. "Expensive," he said.

"100," said Max. "US."

The man shook his head. "500."

Eventually they settled on $250. Max paid cash—no receipt for the expense people here, he thought, dourly—and left. As he strolled through the market downstairs, someone tapped him on the hand. It was the daughter.

"Mr. Max," she said, with a luminous smile. "You forgot your bag upstairs."

He thanked her and she disappeared into the crowd. What a life for a pretty, intelligent girl, he thought, manning the counter up there, scorching heat or deep freeze of winter, when the hangar's tin walls let in every breeze and the only warmth came from the crush of bodies. Outside, he checked the bag: three SIM cards, different carriers. Just in case.

Just as he was about to slip a new SIM card into his phone, it rang. "What the hell do you think you're doing?" It was Dunkirk. "If NNSA doesn't have the manpower to file the papers on

Ostranova, what makes you think they have time to sit around shooting the shit with you?"

"It's in my brief," said Max. "If there are signs of irregularity, I'm bound to investigate."

"For Chrissake, Max! If there were signs of irregularity, you never would have gotten this case. Have you even been to the police station yet?"

Max hesitated. A mistake.

"For Chrissake. Is this a classic Rushmore self-sabotage? It's only because of Rose that I agreed to take you back in any capacity whatsoever."

"Leave Rose out of this," said Max. Dunkirk backed down. He had made a play for Rose a few years into her and Max's marriage. A gentleman's foul. And Dunkirk was nothing if not a gentleman.

"Have a copy of that report on my desk ASAP or this is your last private contracting gig. Ever. I'm not kidding. And Tippney covered for you—sentimental idiot. Good thing his secretary pinged me."

This time rage kept Max silent.

Dunkirk spoke again, softly this time. "Max, look. I'm trying to do right by you. Help me out, ok?"

10

Max got off at Chinatown. The *babushki* were selling flowers, lined up along the steps, in the sunshine. Their bouquets of daisies and bluebells were wilting in the heat.

Max walked to Red Square, past Lubyanka Prison, then Armani. On the sidewalk a woman sold ice cream cones from a little glass box. Perfect round scoops, cream-colored, packed in dry ice. Further on, an old, twisted woman in a dirty blue dress, dirty wool sweater, and dirty woolen shawl over her head knelt and rocked back and forth, back and forth, her hand out for change, moaning an incantation. He couldn't see her face. A few feet away, *kopeks* were strewn on the sidewalk. They gleamed in the sun.

Max walked. He felt the grime of the city in his eyes, his pores. He needed to think. Old Moscow was good for that. Its quiet, genteel streets, shabby and lovable. He bought a birch swatch from a lone hunchback wandering slowly back and forth on the corner. Her smile was mirthless.

A few minutes later, he reached the Sanduny Baths. At a wooden booth, he bought a ticket, then took the broad marble steps two at a time. Past the first, then second attendants—big silent men in towels—he located a free spot on the high-backed wooden bench, padded in faux burgundy leather, and stripped. He hung his clothes from the plastic hangars. Max wrapped himself in a white sheet and made his way to a marvelous, white-tiled room whose cracked pools shone green. The room echoed with the sound of running showers, like a waterfall. He entered the wooden *banya* and took a seat on the bench. The door shut heavily below.

Max pulled his woolen hat down over his head. A shuffling attendant opened the oven doors with a loud, metallic clanking. The coals hissed as water poured mercilessly over them. The heat pricked, then burned, then seared. Nearly intolerable. "Gentlemen, close your eyes!" shouted the attendant. A naked elderly man sprawled back, head loose against the boards, his narrow white thighs marked with burst blood vessels, purple veins, and white hair. Next to him, one of his cohorts groaned. The attendant beat the air with the leaves so that the heat intensified again and again, short, unbearable blasts. Max felt a weight descend on his chest, struggled to use his lungs. One-two-three, one-two-three, he counted. The body can adapt to almost anything. Another blast. His lungs opened, all at once. Get through the pain. Find release on the other side. The attendant left, closing the door behind him. The heat was different now. Heavy, like being buried alive.

The three of them sat perfectly still. One of the old men leaned forward. He rearranged the folds of his belly, crossed his legs, turned towards his friend. In low whispers, they began discussing their girlfriends. Max dozed, letting the lessening heat sink into his bones. "Ah, these young ones!" he caught. "Jewels." The other clucked in sympathy. "And it isn't like the old days ... real from fake." A chuckle. "I tried to give her a ... my wife would have ... when she was eighteen ..." The man paused. Then Max heard quite clearly: "I thought she was going to kill me." The other man shook his head. "Never ... a woman so angry ... in the river ..." The two men rose, in one movement, to leave. "The young, the young," said one. "Different than we were ..." said the other.

Max exited. He stepped into the freezing blue-tiled bath, submerged himself completely. He inhaled the harsh, clarifying eucalyptus. He felt his body shock, numb, adjust. The eucalyptus reached his brain, moved through it, cleaned it, emptied it. When

Max left the pool, he was a pristine vessel. A pure, crystalline being.

After the baths he felt better. Lighter. Clearer. He walked outside, into the city. Unbidden, the image of the old men in the *banya* rose up in his mind. Shriveled bodies like a memento mori. Max grinned. He rumpled his shirt and patted down the fronts of his slacks.

Then he sidled (nonchalant, he thought, nonchalant) into Cartier. His plain gold wedding band shone from his left-hand ring finger. Max was dressed too casually, but he waited, exuding entitlement. The American ease that comes from not fully understanding one's surroundings. A conqueror in khakis. A Russian clerk walked past, pretending not to notice him.

Max didn't hesitate. In English, a broad, loud drawl, he said, "'Scuse me, I have a question." Then he took out his phone and pulled up the snapshot he'd taken of the ring the night before. "I'm looking for a diamond that's comparable to this," he shrugged. "For my," he winked, "lady friend."

The man looked him up and down, reassessed. Max let him look. Friendly oblivion—a sign of power. "One moment," said the salesman. Then, according to some complex back-room hierarchy, he lied. "My English is not so good."

He disappeared behind a small door and emerged with a much more elegant salesman, small and dapper, with black hair combed in a single, gelatinous sweep over a bald spot.

Max grinned and repeated the manoeuver. The man glanced at the wedding ring on Max's hand as he took the phone with the image. He studied the picture again. "A woman who only wants what she can't have, I see," he said with a chuckle.

"Whaddya mean?"

"Did she send you this?"

"Yeah," said Max. "Why?"

"It doesn't exist. Not for sale, anyway. You see the blue lights, here, and here? This is a Siberian diamond—one of the clearest

stones in the world. There was an exhibit that came to Moscow..."
He looked more closely. "She probably took the photo from the newspaper. Let me see ..." Max became nervous: the photo was clearly not from a newspaper.

The man seemed to realize this at just the same time. He handed the phone back to Max. "Maybe in the back I have something..." he said. "If you'll just wait."

"Sure," said Max. "I'll have a gander at the rubies. She's crazy 'bout those."

The man nodded. As soon as he turned away, Max made his way out the door and out into the shopping street.

A few minutes later, another conqueror in khakis entered through the store's silent glass doors. He was older than Max, heavier; his oblivion to his surroundings more complete. As he walked, the man kept his head down, his belly thrust forward. He whispered something to the salesman. Then the man with the gelatinous sweep of hair emerged and ushered him to the back room.

11

The woman called Dasha stared, yet again, into the brown eyes of the photo on her passport. They were deep, and thoughtful, and held more than a note of reproach. It was this reproach, she thought, that drew her own green eyes to look at the eyes in the picture several times a day. What about my family, those brown eyes seemed to say. What about my mother, my father? My husband, my lover? My daughter, my son?

Don't you think they would like to know that I am gone? Not to wonder? The green-eyed woman shivered, despite the warmth of the day. "Hey!" A voice startled her. She quickly put the passport into the large front pocket of her blue work apron. Then she looked up. A slovenly female figure was balancing in one of the hotel's doorways. An orange-colored wig hung askew over unfocused eyes. Her voice was rough. "You got the sleeping sickness, or what?"

The woman called Dasha shook her head, no. The hotel prostitute cackled, slammed her door shut, and was gone. Dasha sighed. She glanced at the photo one more time. Soon, she promised. Soon. Then she put the passport back into her bag. She pulled her flimsy cardigan sweater tighter across her thin chest. Then she grasped her mop, wrung out the cloth, and, inhaling the mildly toxic smell of cleaning fluids, began to clean the long fourth-floor hallway.

12

A creeping unease came over Max as he headed home. The metro car shook. Steady, violent, metallic. Max scanned his fellow passengers. A pair of exhausted peasant women with bad teeth and red print aprons, a half-empty sack of potatoes sat, caked in dirt, between them. A pretty girl, staring at the ground. The straps of her shoes had left angry red welts on her ankles. A drunk. Commuters, tired.

The drunk had passed out in the back, swathed in layers of rotten clothing. His face was cracked and battered. He sat upright, mouth open, eyes closed, vulnerable yet untouchable. The car emptied, stop after stop. The drunk's smell grew stronger. Everyone was sweating in the heat.

Max suspected all of them, each of them, in turn. Even the big mangy dog, alone at the very end of the car, lying on the floor with his paws under his head and his eyes closed, pretending to be asleep. In Moscow, the stray dogs lived in the suburbs; they'd learned to take the subway to the center in the mornings, where the begging was better. In the evenings they took the metro back home. Sometimes they fell asleep and missed their stop.

Max's stop was the end of the line. He walked towards Olga's. The street was wide. Long. Lined with high rises. A Volga was shadowing him. Breathe, Max, breathe. He walked faster. The sun had sunk to a low orange over the sky, and a sickly yellow harvest moon had risen between the apartment blocks. He ducked behind a cement mixer and waited. The Volga stopped, then drove on.

When he saw it move out of sight, he realized how overwrought he was. He walked on, slowly.

The night was hot, really hot. Much too hot, for this time of year. A group of men and women sat on the benches in front of the *Produckti* near Olga's building, drinking beer from bottles and sweating. The women in thin-strapped tops, bellies bulging, like the tropics. Max jumped the short fence, cut through the deserted 'auto-service' yard, jumped the fence again, and came out at the foot of the building.

He punched in the code and, with a high-pitched beep, the metal front door unlocked. Max had a funny feeling as he took the elevator, which smelled ever so slightly more intensely of urine, to the twentieth floor. He stopped in hallway, went to the window. Something whooshed down the pale blue trash pipe.

He let himself through the three doors to the apartment. He sighed, relieved to be inside, in the relative cool, and in the darkness. He took a step forward and heard something crunch underfoot. Max flipped on the light.

There was glass everywhere. Glass, and books. Pages torn out, spines broken. Max opened the door to the next room. More of the same, plus the couch torn to shreds, stuffing bleeding out, white and yellow. Like guts, he thought. Max tread, softly, to the bathroom. He looked. The toothpaste had been emptied out into the basin, his shaving things were on the floor. The shampoo bottles lay in the bathtub, emptying their contents. And next to them lay the soap. Untouched. With the ring still hidden inside.

Max picked it up, wrapped it in a piece of toilet paper, and slipped it into his pocket. Dmitry's old suit coats had survived the chaos, still hanging on the coat rack. Max took one, folded it up and stashed it under his arm. Then, muttering a silent apology to Olga, he locked the door of Dmitry the ex-code breaker's apartment behind him for the last time.

13

The Paris headquarters of Dynacorp Internationale were not far from the Gare de Lyon. Gerard took a taxi down the stone streets. He hurried across the modern glass lobby. Video screens played advertisements for Dynacorp's different energy products from all over the world. One caught his eye as he tapped his fingers on the receptionist's glass desk: a lovely Spaniard in a jogging bra tilted her head back and drank deeply from a bottle of water.

The Old Man met Gerard in one of the smaller conference rooms. The meeting was brief and perfunctory. "The Supér is progressing," said Gerard. "It's behind schedule, but I think we should be seeing results soon."

The Old Man nodded, folding his large, papery hands. With his milky blue eyes he gazed at Gerard. Waiting. It occurred to Gerard to tell the Old Man about Sonja. Had she seen the papers he left out? The ones that detailed Dynacorp's switch from Red River to Atom Town as the depot point for disposing of processed French waste? If she had seen it, would it matter?

Gerard was on the verge of confessing his sloppy mistake. How could he have left those papers on the desk? Alright, he hadn't expected her to arrive early. Still, it was no excuse. Then he recognized that old desire for absolution, remembered that you never get it, that it's pointless. After all, church is a place to see—and be seen. Only a fool goes there to be saved. Gerard was no fool. He smiled.

"Good," the Old Man said. "By the way, I want to congratulate you on your engagement to Eloise. A wonderful woman. *Exactement comme il faut.* And of course, it means you will finally be one of the family."

Gerard thanked him. But the Old Man's thoughts were already elsewhere. "And our ... Russian venture?"

"There are no problems," said Gerard.

14

Friday night. Very good. Max hurried through the rose-colored station, with its marble columns, his echoing footsteps taking the place of the thunder of the trains. The station was built during the war. Heroic, triumphal. Like an underground ballroom. He took the stairs two at a time, then dodged oncoming pedestrians under the cut-glass murals: glittering revolutionaries taking the Reichstag. A mosaic, thought Max. More than the sum of its parts. The escalator bore him up, but he still took the steps two at a time.

At the ticket counter, he asked about the 11pm slow train. "Sold out," said the surly woman behind the glass. Max smiled. 10:53. He had to act fast.

He sprinted to the 11 o'clock platform. At each car's door stood a sturdy woman in navy blue. There were very few people on the platform: most travelers arrived early, made their beds, and changed into pajamas well before the train pulled out. The first strains of 'Moscow Bells Chiming' began to play over the loudspeakers: a military march with a melancholy undertone. Tinkling bells. He had to hurry. Scanning the navy blue ladies, he picked the second oldest and hurried over to her. Her face was jowly and impassive.

"I need to take this train," he said.

"Sold out," she said.

"My—wife," he said.

"You got a wife," she said, and Max thought he detected the possibility of humor in her eyes. "Good for you."

"I need to see her," said Max, throwing himself into the role. His voice sunk. "She's having a—a—depression."

"Uh huh," she said. "You a doctor of psychiatry, or what?"

"Let's just say that I have a firm grasp of human psychology."

She grinned. "10,000," she said.

Max handed her the notes, blocking them with his body so no one could see. It was an exorbitant sum—yet again, with no receipt. Max shook his head. It would take a while to get used to this new order of things. He decided to look at the money as an investment in his career. The woman, grinning, used both hands like a shovel to usher him on the train.

Just then, the conductor whistled, and she turned back to yank the metal doors shut. Max waited in the corridor. Inside, Max followed her to the door of her narrow personal compartment. "Make yourself at home, doctor," she said. "Best regards to your wife."

The door shut, Max looked in satisfaction at his illicitly acquired private chamber. It was tiny, smaller than the regular cabins, with two beds stacked along one wall and a miniature desk next to them. It was decrepit—lived in, but not uncomfortable. Photos from a magazine—faded flowers, a lurid sunset—had been tacked up on the wall—a homey gesture, two little odes to the capacity to dream.

Max rolled Dmitry the ex-code-breaker's jacket into a pillow of sorts, one with a distinct smell of old man, laid down, and, watching the sodium lights flicker through the window, felt the train pull out of the station. All in all it was a successful transaction. She would have to spend the night in the hallway on a pull-out seat too small for her rump. But she had sold her bed at a good price and would be able to buy her grandson shoes for the first day of school. And Max had secured passage out of Moscow without once flashing an ID.

*

Max slept remarkably well. He woke only once during the night, with a stab of fear, as the light from the corridor shown in his face like an interrogation bulb. Then he made out the square lines of the babushka. Behind her stood the outline of a doe-like young woman. "Don't worry," muttered the babushka to the girl. "He's a medical man." The girl clambered with agility into the top bunk. In the morning, Max left the cabin early to give her privacy.

Wearing Dmitry the ex-code breaker's rumpled, threadbare jacket, Max stood in the corridor, looking out the window. He gave the babushka 100 rubles, and she shuffled off, her legs painful and swollen with sitting in the corridor all night, and brought him black tea with sugar. The glass cup was set in a metal holder. Old fashioned, like a polio brace. The tea fogged the window, then cleared. The morning was overcast. Cool. The train had left the heat wave behind with the capital as it traveled north in the night. A heavyset man in a tracksuit took up position next to Max. The faint outlines of two tobacco-colored moons under his armpits. He said that he had played Eugene Onegin on stage. That life was hard. That family was everything. Using his perfect Russian accent, Max, himself clothed in an undershirt of secondary freshness, agreed: life would be meaningless without poetry. Satisfied, the two of them watched as the tall gray outskirts of St. Petersburg came into view.

"This city has a soul," said the man, as the wheels began to slow. "It either accepts you, or rejects you. My wife, the first time she came here, she couldn't stop crying. For three days she cried. She won't come back. But me, I love it. Sometimes the place talks to me. That ever happen to you?"

"Once," said Max. "The city whispered 'You won't be back' to me."

"Huh," said the man. "To me, the city just talks. Regular volume."

15

Max's heart rose as he walked up Nevsky under the pale, high early-morning sky, past the plaster cherubs and the sea gods. A bracing northern breeze pierced him through Dmitry's thin jacket. The dented eyes of the facade girls, whose melancholy gazes were fixed, for eternity, over the street. Like walking through someone else's dream. The unstable feeling of the swamps beneath the streets. Then the Neva, dark blue, and shining brightly as the golden domes, the golden spires, like a revelation. Max made his way happily over the bridge to the university embankment.

"I'm John Smith, from the Cleveland Art Institute," he said in English. "I'm looking for Professor . . ." He pulled a piece of paper from the pocket of the khaki pants and read, "Volkov."

"Masha!" the woman called, and a full-figured brunette in a clingy red mini-dress sauntered into the room. It was, Max noticed, extremely warm here, despite the open windows. The older woman rolled her eyes at Max. "This joker speaks English," she said in Russian.

The brunette fanned herself with her hand and turned to Max. He repeated his introduction.

"Professor Volkov is not at the university today. He has holiday," she said pertly, then turned her back on him. He saw her thighs had left damp ovals on the clingy fabric.

"Aw, jeez," said Max. "I'm only here today, and my museum has got $15,000 we want to devote to your department's research in exchange for a little help with our exhibition."

The women consulted. It seemed the heating was broken. At present, there was no way to turn it off. They feared, however, that when winter came the system—well known for its perversity— would refuse to turn on. The older woman wrote a number down on a piece of paper. She handed it to the brunette, who passed it eagerly to Max. "This, professor mobile," she said.

Outside, Max looked across the river—from here it was powder blue—at the English Embankment. Using one of his new SIM cards, he dialed. After several rings, the professor picked up. In Russian, Max said, "This is John Smith from the Cleveland Art Institute. I wanted to meet today to talk about your research."

"I am sorry," said Volkov. "I am at the *dacha*."

"I could come to you," said Max. "I'm afraid it's very urgent. Sonja Ostranova said you were the only person who could answer my questions."

There was a pause on the line. "I see," said the voice. "Very well then, I can meet you at the train station. Let me know when you arrive."

*

The electric train's benches were wooden. A man in a suit and hat was fast asleep across from Max. They went further and further into the woods, and the day became grayer and grayer.

Forty minutes later, Max disembarked. There was no train station to speak of, just a Tolstoyan one-room shack and a dirt path leading into the woods on either side. Waiting at the edge of the woods was a sturdy man, not tall. He may have been an intellectual, but he had the strong shoulders and boxer's stance of a man who knew how to handle himself in a fight.

"We'll go to the beer garden," he said. "We can talk there." They set off into the woods. It was so lonely that Max wondered if there really was a beer garden.

They came upon it suddenly. Volkov motioned and Max sat at

one of the tables set in gravel. He came back with two large plastic cups. Strong. Twice the proof in the West.

"To health," he said.

"To health," Max said, and switched to Russian. "I'm not a professor."

"Ha!" said Volkov. Then he laughed, a long, low laugh that seemed to originate not in his body, but somewhere deeper, near his feet, in the ground.

"I'm a colleague of Ms. Ostranova's," said Max, warily, when the laugh stopped. "She hasn't come back to work, and the company asked me to step in. They don't want to involve the police."

Volkov had a battered, hang-dog face. He looked out at Max from large, dark brown, intelligent eyes. The set of his mouth was such that, in reverse, it would have been a smile. He started laughing again, a long slow, heavy, hearty laugh. One that, Max imagined, girls liked, wanted to tame, couldn't. A laugh that spoke to men, too. Let them know that he was one of them, but also just a little bit better.

"Do you mind?" Volkov said, switching back to English. "I seldom get to practice. I spent two years in London. In the '80s. I think I can say they were the best years of my life. Of course, they were training us to be spies," he shrugged. "There wasn't much choice. Men my age were disappearing into Afghanistan. I studied to stay out. When I got the summons to come down, it was the most terrifying experience of my life. I told them I was a drunk. I told them I couldn't keep a secret. I was a womanizer. I told them—anything I could think of. And they left me alone. I had some friends, though, who took them up on their offers. I don't even want to know what they are doing today."

Max thought: we might be friends, in another life. The wind blew through the trees, and the silvery leaves made a sad kind of sound, like a mother hushing a sick child. The sky was overcast, high and light gray, and there was a chill in the air. It was not a good day for swimming.

Finally Max started again. "Ms. Ostranova is a highly valued colleague, as you can imagine. And we are all very worried about her."

"Perhaps you did not understand the point of my story," said Volkov. His voice contained an animal warning. He began again. Slowly. Carefully. "Do you think"—he paused—"that I"—he paused again, as if he might cough—"have lived my entire life in this shitty system"—he looked up again, those deep brown, intelligent eyes trained on Max—"and that I don't know exactly what you are?"

Max watched as Volkov lifted the partially opaque plastic cup to his lips and drained the beer to the end. He set the cup down and slowly stood. Only then did Max realize that the professor was drunk. Perhaps he had been drinking since Max's call. Perhaps he had been drinking for days. Or years. Decades. A half-wasted lifetime. He thought of Chekov: only Russia could produce a man like this. And only Russia could destroy him. The professor's step was heavy, and he faltered for a millisecond.

"They might be worse," Max said finally.

"Who?"

"Whoever has her," said Max.

The professor swore. "Let's walk," he said and stood, striding resolutely off. Max followed at a distance. The path was sandy. On either side the birches rose up, sparse pines in between. There was a clean smell of fresh air and, in the distance, saltwater. Their feet fell softly. After a good while, the two men were side by side, and they continued, like this, step matching step, for a good while.

"Is it true," said Volkov suddenly, his deep voice breaking the silence of the soft, high-pitched crackle of pine needles muffled in the sandy earth, "that everyone in the West has a psychotherapist?"

Max thought back to the basement office of the Feeling Eater. The windows, mottled, criss-crossed with thin silver wire embedded, 1950's style, in the panes. The therapist's big blue eyes, set like two crystal balls in the unlikely frame his thin face. How he turned those twin orbs on Max and asked if there was anything—anything—Max wanted to tell him. How Max considered, for one, solitary instant, breaking down, telling him how much it hurt to be "downsized." How he didn't understand it. How he had done his best, always. Rose's sadness. The sleepless nights. The little rented apartment in Bethesda, with the rented furniture. How his days and nights were all the same color (beige).

Then Max remembered the rumors: that the Feeling Eater's offices were in the basement, but his influence went straight to the top. That whatever you said down here would be with you forever. And Max had straightened up. Looked the Feeling Eater right in those big blue orbs. And said, no. Everything's fine. Just fine.

The Feeling Eater kept his stare trained on Max for another moment. Then he shook his head, like an old cat who knows the mouse is in there, quivering, but has decided the hunt isn't quite worth the exertion. Not today. Those blue eyes flashed as the Feeling Eater looked up from his stuffed chair, so at odds with the sterile bureaucratic room. He laughed, and, like a curtain lifting to show what was really behind the scenes, he broke character. "You're a lucky man, Mr. Rushmore." Then it was over, and the smile, the empathy, gluey, returned to his eyes.

Now, in the still of the pine forest, Max laughed in spite of himself. "Yes," he said.

"Do you?" said Volkov.

Max laughed again. "In a way, yes. I suppose I do."

"But why?" said Volkov. "Don't you talk to your friends, in the West?"

Max considered. "Sure," he said. He remembered a trip he took to the supermarket with Rose, on the way home from the doctor. They had pulled into the parking lot, left the car. She was walking strangely, his Rose. Like her legs didn't belong to her. As the automatic glass doors slid open for them, Max had the feeling they were crossing over. Under the florescent lights, in front of the vegetables—even the vegetables, he thought, were perfect, totally unblemished—he had had the feeling that he was a visitor in the land of the living. A place for the flawless and the strong.

"In the West," he said. "There's not much room for death."

"Ah," said Volkov, as if he understood just what Max meant. "Here, it is different. Someone is always burying somebody." He paused. "If you couldn't talk to your friends about it, you would go crazy."

The two men continued walking. Suddenly, just beyond the trees, the sea appeared. A line of dark blue under the lighter blue of the sky. Max felt a strange stirring, a lifting of the soul. "It's beautiful," he said finally.

"Yes," said Volkov. "It is."

They walked to the beach and Volkov continued. "This is a very important time for the Finns. They say this, now, is the time when the goddess rises up from the sea," said the professor. "She gazes on mankind and passes judgment. This judgment determines if it will be a hard winter—or an easy one." He shrugged, changed his tone. "They are very spiritual, the Finns. Very close to nature. This is a very sacred time, for them."

Max said nothing.

"Yes, she came to see me," said Volkov, suddenly. "Twenty years. Twenty years since I saw her last. But it was as if she had packed her bags yesterday."

Max waited. They walked on, came to a café that had been crudely constructed on the beach. The professor stepped up onto the wooden platform, took a seat at the plastic table. Max followed. Nothing happened.

"Hey!" shouted Volkov, half turning his strong, stiff torso. "Two teas," he barked, when the skinny, surly teenager emerged from behind the makeshift wooden counter. "She wanted—," said Volkov, interrupting himself as the boy emerged and placed the teas on the table.

Volkov lifted the little white plastic cup from the handle that emerged like a tail. He grimaced at the sweetness.

"She wanted to know about some Siberian tribes. In the north. She didn't say why. She didn't stay long." He finished the rest of the tea, shrugged. "She asked if she could stay at the *dacha*. I said yes, of course. When she came back she wanted maps. I gave them to her. She left. And now," he looked Max full in the face, "I suggest you do the same. There's a train in ten minutes. You'll just make it."

He got up then and began to walk off. Max hesitated. He watched Volkov disappear. He took a step in the direction Volkov had pointed. But then, Max turned away from the train station, and, moving stealthily through the trees, the pine needles masking the fall of his steps, Max set off after him.

*

He thought he had lost the professor, but luckily for Max, Volkov had stopped to relieve himself, somewhat shakily, in the bushes. Max trailed him back to a little wooden house in the trees. Voices—men's and women's—raised in greeting when Volkov reached the little wooden stoop. "Wonderful! Wonderful!" came a chorus of men's voices, deep and guttural. "*Vofka!*" A woman said, "Precious!"

Volkov responded: Max couldn't make out what he said, but he heard laughter, the clinking of glass. "To health!" And Max felt a hole in his heart: a real, physical sensation. Max paused, breathed deeply. He crouched at the edge of the forest and circled the clapboard cabin. Everyone was in the kitchen.

The lights were on, glowing softly, and a group was gathered around the table, eating brown bread and drinking. The curtains in the windows were frilled, at odds with the scruffy, rough-edged men inside. A jolly blonde woman was serving something from a large, enameled pot, black with red flowers. Volkov took his place at the table next to a raven-haired girl, lovely enough to be in a magazine, young enough to be one of his students. He put his arm around her absent-mindedly. Then, as if he had just realized she was there, he leaned in and said something to her, and she beamed up at him.

One of the long-haired men picked up a guitar and they all started singing. Max squatted outside, in the dampness. Storm clouds gathered and the night grew dark because of them. An hour passed. Two. Max's legs grew stiff, sore, and then he couldn't feel them anymore. This eased the pain: he was back, he was in action.

In pairs, the group left. The guitarist and the jolly blonde in the car. Another pair set out on foot into the woods, towards the station. The beautiful student pulled rubber gloves over her long delicate hands and stood over the sink washing the dishes.

Through the window, Max watched as Volkov stood, said something to her. She nodded, smiled, and he came outside. He stood on the stoop and, setting his beer bottle down on the porch railing, lit a cigarette. He inhaled, the cigarette glowing orange in the shadows. Then he picked up the bottle and walked out to the woods. A few feet from where Max was, he called out. "Hey, you."

Max was damp, and cold. His knees had stiffened into place, bent, and it took a few moments before he could straighten them out again. When he did, he joined the other man. They sat, almost of one accord, under a birch, whose white bark gleamed, hard and white, in the gathering dusk.

"Cigarette?" said Volkov.

Max took one, and the two men smoked in silence.

"Beer?" said Volkov.

Max nodded, took the bottle. It was green glass, worn, like it had been at the bottom of the sea. He took a long draught. Strong. He passed it back to the professor.

Finally it was Volkov who spoke. "In the West, you've forgotten how to live. We are losing this, too, of course. But we have still not forgotten entirely. It is well known that if a Russian goes to Paris— well, everyone falls in love with him immediately, because he hasn't forgotten. I don't know anything about it, but I imagine America is even worse." He stubbed out the cigarette, took a drink. He gazed into the distance and Max felt as much as saw the glazed look of the alcoholic overtake him. That shuttering of the soul. Then the man was back. "I heard her on the phone," Volkov said, lucid. "A nightclub—she was going to a nightclub. It had an English name. Nighttime, or—Midnight. Yes, Midnight. That was it."

"That could be helpful," said Max. "Thank you."

Volkov stirred, sober again. "There was a child," he said.

"What?" said Max.

"She told me. My—child. I never knew. Sonja kept it secret. I—" The moon had risen, and in its light, Max saw that there was a dampness in the other man's eyes. The Russian started to laugh: a deep, tragic sound that ebbed and flowed like a force of nature. Maybe, thought Max incongruously, it will be a hard winter. He shook his head. "A little girl. She was born with three kinds of cancer. She was just three weeks old when she died. Sonja emigrated after that."

Max was silent. Volkov reached into his jacket pocket. He took out a piece of paper, folded over and over, and gave it to Max. An offering. Even in the twilight, Max recognized it instantly. A map.

"In Russia," said Volkov, his voice trembling, "we think that time is a river. Always moving forward. Sonja wanted to know about this area." He indicated the map with a nod. "Here there is an ancient tribe. They say that time is a landscape, you can walk, back and forth, across."

"Ah," said Max.

Volkov's voice grew more even. "Some people say that the Russian Cosmism—the belief that once space travel was invented, all the souls of the dead could populate the new territories, planets, moons—actually originated here, with these native peoples."

In the darkness, Max held the map close to his face. A circle. Marked in pen.

"Maybe that's helpful to you," said Volkov.

"Maybe," said Max. Then he stood. "Good luck to you."

16

Night had settled, inky over the streets, by the time the electric train reached the city. Max hailed a car with a dented plastic taxi sign taped to the hood.

Pasha the Playwright was a tall, burly man with a beard, who huddled into himself girlishly. The room was low, dark, and cavernous. The lamps were made from gilded Kalashnikovs. On expensive-looking velvet benches sat expensive-looking silky blondes. From their plates, it appeared that the only thing served here was steak.

"What happened to the Number One Club?" said Max.

"Ah! That was a terrible place," said Pasha, fondly. "But the caviar was good. Did I ever tell you about the gunfight? I was meeting a producer one night. You remember of course, the casino's snow-white décor. Well, in the middle of my pitch, bam, bam! Blood all over, splattered on white sofas, white walls, a waiter in tails. Very dramatic, visually! The producer bought my treatment immediately. Naturally—those types love gore. Now it's a coffee shop."

Max shook his head. The two men toasted. "To change!"

Pasha ordered more vodka. Pasha and Max had, in fact, been brought together to trade secrets. Pasha was 'recruited', if you could call it that, by Dunkirk's predecessor. In the chaos of the early '90s, before Russia had become more or less obsolete, there had been a good deal of prophylactic trawling, particularly by the generation that didn't believe the dictatorship wouldn't revive and saw this as the moment to cash in on America's soft power and breed a generation of new recruits.

Pasha came to them accidentally. Hung-over and depressed by what he saw (correctly, as it turned out) as the beginning of the end of his career as a poet, in the form of a very poorly received reading followed by a night of extreme inebriation—'Leningrad drunk' it was called—Pasha had decided to chuck it all, all of it, and delivered himself, still fairly woozy, unto the visa application waiting room at the American consulate. If no one appreciated him in his country, he would find himself a new one.

He had already been imagining his reception, in Hollywood perhaps, as a Great Poet, when a portly gentleman (Dunkirk's predecessor) appeared in the waiting room and asked Pasha into a small office. Pasha vaguely remembered agreeing to something or other, thinking all the while of his triumphant American debut—a scenario in which swimming pools played a key role. A few weeks later, his first official meeting took place—disappointingly, in a flat not so very unlike his own communal one, except less crowded—and was devoid of specifics. It was suggested that he, Pasha, 'keep his eyes open' and 'report anything unusual' in student circles.

When Max first arrived, Pasha got a note under the door and, having nothing more pressing to do, trotted off to meet the new American. The cover—that he should befriend Max—wound up being the only relationship that ever transpired between them. By now, they had both more or less forgotten the origins of their acquaintance, and Pasha, who had grown into a happy cynic and had, against the odds, carved out a reasonably lucrative niche for himself and his young family in the New Russia, would have been aghast if anyone had suggested that these meetings had anything remotely ideological about them.

Pasha ordered a bottle of Riesling ("You know this German wine? Wonderful, wonderful, I am preparing for my new life in exile.") and began telling Max about his current projects: something for television and two new plays. One was about a bug who wakes up to find he's a man, the other was about a doctor who, vacationing on a tropical island, meets the patient whose limbs he accidentally severed twenty years before. "It's about the past," shrugged Pasha.

"Sounds great," said Max.

"Yeah," said Pasha. "By the way, can you believe it, we are getting calls from censors at the TV station. Like Hezbollah! Who would have thought. I didn't realize I had moved to Gaza!" Pasha shook his head. Then he shrugged. "Anyway, I don't want to talk about it."

Just then a small man with a large backpack and sad eyes, who had approached stealthily, skirting the low, arched wall, reached the sofa and slid into place next to Pasha. He tried to fold himself into the darkest corner. Only then did he look around, with those sad eyes.

Finally, he spoke. "Pashchik! If you choose to drink in places like this that is your affair. But why do you insist on involving perfectly innocent friends?"

Pasha grinned, threw his arm around the new arrival. "Wonderful! Wonderful you have come!" He turned to Max. "Max my friend! May I introduce St. Petersburg's number one critic of rock music since twenty-five years."

"Nice to meet you," said Max, stretching a hand across the table, which the critic regarded dolefully before giving it a half-hearted shake.

"You realize," the critic said when he recovered his hand, "that we are sitting in a morgue?"

A beautiful waitress arrived at that moment with three steaks. The girl started, a little, at the word morgue.

"That's right, my dear," said the critic, addressing her. "Generations of corpses."

"Ew," she said, her blonde hair falling over her shoulders as she set down the plates. Max caught a glimpse of lace beneath her short dark skirt.

"By the way," muttered the critic, "I am a vegetarian."

"Ignore him, my dear!" said Pasha. "Live happily, content in the knowledge of your own perfect beauty!"

The girl rolled her eyes and walked away.

"My friend here is absolutely correct," said Pasha, tucking heartily into the meat, which gushed, dark and bloody, under the knife. "The other fine-dining option is a former public toilet! Very expensive, though of course the service is terrible." He laughed, threw his hands up. "This is it! Our 'Russian Dolce Vita!'"

"Don't joke," said the rock critic. He turned to Max. "Of course the situation here is absolutely terrible. Anyway, I don't want to talk about it."

"He has a borzoi named September," noted Pasha, nodding at the rock critic. "He is a wonderful individual."

The critic nodded, sadly. He drank but did not cheer up. Instead, he cast his sad eyes around the former morgue, and sighed. "I am not leaving. You will leave, Pashchik, and everyone else will leave, and in the end it will be only me. Here. All by myself."

"Many illustrious corpses have passed through here," said Pasha, who began to laugh.

After that, they drank. Max watched the room buckle a little, and sway, as if warped by the incandescent dead. Let them dance! he thought. He felt warm and content, vaguely inspired. He decided the time was right to ask his question, the one he had called Pasha to ask. Nonchalant, thought Max. Nonchalant.

"Heard of a place called 'Midnight'?" he said.

"In Moscow?"

Max nodded.

"Sure," said Pasha. "Place like this—same owner, actually. A man called Fuks. Constantin Arkadyavich Fuks. Nobody knows where he gets his money—and we all know what that means! 'Midnight' ... The trick is that something special always happens at midnight. Midnight at midnight, that kind of thing. Not very sophisticated, but what can you expect from a bunch of peasants dripping with diamonds?"

"Fuks," murmured the rock critic. "Fuks, the fox. Foxy Fuks."

He and Max drank to foxy Fuks .

"What I need," Pasha was saying, "is a village. With serfs. I don't need a lot—just one village! To do what I want. Just one!"

They drank to having a village with serfs, although Max thought the rock critic showed very little enthusiasm for the prospect.

17

Max opened his eyes with great effort. Through a fog he saw a little pixie, whose face was centimeters from his. As his eyelids fluttered, she gave off a shriek. "He's awake!" shouted one of Pasha's little daughters, running off then returning. She placed her face a few centimeters from his again. "Would you like some tea?" she asked, very seriously.

"Yes, please," managed Max, forming the words with difficulty on his sandpaper tongue.

He rose, gingerly, then lay back down and groaned. He was still dressed. He tested each limb, felt something like terror in his belly-lining. The pitter-patter of little feet heralded a cup of strong dark liquid, which he accepted gratefully.

At the breakfast table, Pasha sat, looking just a little seedier than usual. His wife, Marina, was in fine form: blonde hair pulled back, lipstick applied just so. She was the kind of successful Russian woman, thought Max, who, having imagined the rest of the world as an anti-Russia, would always be disappointed abroad. Paris would be dirty like Russia, Berlin ugly like Russia, New York full of Russians.

Max complimented her on the apartment, which gleamed with its renovation. "Yes," she said. "We bought it room by room, each from a different family. But we just looked at a place in Tallinn. A three bedroom, nothing special."

"You know, if you're a property owner, you have residence rights in some of these Baltic states," said Pasha, helping himself to porridge. "Darling, did you get the tickets for Corsica?"

They started talking about flights, and airports, and waiting times, and headaches, when Pasha's wife said, "Isn't it hard to believe how much the airport has changed for us? Now, it is, 'oh, what a pain!' But before ... do you remember?"

"Yes, of course," said Pasha. "Now that you mention it. That was something to do, on the weekend. Walk to the airport—it took a few hours, by foot."

"And when you got there, you could drink coffee in the lobby."

"Just to have the feeling," he said. "As if you could touch the outside world."

She turned to Max. "So you are going to see Papa?" she said.

Max nodded as the conversation from last night came back to him: he had asked Pasha if he knew anyone who could tell him about jewels. "Someone discreet." Pasha was an artist by vocation, but he took an engineer's satisfaction in solving problems. Through his headache, Max heard Pasha speaking again. "My father-in-law!" he had said. "My father-in-law! My father-in-law!" The line echoed in Max's ear. His head began to hurt more.

Now, at the breakfast table, Pasha was still talking about his father-in-law. "He would have been a physicist if he hadn't had the bad luck of being Jewish," he said, as Marina poured more tea for everyone. "He graduated with all honors. But the Soviet Union's officially unofficial anti-Semitic quotas were filled. So he went to work at the Hermitage, dusting the exhibits."

"He lives in his old *Kommunalka*," said Marina. "He refuses to leave."

Pasha and Max set out a little before noon. They walked up the dirty stairs, under the boarded-up window that had once been grand. Gennady lived on the top floor, in a room at the back of the apartment's long hallway. A shuffling man let them in. Two children, a boy and a girl, screeched past, then disappeared into another room. They heard bumping upstairs. Gennady looked up and curled a lip in disgust. "A heroin addict lives in the attic. At night I hear him, usually. As if he is moving furniture. Maybe he is. Probably!" he laughed. "Probably only a heroin addict can afford new furniture these days!"

"He could move in with us, but he doesn't want to," said Pasha, sotto voce.

"This is my home," said Gennady, simply. "As you know very well, Pashenka. Now," he said, turning to Max, "what did you want to show me?"

Max took the soap out of his pocket and slowly broke it open.

"Ah," said Gennady. "This is very interesting. The setting is very fine. That's to say: good quality, but not terribly spectacular. The jewel, however—even to the naked eye, the jewel is stunning."

He took out a jeweler's glass and, shuffling over to the window, peered down. His shoulders, draped in an old sweater, were coated in dandruff. "Yes," he said, finally. "I believe—" He laughed. "Now ... either you have robbed Catherine the Great's tiara and no one has noticed"—he laughed again—"or it is a figment of our collective imagination."

The door to the room flew open, and a bent old man in his underwear and suspenders addressed himself to Pasha's father-in-law. "Have you an enema?" Then he looked, in surprise, at Pasha and Max. "You have visitors! Pardon. I'll come back later." The door slammed and he was gone.

"My neighbor," said Gennady, with a chuckle. "Now, back to your diamond..."

"It belongs to a friend," said Max. "I'm—I'm trying to find her."

Gennady waved his arm, as if to say it was none of his business, and resumed studying the jewel through the eyepiece. Then he held it out to Max.

"See the blue lights?" he said. "This diamond is identical to the ones in the tiara, which Catherine received as a gift from a high German court." He considered. "Of course, there were always rumors about that piece. For one, the diamonds looked different from the other pieces—at the time, diamonds all came from riverbeds in India or China. And the tiara was missing for several years. Some said it was in France, after the war, that the French had plundered it from the Germans and sold all the original stones. Then, to avoid a scandal, they replaced them with new ones and gave the tiara back. This didn't make too much sense as the new stones—if they are new—are really first rate. Beauties, they are. You should go see them, if you can. There's a wonderful exhibition in the museum."

"My friend's just a regular girl," said Max. "Unless she's gotten mixed up in something."

"Yes, it is exceptionally strange," said Gennady, as the occupants of the room next door had a loud disagreement about the merits of prose versus poetry, and whose turn it was to go to the liquor store. The argument ended with the slamming of the door that shook the tiny room to its foundations. Gennady cocked his ear. "In the old days they used to make their own liquor and sell it. It was terrible! Drunks coming all night to pick up their orders."

He shook his head. "Anyway, back to your lady friend's jewelry. If I remember correctly, another theory was that the French never had the tiara at all, or the Germans for that matter. After the war, Comrade Stalin needed diamonds for machine tools, to rebuild the country. So Stalin said to his geologists, 'Find me diamonds!' And they did! But it took a little while. Some people think that, in the meantime, they used the Czarina's jewels. Later, once the Mirny mine opened, they replaced the tiara's jewels with Siberian ones. And it 'miraculously' reappeared in Russia."

"Ok," said Max. "So it could be a new—or new-ish—Russian diamond. That makes me feel a little better."

"I'm not sure that it should," said Gennady, slowly. "If anything, these diamonds are more valuable—one could say, invaluable—than the originals." He paused. "I knew the woman who helped find the first Russian diamonds, from a Leningrad lab," he said. "If you wanted the whole story, she might tell you. I'll have to make up a good story. Tell her you're some kind of big shot. Yes ..."

Shuffling in his ancient felt slippers, he left the room, shutting the door, and went down the hall to the *Kommunalka*'s single telephone. Pasha and Max sprawled on the sofa that was also Gennady's bed of one accord, giving in to their headaches, as the old man's voice floated down the hallway. From overhead came the sounds of furniture being moved, dull and then screeching, followed by a resounding, hollow thud, then silence. Hearing the click of the receiver—a big, heavy, plastic contraption, Max had noticed it immediately when they came in—the two younger men stood up, to attention.

Gennady said that Larissa's grandson would meet Max in an hour at the Square of the Revolution. "Of course," he said, eyeing the diamond still sitting on his work desk, "she's almost totally blind. So showing her wouldn't do much good—even if it were a good idea, which I don't think it would be. You never know who she might tell. She always did have good connections with the KGB."

Max nodded. "Thank you," he said, bowing a little. "Thank you so much."

"If you like," said Gennady, "we can put it in a new setting. Something cheap." He walked to the back of the room and rummaged through the drawers of a workbench. Then he found something, placed it on the counter, popped out a shiny object, lit a blowtorch, and fixed the diamond. He returned holding a tacky metal pocket knife decorated with a naked girl. The diamond twinkled from the V of her legs.

Before Max left, Gennady took out a candlestick. Slowly, lovingly, he rubbed the diamond with it. He handed back the dulled jewel to Max, who slipped the knife in his pocket. "It won't hurt," he said, "if it is not quite so shiny."

*

On the landing, Max said, "Let's take the elevator." Pasha looked at him a little strangely but followed. Max pushed the button and the contraption rattled up. Even noisier, thought Max, than he had hoped. The doors heaved open. It was really only big enough

for one of them, but the two men stepped in and arranged themselves shoulder to shoulder, head to head. The elevator was black,
and wedged into the ventilator overhead was a needle.

The addicts in the attic, thought Max. He gave Pasha the up
and down once more as the door rattled shut. Height, weight, age,
hair color. Yes, it would do. With a groan and a slight, quick slip
of the gears, the car dropped, then caught and rattled.

"Pasha," whispered Max, as soon as it was loud enough. "I
need one more favor."

"Another one!" said Pasha.

Max nodded and whispered something. There was a loud
clang, the elevator paused, then dropped again. The gears caught
and Pasha sighed. "Let's hope I don't decide to emigrate to Paris
this weekend," he said, reaching into his pocket and drawing out
his identification papers. By the time the doors opened onto what
had once been a stately German merchant's entryway, guarded by
a host of heavenly creatures who, from the point of view of the
merchant, at least, had entirely failed in their capacity as guardians,
Pasha's identity card was securely placed in Max's coat pocket.

"Don't forget," shouted Pasha, after they said their goodbyes
on the sidewalk. "I'm taking my wife to Corsica in three weeks!"

*

The car—a souped-up Lada, post-Soviet make, with a bumper
attached with tape—would have mowed down a less alert man.
"Climb in!" called the driver, a man with long blonde hair pulled back
in a greasy ponytail. "You're one of these arty friends of Pasha's, huh?"

Max nodded. On the highway, piles of stone appeared without
warning.

"Making a documentary film about our Soviet diamonds?"

So that's what Gennady told them, thought Max. "We're in the
research phase," he said. "Don't know if we'll get the funding yet."

The car slid to the left. Larissa's grandson—as he introduced himself—drummed his fingers on the plastic dashboard. "If you do get the money, you'll pay the people in the movie, right?"

"Documentary," said Max, for credibility's sake. They passed a new roadside diner in a plastic log cabin and an old, polished red stone sign for a shrine to Lenin. "And, yes. Not a lot, but something."

"Good, good," said the grandson, speeding up as traffic thinned. "My grandma, you know, she could use the cash. She's nearly completely blind, you know. It's not easy."

"Very hard!" said Max, shouting over the noise of the car. The trees lining the highway were dusty with exhaust.

"Still sharp as a whip!"

"Gennady told me!" Max tried not to wince as they overtook a swerving truck. Without warning—or slowing—the car pulled off the highway onto a service road. The car thumped over a dirt road. It was quieter here, and the grandson continued in a normal voice.

"You know the chess player, Karimazov?" he said. Max nodded. "Well, his *dacha* is right next door. He has a grandson, about my age. We've known him for years. He was always a little funny. Very intelligent! But had a hard time 'fitting in.' Anyway, a few years ago, he decided to become a Viking. So he moved to the *dacha* and set up an internet connection. He downloaded instructions on how to build a Viking boat from a tree trunk."

Larissa's grandson pulled onto a dark, verdant path, and shut off the engine. They climbed out. "Then, when he was ready, he left!" the grandson continued. "He rowed all the way to Finland. In the middle of the ocean, guess who he met? A Finnish Viking! In a carved tree boat! On his way to Russia! It just goes to show, you are never alone. After the guy got back he became very anti-American—no offence. He decided to join Al Qaeda, and no one has heard from him since."

Max whistled, appreciatively. They drove past a little lake. Its surface was entirely black, like a mirror in a dark room. "These lakes are full of magic, you know," said the grandson. "Maybe you could make a movie about that."

Through the trees, the first *dachas* appeared. Small and wooden, almost handmade, set back in small, overgrown plots. They walked through a rambling garden to a narrow, two-story house. Flowering vines climbed up the weathered gray wood. Devouring.

A feeble woman's voice called from behind the house. They followed it. In a natural bower, a tiny old woman with a halo of white hair presided over an ornate, wrought iron table, painted white. There was a samovar to her right, and plates of berries and cream in front of her.

"Sit, please," she warbled, her eyes focusing on nothing in particular.

"Babushka!" shouted her grandson, as if she was deaf, not blind. "He's a big star, from Hollywood! He wants to know about the diamonds!"

"Well, actually we're a small production company—," Max said, before Larissa cut him off.

"Yes, yes," she said. "Gennady told me on the phone."

Max had brought a bottle of wine, which he placed on the table. The old woman reached out and felt for it with her hands. She nodded her head in thanks. Max took a seat on the hard metal bench.

"So I was wondering," he said, "If you could tell me a little bit about those days. For our film. When you discovered the Siberian diamond. It must have been very exciting."

"Yes, it was a wonderful time," Larissa said, nodding, with her eyes half closed. Then she turned her filmy eyes directly on Max. "Well, I was young," she said, dropping her head again. "And when you are young, it doesn't matter how poor you are, you are excited about life."

"Yes," said Max.

She poured tea with a shaking hand, and the sun shone out from behind the clouds overhead, turning them silver and gold at the edges. "The war had ended, and Stalin realized that if Russia was going to industrialize, we needed diamonds. For machine tools, that kind of thing. Russia, you see, was dependent on the South

Africans for diamonds, and with the Cold War in the offing—you could see it coming even then—we were afraid that the supply could be cut off. There were two options when Stalin said we had to find our own diamonds: either we discover them—as a geologist, that was where I was involved—or we create them artificially. So a team in Leningrad began to study our options. We saw that in Siberia, in Yakutia, there was a 'shield'—a kind of geological formation—that looked very much like the South African 'shield' where diamonds had been found. Well, it was a long shot—there had never been any Russian diamonds, ever. But in the winter of '47, a team of explorers set out. They were terribly unequipped, temperatures can be negative eighty, and nearly everyone died."

"Very sad," said Max.

Larissa shrugged. "Six months later, they tried again. This time Moscow spared no expense. They sent soil samples back to us in Leningrad. But they didn't find any diamonds. We felt terribly hopeless. Then one night, I was in the lab. And I noticed that the samples sent that week showed traces of a blood-red garnet. This reminded me of something."

The old woman sighed, and the sun passed behind a cloud, throwing the garden into shadow. Max watched her, intently.

"So I went back to the books," she continued. "And I found what it was. In South Africa, garnets were found near diamond pipes. So I told them—follow the garnets! A few weeks later, Moscow received a radio message. One of the geologists had come across a foxhole. The earth, where the fox dug, was blue—the result of garnets in the soil. At the bottom of the foxhole, he discovered it: the diamond pipe. 'The pipe of peace is being smoked,' he radioed. That was the code, and when we heard, how we celebrated! Someone's mother had sent a suitcase of smoked fat on the train from Chisnau and he ran home to get it. The director brought out a bottle of champagne and we made quite a night of it. Later, of course, that spot would be the Mirny mine. Surpassed in quality only by the smaller Diamant mine, which ran out quickly but produced absolutely spectacular jewels. A few months later, I joined the expedition. The journey alone! But I wouldn't have missed it. I saw the first digging. I saw it all. The clearest diamonds in the world! And I helped find them. I will always be proud of that."

"Very interesting," said Max.

Larissa smiled with satisfaction, her filmy eyes moving back and forth.

"But there is more!" she said.

"Really?" said Max, to be polite.

"This is a very strange story—perfect, perhaps, for your Hollywood movie! Would you like to hear it?"

"Very much," said Max.

"I imagine!" said the old woman. "And if you make the movie, you will pay me, yes? You cannot even imagine what we live on, now that the Soviet Union has disappeared. Fifty years I worked for my country. In dollars it's—oh, fifty dollars a month, is my pension."

Max shook his head. "Well, if I can sell this film, we can give you more than that."

"How much?"

"A couple thousand dollars. If we sell it."

She nodded. "A couple thousand dollars ..." She sighed. "It's better than nothing. Although I expected more—from Hollywood!"

Max was silent. The grandson poured tea from the fat samovar sitting beside the table. She accepted a thin porcelain cup with a golden ridge, inhaled deeply, sipped.

"At first," she said, "the mine behaved normally. That is to say, it produced spectacular, one-of-a-kind diamonds. Not the off-color ones suited for machine tools, but jewel quality. And not just any jewel! These were wonderful, distinguished by a particular blue light. Of course this was as good as currency—the head of the Diamant mine used to call himself Russia's department of the treasury. The odd part came later. Most diamond mines—which, by the way, operate in arid climates, not in a deep-frozen landscape that shatters rubber like glass—yield the most in the first years. After that, production drops off. But Diamant, which was actually quite a bit smaller than its counterparts in South Africa, produced more and more with each year. The quality tapered off, yes. There were no more pure stones, with blue light. Instead, the diamonds had a greenish hue and were so alike—down to the size, shape and cut—that they became known as the 'beer-bottle bears'. It was as if they had been manufactured, like beer bottles. Naturally the South Africans were upset. They had to buy these beer-bottle bears, or risk having the Russians undercut the market. But every year they predicted an end to the supply. And every year the Russians had more for them."

"How was that possible?" asked Max. "Were the Russians manufacturing the diamonds?"

"That would have been an even bigger mystery, of course! Since the West had, at that time, no technology even remotely capable of 'making' a diamond. There were rumors, of course, that Russian physicists in Kiev had built a ten-story-high crushing machine. And that they were able to make diamonds from carbon with this. Others said there were secret mines and that the diamonds were from the hordes left behind by an ancient civilizations, that the USSR was in touch with mystic beings. There is a tribe there, in this area, that believes that time doesn't move in a linear fashion. They say time is a field—something like that—a plane, that you can traverse at will. In any direction. I once met a lovely young man, a government physicist working in those parts. Anton Samodelkin was his name. He had gone into the woods and lived with one of the tribes there. They were known as 'time travelers'—supposedly they had an understanding of the energetic world that allowed them to traverse time and space freely. 'Time is a landscape that you can walk back and forth, across,' Samodelkin told me once."

She laughed, a tinkling, pleasant laugh. Max caught the scent of sage wafting from the teapot. "Of course," she said, "he was completely mad. But a very nice man. He shared with me an entirely novel theory regarding the Diamant mine: the USSR, he said, was most probably getting these diamonds from the future!"

This time, Max joined in her tinkling laughter. If she had cried, he would have wept with her. Was it hypocritical? He never asked himself that. Back when he started, and Rex was still in charge, the older man had pulled Max aside one day. "Your empathic approach is effective," Rex said in his gravelly voice, his cheap suit reeking of old cigarettes. "That's what counts. That's all that counts."

Of course there was no point in 'what-ifs'. But sometimes Max did wonder—what if Rex hadn't wrapped up a twelve-hour meeting about intelligence leaks by going back to his office and dying in front of his computer from a brain aneurism? Sure, for someone who loved his job the way Rex did, it wasn't the worst way to go. Still, if it hadn't happened, if Rex had lived, would Max's path have turned out differently? Or would Rex have given up on him, too?

As the laughter concluded, Max posed a question. He was wondering how reliable this Larissa was—or how senile. "You don't think this—Samodelkin—was right, do you?"

Larissa shrugged. "'There are more things in heaven and earth, Horatio—,'" she said, and paused. "But it sounded completely unscientific, to me. Have some more tea, my dear."

Max left, shaking his head. He had not learned very much, he thought. Yet the visit had done him good. The beauty of the Karelian countryside. Silver clouds. Black lakes. Wild blueberries.

After depositing Max at the station, Larissa's grandson drove back to the *dacha*. His grandmother was still sitting outside, smoking. "What did you think?" he asked.

She paused, her hair like a pale halo. "He was a good listener."

18

The woman called Dasha stared, yet again, into the brown eyes of the photo on her passport. The green-eyed woman felt, again, a stab of guilt. She had only seen the real Dasha, the woman in the photo, once. That freezing January night in Moscow, the real Daria Denisovna Kedrova had sat perfectly still, clothed in black, as if she was just resting, by Patriarch Pond. Just below the sign with the three figures—a thin man, a fat man, and a cat—that warned against speaking with strangers. Sonja—then she was still Sonja—had always loved Bulgakov. The writer had lived right by the pond, and said it was one of Moscow's most spiritual places.

That freezing January night. It had been dark for hours, and there were hardly any people out. Those that were hurried past, heads down against the snow and biting wind, bundled in scarves. Only Sonja, just in from Washington, jet-lagged and groggy, but alert with her own fear, had happened to pass close enough to the woman on the bench to see something was wrong. The slender, black-clad figure. Sitting. Perfectly still. Much too still. Sonja was in a hurry: she had to find something to wear to her meeting with Constantin. The instructions were very specific: no nightclub dress, no entry. Of all the ridiculous—but she stopped, knelt by the woman, took her ice-cold wrist. No pulse. It was then that Sonja was struck by the similarity in their faces and figures. As if she were a vision from her own future! A ghost! A warning! Sonja pushed the idea away. This was a time to be practical. She searched the woman's purse for her identity papers.

"Really," she explained, yet again, to the photo she saw before her now, with those deep brown eyes that were like hers in size and shape and intonation, but not in color. "I only wanted to know who you were."

But when Sonja found the passport, she had another idea. She slipped Dasha's passport into her purse and replaced it with her own. Using Yelena's cell phone, she placed an anonymous call to the police. "A woman is dead," she said. "Her name is Sonja Ostranova." And then she had hurried away into the dark night. Literally, a new woman.

PART III

19

The Hotel Metropol rose ahead of him, a mournful, curving Beaux-arts apparition tucked away in the night. Red Square was five minutes' walk and a world away. Across the street—six lanes of deadly traffic that could only be crossed underground—the Bolshoi Theater glittered, renovated, bathed in light. But the Metropol was in shadow.

Max had a feeling it would always be in shadow, out of place, a visitor from another dimension. Before he entered the hotel, he scanned the glazed brickwork, the shiny falling tendrils of women's hair, their soft, supine bodies, the giant sea-green lilies. He found it, first the one, then the other. Script so ornate it was almost unreadable. The original quote on the façade was from Nietzsche. 'On Good and Evil'. It ran: "On finishing building a house, you notice that you have learned something from it that you ought to have known before you started building."

The next was added later, in the same delicate, glazed brick-work, but easier to discern. Lenin. "The dictatorship of the proletariat can emancipate all people from the power of capital." Max shook his head. Nodded at the thugs in suits guarding the door. They didn't nod back.

The flight had gone smoothly—he had used the last of his ready cash to buy a ticket at the airport, flashed Pasha's passport. Now, he nodded at the guards, slipped up the weird marble stairs, made his way through the green lobby. Max slipped the plastic key card from his wallet and let himself into his room.

Everything was intact. He opened the closet door. His German suit. Max smiled. He tried the jacket on. Still his size. He lay down on the bed, fully clothed. He had another day before he flew to Novosibirsk for the Canadians.

He reflected peacefully on the positive impact this 'PI' gig was going to have on his income liquidity. Once the payment came through, he would be able to pay off a good chunk of Rose's renovations. Not all of them, but a good chunk. After that he would sleep better. After that, he would tell her about the job. He could already see her blue eyes filling with disappointment, then fear. She would ask if she should go back to work after all. She would say that her panic attacks had gotten better with the medication, that she felt almost normal, sometimes, now. He would shake his head, no. He would show her the paycheck, explain that it wasn't as bad as it sounded. That, sure, the income wouldn't be as steady anymore. but, like Nightshade said, he could actually earn more freelancing.

The sounds of a ringing phone woke Max. He reached over to the bed stand, picked up. It was a Canadian voice, on the phone. "Sorry aboot calling in the middle of the night," said the voice, friendly in a large-handed, wilderness guide's way.

"No problem," said Max. "All set to meet your people tomorrow night."

"Actually, Max, that's what I'm calling aboot. You see, we've been doing some restructuring over here, and from the looks of it our Russian portfolio is being otherwise optimized—which is to say, we won't be needing your services at present."

"At present?" Max said.

There was an uncomfortable silence. "At all, I guess, is the right way to say it. Of course," the voice on the phone went on, "we'll pass your name on to the new owners, with our recommendation. They may decide to re-evaluate the joint venture, as we had planned. But we have nothing to do with it anymore."

"What about my fee?"

"Well, friend, if you read the contract, payment is contingent on work completed. So, under the cancelation, unfortunately you're not protected. We'll pay the hotel through tomorrow, of course. And I suppose you've bought the plane ticket to get on out there?"

"It's bought," said Max.

"That's a darned shame," said the man. "See if you can return it. If you can't, well, that's ok. We'll cover that one then, too. I mean, we're legally obliged to. If you look at the contract. Ok, then. Have a nice time in Moscow, hope to be working with you again."

The phone went dead. Max groaned. He trudged to the mini bar, helped himself liberally to its contents, and went back to sleep.

20

The woman who called herself Dasha waited next to the little metal hut that served the purpose of bus shelter. She was too thin, and sleepy, she didn't know why. Maybe it was this freak Indian summer weather. Everyone said it should be snowing by now. She was wearing the tight skirt she had bought in town, cheap, and a shirt that showed the lines of her bra.

She watched the muddy road. No bus. Instead, a giant swarm of mosquitoes was approaching. The cloud followed the road, almost as if it were driving, or driven, coming nearer and nearer, spoiling the fresh green landscape.

The sound of a motor broke through the quiet morning, a harsh, welcome counterpoint to the chirping of birds. Dasha's heart leapt. A Lada, covered in mud, came into view over the hill, visible through the black cloud of mosquitoes. Then, suddenly, the car burst through them. A purple color was visible under the mud. Her heart sank, again. Dasha stepped back, but it was too late. The driver had seen her. The Lada pulled up to the bus shelter, and the driver—a rugged man with salt and pepper hair and deep laugh lines—motioned for her to get in. She hesitated.

"I am Grigor Borisovich Shagin," he shouted, over the motor. "And you are a beautiful woman waiting for a bus that has been canceled until next Tuesday. Please, I will take you where you want to go!"

Dasha smiled, unexpectedly. It was the first time she had smiled in a long time, she realized, as she felt the muscles of her face contract so unfamiliarly. Stepping gingerly around a puddle in her sandals, as if she were dancing in toe shoes, she climbed, gratefully, into the passenger seat of the car.

"I want to visit the crater," she said. "From the meteorite."

"Ah!" said Grigor. "Our ancient crater! Yes of course!"

In the car, as they bumped and bounced along the road, Grigor laughed and made jokes. He told Dasha everything about himself right away. He was a geologist but also worked as a welder when there were no projects for a geologist. His wife had gotten sick and died. "Sometimes," he said, laughing, "when I am welding, I think it is myself I am trying to put back together. With a blowtorch!"

He was an intelligent man, and kind, and Dasha, to her surprise, found herself liking him very much. She said she was from Moscow, she had been abroad, and now she had come to tend to her sick aunt. Her mother's second cousin.

"You are the cousin!" said Grigor. "We all have been wondering who this is, staying with that old lady all this time. Who would have thought Ancient Olga could have such a lovely cousin! No wonder we are not allowed until now to see her at the town meetings or the dance once a month. Like in a fairy tale, the witch keeps the maiden all to herself." He paused and looked at Dasha. "I suppose she has been telling you all kinds of stories about the local shamans?"

Sonja nodded. "Time is a landscape that you can walk, back and forth, back and forth, across," she said.

Grigor laughed. "Wouldn't it be nice if it were so!" Then he added, slowly, still with laughter in his eyes as if he wanted her to know that he wasn't going to pry, "Though it is a bit strange. Ancient Olga says the whole time it is you who is ill and can't go out. A statement, of course, which all of our housewives have contested, having seen you bargain like a lion with the girls at the market."

Dasha said nothing: she had told the old lady that she was on the run from a terrible husband. That she would be happy to sleep

103

on the couch in the kitchen, and to pay well for it. But that no one could know she was there. To Grigor, who was watching her intently from the corner of his eye, she seemed to stiffen, as if from a deep internal pain. He felt he had hurt her and he was sorry. To make it up to her, he asked why she wanted to go to the crater. Had she read about it? Did they talk about it in Moscow, their beautiful crater? Or perhaps it was in a guidebook?

With an effort, she spoke. (Ah! thought Grigor, so the pain doesn't go away so easily. Well, this was a place that was built on pain, pain that was preserved, decade after decade, in cold. But this moment, now, this brief, precious summer, was the one time when it thawed here, and they, too, could breathe. So he would bring her around, he would!).

"I just want to see the crater," she said, finally. "It must be very interesting. Olga Borisovna keeps a crystal she found there on the shelf at home. It's such a lovely thing, this tiny crystal, very clear, in the rock. All winter I looked at it and imagined I was looking at the place where the meteorite struck, and imagining what it must have been like, all those eons ago. I imagined I could walk across it. And that, at the center there would be something—pure."

"The crater is very fascinating," said Grigor, nodding. "The natives say that it has strong spiritual powers. Both to heal and to destroy. Personally, I am a geologist. In our training we never spoke of such things. It is not scientific. But sometimes, if I am there alone, well … it is easy to imagine." He frowned. "A crystal. That I haven't seen there. No, no. Never. Still, the edge of the crater is not so far. Shall I take you there now?" He looked at her, and Dasha thought she saw something change, soften, in his face. "Or maybe you would like, after so many months of playing the nurse, to go to a place where we can sit at a table under an umbrella, drink a beer and watch the butterflies?"

There was something so gentle, so open in his face that Dasha found herself reconsidering. A fatigue took hold of her, and a desire: to sit and watch the butterflies. But there were practical considerations, too. The crater was enormous. A guide would be immensely helpful—if there was anything to find. She nodded, yes.

"Good! Then that's settled," said Grigor, and the shadows that resided in his face dissipated briefly. "And I'll get myself an invitation to Ancient Olga's flat to take a look at that 'crystal,' as you say. I am very curious about it!"

21

Max slept late. A knock on the door woke him, followed by a maid's voice asking if he was still planning to check out today. "Yes!" Max almost shouted. "For God's sake, yes! Give me an hour. Two." She nodded, retreated. He sat up. His head felt like lead. What was he going to do now? Tell Rose, whispered a voice in his head. No! he countered. No! He showered, dressed and took the fire stairs down to the lobby.

In the cavernous dining room, a cut glass dome of brown and green flowers cast a strange, unhealthy light over the breakfast buffet. Red caviar, blini, pickles, scrambled eggs, bacon, toast. Across from it, on a little raised stage, sat a white harp.

Max helped himself to extra portions of everything. A girl in a white ball down climbed the stage's steps and sat down by the harp.

At one of the large room's empty tables, Max took out the map, spread it on the table. Then he picked up the German newspaper someone had left behind to cover it. The headline caught his eye: '3 Mile Desert: America's Nuclear Disaster in the Making'. The article continued: 'Last week's train disaster, in which three were killed, is a sign of things to come if the United States continues on its current track. The American infrastructure is old and failing, and according to German analysis cannot be entrusted with the transport of highly dangerous materials.' Max scanned to the middle: 'One more sign of an empire in decline?'

Before Max could find out what the German editorial staff's answer to that question was, a voice interrupted him.

"'Scuse me, you speak English?" Max looked up. A big man. Gray suit. Heavy, with a belly that stuck out straight in front of him. He struck Max as familiar, but Max couldn't place him. Probably a type.

"Sure do," said Max. "Can I help you?"

"Oh thank God, you're American," said the man, with a smile. As if smiling didn't suit him. "How d'ya get a coffee around here?"

Max looked around—the waiter was nowhere to be seen. The man sat at the next table over, so close that they were almost side by side. "Mind if I join you?" said the man. "I really need to hear an American voice. I was dang near afraid"—he glanced at the newspaper—"you were a Kraut."

"I don't actually read German," Max said. "Just like to have something to look at while I'm drinking my coffee."

The man glanced at the paper, with its picture of the Yucca crash. "Bunch of Nazi propaganda, I bet," he said.

"Most likely," said Max.

"People don't change," he said. "Say what you like, but they don't. What line of work you in?"

"Computer parts," said Max. "Sales. You?"

"Chicken," said the man.

"Ah," said Max. The Americans had cornered the chicken market soon after the Soviet Union collapsed—one of the few true success stories. Americans liked the breasts, so the Russians got the legs. 'Bush legs,' they were called. 'The Bush family comes and goes, but the legs stay the same.'

"Yeah, the government's making a big stink about us dunking 'em in chlorine. Saying they're going to ban them if we don't stop. Say that's the EU's rule, and that's going to be theirs, too. No thanks for feeding them when they were starving, no, nothing. Nada. Getting angry about a little chlorine! Heck, if it's good enough for my grandkids, it's good enough for these Russkies."

Max nodded, sympathetically. On stage, the girl's hands glide.

107

The harp, Max thought, was quite possibly the most depressing instrument to breakfast to.

"The thing about America," said the man, vehement, as if he had something he needed to get off his chest, "is that we are a country that's accomplished every single thing we have ever set out to accomplish."

A desert. An interrogation room. Max looked harder at the man. Could he have seen him on one of his tours of duty? In the early aughts, a rush of funding had set off a number of interesting projects. One of these was to retrain some of the older people at the Agency whose areas of expertise didn't mesh with post-9/11 needs. This was when Rex was still around—well, right at the end. And Rex had always liked Max. So Max had found himself trundled off to all kinds of places: Libya, Gaza, the Kurdish settlements in northern Iraq.

The fat man was still talking, his voice growing louder and louder. "Whereas your Russian!" the man boomed, evidently unaware of the presence of the waiter, whose nametag read MIKHAIL, and who was timidly attempting to ask if he wanted more coffee. "Your Russian! Wakes up every morning and looks limitation in the face." The man brought his fist down on the table. Then, noticing the waiter, held his cup out for more coffee.

Max shook his head. Northern Iraq? Not this soft, spoiled man. Someone like him, maybe. But with more mettle.

The man finished his coffee and stood. As he handed Max his business card, he reached for Max's suit jacket instead of his own. "Sorry!" he said. "My mistake." Max shrugged. The fine gray wool of the two suits were almost interchangeable. Odd, actually, thought Max. This blowhard had far better taste than your average chicken leg baron. The well-tailored man turned and left, his big belly preceding him. Max watched him go. Glanced at the card in his hand: Bob Dominion, Texas Chicken Inc. Worked his way through the plate of food. He sat back with a sigh of contentment.

Then he closed the broad pages of the German paper. Beneath it, to his surprise, was only the polished surface of the table.

Volkov's map was gone.

Max dashed to the lobby. Husky bellboys paced the dull marble on the balls of their feet, like they were spoiling for a fight. At the far end of the very long brass reception desk, the clerk looked very small and very busy. The clocks on the wall told him what time it was in New York and Sydney. Bob Dominion was nowhere in sight.

22

Max felt energized, almost elated, as he checked out of the Metropol. The excitement of the hunt. Pursuit. It was a feeling Max knew well, even if it had been a while. Not unlike the beginning of a love affair. That sixth sense, that sureness. There was something there. Something to uncover. If he had had any doubts before, the stolen map had a put an end to them.

He crossed Red Square. Quieter, more inward looking, in the cooler weather. He crossed the bridge and turned right, following the river. Roman was the first person he thought of. Oh, Roman. He was a computer-geek turned environmental crusader, a tiny, wild-haired fanatic with a nervous twitch who was so horrified by the mountain chain of garbage circling Moscow that he saw on a ski trip that he quit his job and almost single-handedly created Russia's recycling culture—such as it was. For a few years, his eco-loft in Moscow was the hub of activity: a small group of similarly dedicated environmentalists separated each kind of plastic (bottles, coffee cup tops, cutlery) for Russia's unsophisticated machines, piled the balcony waist high with paper, and collected batteries in jars, then carried them to Europe on vacation.

From there, they had grown into a kind of de facto center for information: mining, energy, cell phone component poisons leaching into the ground. You name it, they knew it. Or knew who did.

In the end, an unhappy love triangle was Roman's downfall.

She chose the other man, the eco-loft disbanded. The eco-loft re-formed without Roman. He moved to St. Petersburg. Started a recycling program there. But Max had heard that Roman was often in Moscow these days. There was even talk of a reconciliation with the girl.

An arthritic wind blew over the river as a hulking cluster of towers loomed. Painted gray. Windows like empty eye sockets. The famous House on the Embankment—the location of the new eco-loft, and Max's destination. Stalin built the place for the most elite friends of the regime. Over the years, Black Marias took most of them away. Now it was a favorite spot for ex-pats—it was generally acknowledged to be haunted, but the apartments were attractive, the views fantastic.

Now, Max passed the complex's defunct cinema, the sushi restaurant that had opened in its elevated lobby, a supermarket chain, and entered behind the theater. The small, interconnected courtyards were packed tight with expensive cars. Large, shiny, foreign. The empty beige balconies that rose all around him felt like observation points; Max felt watched. He knew this feeling from previous visits. It was the architecture. Or the ghosts, take your pick. In the corner, a yellow seesaw moved slowly up and down. But there were no children in sight.

At Stairwell 8, he punched the code into an old-fashioned panel. A long, high-pitched peep followed, and he threw his weight against the heavy wooden door. The stairwell was dusty and comfortable. Broad shallow steps, well lit despite the grime on the large windows. He took the elevator to the fifth floor.

The landing was smothered in potted plants: immense fronds and palms and snaky climbing vines.

A bald man opened the door, nodded him inside, handed him a pair of checked orange house shoes. Max slipped his street shoes off, looked around. This apartment had a view nearly identical to the Norwegian ambassador's: from the vestibule, the Kremlin's golden domes, walled off from the world, shone dully beneath the gray autumn sky, looking close enough to reach out and touch. But nothing else was similar.

Instead of white walls, recessed lighting and Danish modern design classics, this apartment's walls were covered in crude rainbows, trees, flowers, and painted messages. 'Be the change you want to see in the world.' 'Recycling Rules!' 'Batteries here.' The kitchen looked more like a greenhouse than a place to cook food. Hay bales took the place of chairs on the hardwood floors. It was so quiet, you could hear a pin drop.

A young, equally bald woman clutching a pale blue teddy bear had emerged from somewhere within the house. She stood just behind her companion. Very thin, slightly bowed.

The bald man spoke first. "Roman said he's sorry he can't be here," he said, in the firm voice of a natural leader. "There's a Greenpeace demonstration in Murmansk tomorrow, that's where everybody is. We were supposed to go, too," he nodded at the bald girl, "but Masha wasn't feeling well."

Max studied the bald woman with more interest. The ridges of her skull were defined, uneven, like an unstable tectonic plate. So this was Masha! The femme fatale who brought poor Roman to his knees. The bald man must be Roman's successful rival.

As if she could read Max's thoughts, the woman looked up, guiltily, from her stuffed bear. Her fingers were long and narrow, fragile.

"Roman said you're a good friend of his," said the man. "Maybe we can help you."

Max took the seat indicated to him. The hay poked at him. The bald couple sat across from him on a futon on the floor, next to a bin half-filled with empty plastic shampoo bottles.

"Ah, that," said the bald man. "You see how much waste it generates simply to have hair. That bin will be filled with plastic shampoo bottles by the end of the month. All of that goes straight into the ocean. Did you know that scientists just found plastic shards in Chinese sea salt?"

Max shook his head, no.

"We want to show how much more environmental it is not to have hair." The woman nodded. Max's seat was itchy. He looked out over the Kremlin walls—they looked like toy walls from here—at the shiny domes. He guessed you never got tired of that view.

"I wanted to ask Roman about Siberian diamonds. Is there any scuttlebutt—new caches, new mining?"

They looked at each other. The bright green paint on the wall reflected on their pale faces, gave them a seasick look. "Nothing new—there are the working mines, and of course these we would like to see closed, as the majority of what comes from them is only industrial quality. And industrial quality diamonds are made, these days, more cheaply than they can be mined. And of course, whenever you can avoid mining, you should. Mining is one of the worst things you can do for the earth."

"Ok," said Max. Masha stood and came back with a bamboo tray. Three bamboo mugs stood on it, steaming. Max took one and sipped the milky white drink. The smell of vanilla rose to his nostrils.

"Soy," she said.

"Delicious," said Max. He hadn't really thought he would find something, but he was disappointed anyway. And now he had to finish this hippie drink. He took out his wallet and handed Sonja's picture to the bald man. He took it, and made a face.

"That's Gerard Dupres. Dynacorp, the French nuclear power-house. They've been sending tons of so-called 'treated' nuclear waste to Russia for two decades."

Masha had picked up the picture and was studying it. She tugged on his loose shirt sleeve. "Look," she said, pointing at Sonja.

"You know her?" said Max.

"Yes," she said. "Nadezhda Levantal."

"Who?" said Max.

"An environmental activist. From Siberia. She grew up in one of these closed nuclear towns. When the USSR collapsed, she was, what, twenty? And gradually it came out, there was a devastating nuclear accident where she lived, in the '50s. Her father was one of the clean-up crew. He died of it, when she was a teenager. Anyway, the accident had been completely hushed up. She couldn't believe it. She became a lawyer and started prosecuting cases. For example, a baby born in 2004 to a woman whose grandmother was one of two-thousand pregnant women who cleaned up the nuclear accident. The little girl developed liver cancer in 2009 and died in 2011. But the government said she wasn't eligible for treatment or compensation. They said the nuclear accident was in the '50s. So it doesn't have anything to do with a baby born now. Ridiculous, of course. Nadezhda took them to court, and won."

"Now the government says she is a 'foreign agent,'" said the man, looking at the photo again. The happy, beautiful woman in a cocktail dress, neckline a plunging V. The feline European with his arm around her. "I didn't recognize her at first," he said, shaking his head. "But it's definitely her." He looked at Max. "She finally had to flee. She's living in Paris, now."

Masha turned to the bald man. "What I don't understand, is . . ."

"What is she doing with him?"

"Maybe they met in Atom Town," said the man. He turned to Max. "That's where she's from. And Atom Town's not far from Dynacorp's new storage depot. It's supposed to be super safe, but it's just a PR move. There was a lot of bad press in France after a French documentary film showed Dynacorp waste just sitting out in a parking lot outside Tomsk."

"You see," Masha said, "various Russian firms take possession at the border. European courts ruled that Dynacorp can't be held responsible—it's the Russian firms' business."

"None of this is new, but the documentary made a big splash

in France. So Dynacorp made a big song and dance about the new storage facility they're building, out of the goodness of their hearts, out in Siberia."

"The new Dynacorp facility is in Control Zone B," said Masha. "Which means there's no fence. It's off limits. But you can go there, as long as you don't get caught. A couple of our scouts went to check it out."

"Building was just getting started,"—the man glanced at Masha—"what was that, last year?"

She nodded. "A year."

"And we haven't sent another undercover team yet. But we've been getting some strange signals from the ground. There are rumors of a 'sleeping sickness' from Atom Town."

"Could I get into Atom Town?" asked Max.

The man shook his bald head, no. "That's Control Zone A. It's impossible, actually."

Outside, Max reflected on what had just happened. He showed two leading environmental activists a photo of Sonja Ostranova. And they both swore up and down that she was someone named Nadezhda Levantal. How, thought Max, could that be?

23

The science city was in the middle of the forest. Everything was black or gray or white: traveling east, to Siberia, Max had left not just Moscow but the last remnants of the Indian summer far behind. Here, two feet of fresh snow lay beneath the trees; the rest lay on top of the bare branches. The road was white, too. *Marshrutka* vans ran over the white surface. So did cars. Sometimes, you could see a research building, a snowy monument to science, peeking through the treetops.

The main street was short, the Soviet answer to the American 1950s: the same small-bore architecture, the same suburban store fronts, the same dusty optimism. Instead of space-age swirls, the facades were decorated in abstracted Russian peasant geometries.

The taxi dropped Max at the science city's only hotel, on the strip's only corner. In his room, Max collapsed on the narrow single bed. The phone rang.

"I'm here!" said a young man's voice.

"Who's this?" asked Max.

"Maxim, Dr. Samodelkin's assistant. I'll take you to the offices now."

Maxim was a slight, extremely young man, with a healthy complexion and large, almost translucent ears who insisted that they both bow, for good luck, because they shared a name. Max complied, of course. He could use the good luck.

Maxim led the way through the snow to the *marshrutka* stop, apologizing. "There used to be an Institute Volga that we could have picked you up in. Before my time, of course. But unfortunately Dr. Samodelkin's research is not supported by the new administration. As you can see, everything here in our science city is very old-fashioned. I like it very much. There are some changes, of course: the university ... that is where I go to school, I am in my second year, I like it very much ... wants to expand its territory ... just there ... and they planned to destroy a glade of trees."

Max nodded, but Maxim seemed not to need any encouragement to go on. "The environmentalist students protested, and now it is stalled. Of course trees are important," mused the young man, who did not stop talking even as they boarded the *marshrutka* and headed back down the wide, white main road to the research buildings. "In fact, you know they say that is why they built this science city here, in the forest. In case the Americans launched an atomic bomb, the trees would hide the research buildings, and some people even say that there is a special power here, in the birches, that would protect the underground labs. Of course that is nonsense. But I think that trees are not always more important than people, I mean, the university buildings are very old and overcrowded, and they want to improve our standing in the world, so I think the environmentalist students are not correct, in fact. This is our stop, come along."

They descended onto the white road, and set off onto a white turnoff, Maxim in the lead. "I have only just begun to work with Dr. Samodelkin but I find his research very interesting. I believe he is a visionary. But—" They dodged a car, sliding along the icy path, and stepped onto slick concrete tiles, where Max nearly lost his footing. Overhead loomed a concrete office building.

"Dr. Samodelkin will meet us upstairs, he told me. Do you believe in the possibility of eternal life? Not in a religious but in a scientific way." Without waiting for an answer, Maxim continued, his ears shining pinkly beneath his cap. "I am still not sure if I do. But I think the exploration of topics like this is very important!

Unfortunately, it is often neglected in these pragmatic modern times."

The lobby was bare concrete, damp, like a public pool. The white light of day shone in through half-boarded-up stained glass: yellow and red and blue starbursts and organic shapes.

Three turnstiles seemed to be in constant motion, as young men and a few women filed in and out. "Programmers," confided Maxim. "We sublet offices from website designers. They work for Australians, Canadians and Americans."

The elevator bore Maxim, Max and a handful of young programmers upwards, with a grudge. Maxim rattled on. "Dr. Samodelkin used to have an office in the main scientific center, here. You see Dr. Samodelkin's research group was started by one of the original founders of the Siberian Academy of Sciences. A great man. Unfortunately he died last week, before I had a chance to meet him. A loss for Dr. Samodelkin, of course. This founder was, in turn, a follower of the great light theorist and physicist, Kozorev. Kozorev is known as the father of the Soviet space program. Under Stalin, Kozorev spent ten years in the gulag, not far from here. Hard labor, of course. Maybe you don't know, but these were terrible times!"

Maxim looked at Max enquiringly.

"Yes," said Max. "Terrible times."

Maxim nodded, satisfied. "At night, he would look at the stars. And he found, on freezing cold nights, that they seemed to be talking to each other. Kozorev came up with an entirely new theory of the universe—but Dr. Samodelkin can explain better than me—that said, basically, that every object is interacting with every other object at all times. That we are not isolated, but all part of a giant, ongoing dialogue. That my atoms are interacting with your atoms right now, for example. When Kozorev was released, he invented the first Soviet space rocket engine. An amazing man."

The elevator doors opened to reveal Samodelkin. He was a big bear of a man with friendly brown eyes. He wore a fur hat, as if he was about to go out trapping. He shook hands with his whole body. "Wonderful," he said. "Wonderful you could come. An American! All the way here. You are welcome, all the peoples of the world are welcome!"

The three of them walked down a large, neglected hallway. On either side doors opened onto large rooms where young people were staring into computer screens—the place, thought Max, had the feel of a permanent squat. "I hope Maxim hasn't exhausted you?"

Maxim's ears turned bright red. "I was telling him about Kozorev," the boy mumbled.

"Ah yes, his discoveries are very important to our work. Come in, come in." A well-padded secretary stood when they entered. Everything was colored oxblood-red: the patterned plastic floor, the cabinets, the low couches.

"Tea?" she said. "Coffee?"

Samodelkin took off his fur hat and ushered Max into his office, which was colored light brown. Maxim followed on tiptoes. Samodelkin took out a model of a globe. There was a yellow arrow, cut from a piece of paper, glued to the Pacific Ocean, pointing East. A pink arrow over Africa pointed down. Samodelkin spun the globe, absent-mindedly.

"So you are making a Hollywood film about Larissa?" he said, looking keenly at Max.

Max nodded. "If we get the funding," he said.

"Yes," said Samodelkin, smiling sadly. "'If you get the funding.' I know all about this! But I suppose in Hollywood there is lots of money." Max shrugged in non-committal agreement. "And perhaps you can even help us with some of our funding problems."

Max shrugged again in the same way.

"Yes," said Samodelkin, thoughtfully. "You probably know all kinds of people … If you don't mind," he said, "I will give you a little background on myself, and our work."

"Please," said Max.

Samodelkin smiled, happily. His brown eyes held real warmth. "In fact, I am a cardiologist by training," he said. "In 1975, I was sent to the Arctic Circle to conduct government research on the effects of solar storms on cardiovascular health. You see, here, below the Arctic Circle, we are protected by a thick layer of atmosphere. So when there are solar storms, it does not affect us as much. But up there, the effects are quite palpable, like standing under an electric shower. Anyway, it was there, in Dixon, that I met my future boss, Vladimir Ilyich—'the Chief,' that's what we called him. The Chief was a great man, one of the founders of the Siberian Academy of Science here."

Samodelkin gave the globe another spin and sighed. "The Chief was conducting government research of his own. He was looking into an entirely different area: following Kozorev's ideas, he was studying the potential for communication via great distances, as well as what in the West you call telepathy—basically, the ability to travel across time and space in non-linear dimensions. He had worked quite closely with one of our local Siberian tribes, who are known as 'Time Travelers', and he believed that with enough research, we too could tap some of these secrets."

"I see," said Max.

"At first, I was skeptical. But the more I learned, the more I believed he was right. You see," Samodelkin spun the globe again, then stopped it with his powerful hand, held it still beneath his palm, "if you study solar storms, you begin to understand that the Western approach to the universe—that it is a three-dimensional place—simply does not account for reality. We all know that time does not move forward like it does on a clock: at a steady, regular pace. No, sometimes it flies, and sometimes it drags. But it does more than that, too. Time is made up of streams, many of them—something like an ocean, with currents. And you can ride, or 'surf' these currents, if you can catch them, backwards and forwards. Not only across time, but across space."

The secretary brought tea on a tray and set it down in front of them. Samodelkin thanked her heartily. He started spinning the globe again, and talking about vectors and magnetic pulls. Max couldn't follow him, though he tried.

"Let me tell you about one experiment we did, with the Chief. This was Soviet-funded, just before the USSR collapsed. We chose seventy-seven random symbols, which we sent to 5,000 volunteers across the Soviet Union. Then, on a given day, a computer randomly generated three of these symbols. We handed those three to a scientist who immediately took a seat in our 'Time Machine' in Dixon—I'll show it to you in a bit, it's not really a Time Machine, but that's what we call it, for simplicity's sake. We asked the 5,000 volunteers to write a letter and mail it to us, telling us which three symbols they saw. 80% of them saw the correct three. But this was even more remarkable—a third of them saw the symbols *before they were even chosen.*"

"Wow," said Max.

"This just illustrates that our official conception of time and space is totally inadequate. The ancient Siberian shamans have a much more realistic understanding of things, in fact. For example, have you ever had a dream about someone and seen them the next day?"

Max nodded: he had.

"Well, this is actually a very common phenomenon. But our society has no desire to understand it scientifically. It was different under the Soviet regime. But now, there is very little interest in this kind of research."

Outside, a storm had started. Max felt strangely at home here, safe from the cold and the buffeting winds, physical and figurative. He liked Samodelkin. "Another aspect of this non-Einstein-ian idea of the world is that we are all energetically interconnected. Relationships are a kind of energy. They form a bond that is, atomically speaking, real. You can be far away from someone geographically, but if you are bound to them emotionally, you are still connected."

Max thought of Rose, whose moods he could catch, sometimes, from the other side of the globe, and nodded.

"I remember the night that it all became clear to me," Samodelkin went on. "I was in Dixon, and the aurora borealis appeared. And I realized, I could talk with it. It was responding to my thoughts. From then on, I went to work for the Chief. It was as if he had passed me the baton—even then, he was getting older.

"In order to 'time travel' you must change the pull of gravity. Certain places on earth—ancient holy places, mostly, we work a lot in Bulgaria with ancient Thracian sites—have a lower magnetic pull. Of course, certain minerals help as well. Siberian diamonds, they're the best. Thanks to the Chief's connections, we were able to get several of those and conducted a number of experiments. Because of their magnetic valuations, they have a remarkable capacity for transmission—almost like radio crystals."

"Radio crystals," said Max. In his mind's eye, he saw the Agency's little in-house museum, tucked away in the corner of the lobby of The Flying Saucer. "But it must have been hard, to get the diamonds?"

"Yes, of course," said Samodelkin, warming to his subject. "Once, early in our work together, the Chief asked me to test artificial diamonds. Thanks to his connections, I traveled to Kiev, where there was a top secret diamond production facility. Yes, it is not widely known in the West, but the USSR was not only first in outer space. Naturally the diamond cartel was stymied by our mass-produced jewels. They called them 'beer-bottle bears,' because they were all the same. Even after they traced a single seam inside each and every silver bear, they could not understand—maybe they could not believe—that they were not natural. You should never underestimate the power of belief in this world, Mr. Rushmore."

Max nodded. "True enough," he said.

"You see, just as there are places where the earth's magnetism is weaker, there are also substances that, because of the way they are formed, can neutralize this magnetism. The Chief understood this. Diamonds, which are highly compressed, not only neutralized but reduced the magnetism. But of course, the Siberian diamond pipes were, unbeknownst to the world, relatively small and depleted within just a few years. So the question was asked: could the beer-bottle bears function just as well in regards to reducing magnetic energies as a 'real' diamond?" Samodelkin paused. His eyes held a melancholy, faraway look.

"Did they?" said Max.

"The beer-bottle bears?" said Samodelkin, turning back to Max. "No, they didn't work. Not at all. Their effect was almost nil. If only the diamond cartel had been able to apply that test! They would have seen that these were not diamonds made by time and pressure and the earth."

Samodelkin paused. "The Chief had a couple of Siberian diamonds, of course. Or else a comparison would have been impossible. But they were sold, one after the other. Funding, you see. We were trying to stay one step ahead. After the collapse of the USSR, we lost so much. The backing of the Institute, the Volga, our office space. For two years we were homeless. We had to leave behind a remarkable device, 'The Shaman Machine,' because it was too heavy to remove from the Institute's basement. It was a long, horizontal cylinder. When you lay in it, it changed the magnetic pull of the earth, and you could experience what Shamans experience: visions, mostly. And a deeper understanding of the pulse of the universe. It was a wonderful machine. With a fur-lined sleeping bag for warmth." He shook his head.

"Now, I wish I could have just one of those diamonds back. You see, diamonds are perfect for these sorts of studies. They are not just hard, but they have a stiff crystal lattice … in the Netherlands, a university physics department just proved that 'spooky physics' is real, using two diamonds they had 'entangled.'

The Dutch scientists placed one at either end of the campus, and the two diamonds vibrated at exactly the same time. As if they were not two objects any longer, but one."

"Wow," said Max.

"Yes!" said Samodelkin, rubbing his hands together. "Siberian diamonds, of course, are much more special. My own research has convinced me that the money we received in the sales of those diamonds is nothing in comparison to the progress we could make if we had the diamonds themselves. If we had a diamond, we could concentrate our work in a way that would get the attention of Western financiers." He shrugged and sighed. "In the meantime, we are developing a water that prevents aging, for sale in Germany."

"That sounds like a winning idea," said Max, thinking of the unbelievable bills that arrived for Rose's Pilates training. Had he paid them all? "People get out their credit cards for the fountain of youth."

Samodelkin smiled, ruefully. "We're banking on it," he said. Then he grinned. "Would you like to try the machine?"

"Uh, sure," said Max. "I mean, please."

With a long, heavy stride—as if he was walking through the forest—Samodelkin led the way through a beige plastic hallway through another door to a large, empty room with a low ceiling. A row of windows along one wall showed the treetops, bending and blowing in the wind. Covered in snow, the black boughs whipped up and down against a pale gray sky. Max thought, not for the first time, that it was no wonder the Russians were such avid explorers of the universe. They lived halfway to outer space most of the year.

At the center of the room stood a tall, round metal structure. It looked like a giant tin can, if you removed the top and bottom, then sliced it along one side and rolled it a bit into a kind of spiral.

"The metal spiral decreases the earth's normal magnetic pull—like a Siberian diamond would, but to a lesser extent. Still, the

124

spiral makes it easier for the person sitting inside to 'catch' a time stream, and ride it," said Samodelkin. "However, you have to be prepared. Meditation, yoga—we test when you are most susceptible to the pull of the moon. Going in cold, as you are, means you might not experience anything."

"Ah," said Max. He stepped up to the gap that was the entrance and jumped—a deep throated, animal howl sounded from the spiral's center.

Max quickly stepped back. His heart was racing. He looked over at Samodelkin, who was watching him quizzically. "Perhaps that is an invitation."

"Or the wind," said Max.

"Or the wind," said Samodelkin, with a smile.

Max approached the entrance again. Again, a howl rushed from the center of the spiral. Something—some kind of fear—resonated, like a guitar chord being strummed in his chest. Max walked inside.

At the spiral's center was a black office chair, on wheels. He sat. Overhead, he heard the howling, as if it was a storm passing over an ancient dwelling. Max stared at the aluminum wall in front of him. He heard Samodelkin switch off the lights and leave the room. Max began to feel very relaxed. At any rate, this was something to tell Rose about when he got home. His eyelids drooped. Suddenly, he saw a woman in front of him. She had a narrow back and a long elegant neck. Slowly, she rotated towards him. Max was not afraid. But his body was paralyzed. He could not have moved if he had wanted to. She looked up at him, from deep green eyes. Then he knew: it was Sonja Ostranova.

"Moscow," she said, her mouth moving slowly to form the words, as if she was underwater. It was her eyes rather than her mouth that said, "Help me." Max shivered. She said, "Midnight."

The lights went on and Max heard Samodelkin's deep, friendly voice. "All right in there? Twenty minutes, time is up."

Max noticed he was gripping the penknife with the embedded

diamond. He forced his fingers open, one by one, slipped the knife back in his pocket, and stood. As he emerged, he was trembling. "Did you see anything?" said Samodelkin.

Max shook his head.

Samodelkin laid a paw on Max's shoulder and thanked him for coming. "Normally, we would test you now, using an electromagnetic brain scanner," he said. "And this would tell us if 'nothing' really happened. But we are a bit low on funds at the moment and so…"

As the older man led him to the office's main door and held it open, Max caught sight of a bulky, muscular figure striding into one of the web designer's offices. Max shook Samodelkin's hand and said a quick goodbye. Then he made his way down the deserted hallway. At the door where he had seen the man go in, he sidled up along the wall. From the hall, he glanced into the room, hoping for luck. The man was talking to one of the programmers. As Max walked by, the man smiled. His teeth were gold, and a tiny jewel glinted in the front left tooth.

24

Gerard was getting nervous. It was a sensation he particularly hated, one that started in his bowels, a kind of ticklish sensation, then mounted, intensifying into a discomfort not unlike cats' claws, into his intestines. Indeed, when it got that far, Gerard had the feeling he could picture each part of his anatomy as clearly as if he were standing before a chart, like the one at the *lycée*, with each of the biological mechanisms that make up the human being clearly depicted in a colorful, old-fashioned pen-and-ink drawing.

Gerard seldom let it get that far. In fact, his entire life had been constructed, he could say, around the simple goal of not experiencing this sort of discomfort, which took him back to a helpless childhood state, made him again very short, unable to tie his own shoes, and subject to the every whim of his beautiful mother. His beautiful mother who, often as not, left him alone with the musty concierge or at the coat check for hours on end as she pursued her trans-European love affairs in hotels and *auberges* of varying quality, depending on the state of her relations at the time with her rich but estranged husband (Gerard's nominative father, though no one with any understanding of the situation—Gerard, from a very young age, included—could have much illusion that M. Dupres was the actual biological progenitor).

From his early teens, Gerard had carefully cultivated a life that would provide as few possibilities for anxiety as possible. He had wooed his aged father, who died when Gerard was sixteen and left him everything, thanks in large part to his son's assiduousness. He had been careful not to care very much about the women he was involved with, or for the friends he had made along the way. He had learned to play tennis well. He had chosen a route (business) that would ensure a certain standard of living without (thanks to his connections) much exertion on his part.

The thing about luxury, of course, is that one needs more and more to maintain an acceptable level of non-anxiety, and in the past years, he had forgotten himself a little. He had gotten in over his head, that was all. Then Sonja—that was a mistake, too. He saw that now, clearly. Eloise's fortune would very much supplement his own, rather diminished one. Why he hadn't seen earlier that this was the best route—! Some secret, adventurous, unsettled part of himself, perhaps the remnants of his maternal genes, had resisted it, but the scare he had gotten was more than enough to tamp that down, perhaps out of existence.

Why had he gotten involved with the Russians? Because he wanted a piece of PLUTO. Who wouldn't? But these double-crossing, good-for-nothing ... he was out of his element. He knew that now.

When he had gone to visit the storage site—that meteor crater—in December, everything looked fine. But 'Looks can be deceiving. – C,' as the first anonymous email had read. And they kept coming! Each more specific, and more disturbing, than the last. They talked about untreated plutonium, cancers, sleeping sicknesses. Always signed '– C'. Sleeping sicknesses! Gerard didn't know anything about 'C'. Or sleeping sickness. But he knew a lot about untreated plutonium. And if that came out ... it would be the end of PLUTO, and his career.

Gerard remembered a joke he had heard at the French Embassy in Moscow. How did it go? In Moscow, a government official is supposed to build an office. He goes to the Germans. They say, 'Two million.' So he goes to the Turks. 'One million.' Then he

128

goes to the Russians. 'Three million,' they say. 'One for you, one for me, and one for the Turks.' The Russians get the job.

"Darling?" It was Eloise. "Are you crying?"

She entered the living room of their Paris apartment like a cat, stood in the middle of the large, quiet room with the endless white walls, the white sconces, the wooden floors, and surveyed her domain. "Tell me," she said, finally, as Gerard failed to look up from the yellow divan across which he was lying, supine, dejected. "Tell me, what is the problem. I will help you fix it."

Gerard threw his hands over his face and groaned. Eloise stood, perfectly still. The sensation mounted, up into his gizzard. It was almost unbearable. He felt, then heard, a second groan emerge from his body. In his own ears, it sounded like 'PLUTO'.

Eloise had not moved. The white, quiet room was white and silent again. Gerard pictured Eloise, in his mind's eye: pink shirt, collared, buttoned down, white skirt. Her white silk slippers. The cashmere sweater thrown over her shoulders. Pearls, a single, exquisite strand, lying tranquil as the bottom of the sea along her pronounced collarbone. She ate almost nothing, and her skeleton showed, bird-like, through the smooth skin, bronzed, thanks to migratory trips around the world, all year. She was an excellent tennis partner.

The clawing grew worse. Then Gerard realized: Eloise. Of course. Eloise. Gerard saw, suddenly, his future before him, and it seemed to him to be a long, flat, open field, wheat colored, like the ones you see from the train on the way to the south, except that he was not looking down from a train window, not speeding past it, but standing on a dirt path, in the middle of this life that was ripening, ready for harvest, all around him.

Eloise, cool as a sprig of mint suspended in a pitcher of ice water, was somehow infused in every atom of this vision. And Gerard realized, for the first time, what it was to join his fate with hers, and he realized, at the same time, why he was doing it. Her coolness, precisely what had repelled him for so long, would get them through this. Would get him through it. That was why he had come to her, finally. And she had waited, she had waited because she knew he would. Gerard let a deep breath out, and took another in. Slowly, without moving, he resolved to tell her the entire story, from beginning to end. He would leave nothing out. Not even Sonja.

25

The room was brightly lit, and everything in it shone with a high polish. It might have been underground, or on the top floor of a skyscraper; like all rooms of its kind, it had no windows. It could have been in Beijing or Vancouver, Cape Town or lower Manhattan. They all looked alike.

Up and down the room, men in black suits bent over black velvet cloths. A constant mumble could be heard: "*Mazal und Bracha*," "*Mazal und Bracha*."

A man with a large belly—rumbling, thanks to the unfamiliar shrimp gruel breakfast—entered. He was special. A dapper Japanese man met him (this room happened to be in Tokyo). The proprietor of the business moved quickly and silently, and when he reached the large man he bowed. The two retreated to yet another room in the back.

"You wish to buy?" said the Japanese dealer.

The American nodded once. Yes.

The proprietor spread a handful of diamonds on the moss-colored cloth. They were stunning: large, pure, they caught the light, shone with all the colors of the rainbow, but with a mysterious blue flash at the end of each sparkle.

"Wonderful," said the Japanese dealer.

The big man across from him seemed to soften, ever so slightly. As if he was pleased. Then he offered a tenth of the market value—a laughably low sum. The Japanese dealer accepted, too quickly. "Normally, I would not sell for so little," he said. "But we have seen a good deal of these on the market lately."

The American's eyes shone with anger, but he said nothing. He paid, collecting the jewels in a mouse-gray chamois purse.

"*Mazal und Bracha*," said the Japanese dealer, using the phrase that concluded every diamond deal the world over. "Good luck, and blessings."

Mazal und Bracha, indeed, thought the fat man as he left. Someone is going to need more than good luck and blessings before I get to the bottom of this. It was his job, after all, to make sure that diamonds, the world over, maintained their proper price. And the only way he could have bought these specimens for so little was if there was a glut. And the only way there was a glut was if they were coming from the black market. And actually, the black market had been eradicated. If it hadn't been, the bottom would fall out entirely. There would be no money for anyone. If only that Ostranova woman hadn't died! It was really very inconvenient.

As the American left, one of the establishment's employees nudged the trainee standing next to him. "Do you know who that is?" he said, indiscreetly. If any of the higher-ups had heard, he would have lost his job. The trainee, no more than a boy, shook his head. "That's Mr. Diamond," said the older apprentice. "He rules this world. You've just seen the Emperor of the industry."

The trainee was impressed. The proprietor emerged and cast a glance in their direction. Both men went back to work.

26

Grigor stood in the predawn coolness looking up at the balcony, the line of glass panes like a set of crooked teeth. Fitting together, but you couldn't quite understand how it worked.

The moon was nearly full and cast a bright, otherworldly light on the street. It was a street he knew well, too well, probably; on every corner, in every doorway, he had a memory, if not many, layer upon layer. The math teacher's family lived there, Pasha, his childhood friend there, he and Masha had kissed there, once, before her exams. But in the moonlight the street felt as alien as another world, another planet. The puddles reflected the light back up, intensifying it, and he had to step into the shadow cast by the building for a minute to collect himself.

Grigor was happy. It was a feeling he was not used to in the last few years, since Masha died. Excitement, adventure—these things he had given up with his marriage as not suitable for a man with responsibilities. But Masha's death had released him from those vows, without giving back the impulse to behave like a young man again. What he wanted was what he had had, and it was gone.

Tonight, though, he was embarking on an adventure. There was no other way to think of it. An adventure! Even better, with the beautiful Dasha. She had come into his quiet life like a ... like a ... his mind searched for the right image, then settled on the full-page color photo of the first signs of a monsoon in Bangladesh in the science magazine he thumbed through down at the library. Those drops of rain, big enough to register in the photographer's lens. The wind whipping through the village, driving everyone ahead of it. The trees, long green leaves splayed out against the clouds. The darkened sky with a just a thin bright strip of gold in the distance, where the storm had still not reached. Like a monsoon! Kicking up air and dust and bringing water, water, water, transforming his world into ... he wasn't sure what. A river? Sludge? Something new and fresh? What did it matter! He gave up the monsoon image, stared up over the concrete roofs of the village's apartment buildings towards the moon, waited another moment, enjoying the night, the empty, tingling sensation in his chest, the little tickle, like the beginning of a laugh, at the base of his throat. She was like an alien, and the night was like another world, and Grigor picked up a handful of pebbles, just as they'd agreed to, and threw them softly against Dasha's window. *Taptaptaptap*, they sounded like falling rain. Or something less substantial—moonbeams, an astral storm. Then he waited.

*

Taptaptaptaptap, heard Dasha, a friendly patter against the window. Thank God. She knew he would come—still, knowing and experiencing were two different things. Silently, she stood up. She was already dressed, ready. Her landlady was snoring. Dasha slipped past the old woman and shut the door behind her. She walked downstairs, and there, outside, was Grigor, beaming. They greeted each other with their eyes and made their way to his car.

Only when they were inside, with the engine running, did they speak.

"Did she hear you?" asked Grigor. He was earnest, but he couldn't conceal his delight at their expedition. She smiled again, in spite of her nervousness. She thought, fleetingly, of Gerard—Gerry. He was so smooth, so elegant. She had really thought that she was in love.

"No," said Dasha. "Snoring."

Grigor laughed.

They drove in silence. Grigor knew his way along these uneven roads by heart. The moon was still so bright that the rutted lane, the trees in the distance, the wide swaths of field, were outlined around them. The sky was like nothing Dasha had ever seen, not even out on her old horse farm in Maryland. She bent forward to look up through the windshield, and Grigor did the same. Overhead, the light splashed across the sky, bright pinpoints that seemed to make the heavens transparent, full of depth, something weighty, but also light. Not the blank darkness of the cities in which she'd lived: Moscow, DC, in which the night sky was just an absence of sun. No, this was like a being, like a god, a universe unto itself. She sat back in the Lada's rickety passenger seat and sighed.

"Beautiful," said Grigor, his eyes again on the road. She nodded. After an hour, he turned suddenly to the left. He drove straight across a field and emerged onto a road of an entirely different sort: wide, well-paved, brand new.

"Ah ha," said Dasha. He nodded. After fifteen minutes, he pulled the car off the road and parked it out of sight behind an old shed. They continued on foot through the woods, an hour, then two hours. The birch trees—Dasha had forgotten how beautiful they were. The bark caught the moonlight and seemed to glow, like guideposts, showing them the way. Suddenly, their way was blocked by a fence. The fence was ten feet tall, brand new, chain-link.

"Don't touch it," said Grigor. He turned to the left and she followed. Here, they came upon a gap in the fence, small and round, like a human-sized mouse hole. "This is where the boys take the extra firewood home when the bosses aren't looking. And metal scraps. Anything they can get their hands on. They're paid decently, ok. But there have hardly been any jobs here for years, they've all got mouths to feed, and they don't know when the work is going to dry up. We'll go through—but it's electrified, or at least, it's supposed to be. Sometimes the electricity fails, anyway. But we don't need to find out."

She nodded and followed him though, lying down on her stomach and pulling with her arms. On the other side, they stood. Grigor whispered, "Wait." He disappeared into the woods, then came back, holding two navy blue work suits. He laughed. "The boys hid these in case they need to come back. Smart, they are! This should fit you, or nearly." Dasha pulled the suit over her jeans and sweater, and Grigor did the same. He nodded to her, and winked. They continued another hundred yards. The wood ended all at once. Grigor held up a hand.

"Follow me," he said. "First I will show you our most impressive local sight. Hold on to your hard hat!"

The sky was growing lighter overhead. Dasha shivered: the morning was cold. Grigor slowed, walking cautiously. Dasha had an eerie sense, as if the blackness ahead of them held a secret better left untouched. She hesitated for an instant. Then Grigor ducked and began to crawl on his hands and knees. She followed. When Grigor stopped, she stopped. They put their heads over what seemed to be a dirt rim. Below them yawned a vacuum. A black hole. An absence. It was unnatural, repellent. Yet, at the same time, it held an attraction, a fascination, as if it wished to suck everything that came near it down into it. She shivered.

"Well?" said Grigor. "What do you think of our top-secret local crater pit?"

He glanced at her—even in the dawn's pale light, she imagined, her face must be pale, slightly green—and he laughed. "You are impressed! I see! For a geologist of course it is interesting, even if they dug like cretins with no respect for maintaining the integrity of the mineral strata, et cetera. Still, you can make out certain things—for instance, if you look down, there, you can see a line of red. That is an iron deposit from the paleo age. If only we were officially allowed to study this instead of sneaking down here in the middle of the night! Oh, the theories we could refute! But we must be satisfied with what life gives us."

He stood and walked around the lip of the hole. Dasha followed. He took her, firmly, by the arm. "Be careful here—nothing is secured. Sometimes there are little landslides. If we fell in, no one would come for us, not in a hundred years."

"And now I will show you something interesting," said Grigor. He led her back into the woods, then across to another section of the mine. Below them, in a subsidiary pit, they saw what seemed, at first glance, to be a construction site. Cranes at the bottom. Metal pilings were stacked along the pit's outer edge. Three cement mixers sat at the bottom. Slowly Dasha started to see what it was that was wrong. Even though the lights were on, the place was deserted. More than that, everything was covered in dust, dirt, and grime, as if it hadn't been touched in weeks, or months, maybe longer.

"The boys were glad they'd been stealing in the end," whispered Grigor. "They stopped work one day nine months ago—just after the new year. Just like that." He paused.

Dasha nodded. The site's function was clear. But why had they stopped building? Where was the waste?

"They stopped building after the new year," she said. "Are you sure?"

"Of course I'm sure," said Grigor. "It's not such a big place, here. At least not as far as people are concerned. Even secrets are well known."

He motioned for her to follow him. As the sun rose over the gray, misty site, Dasha shivered. Finally, they stood in front of another pit. Here, concrete-covered waste containers were piled. Haphazardly. Even this far away, the heat they generated was palpable.

"We should leave," said Dasha. "Now."

Grigor nodded. "It's dangerous, yes?"

"Yes," she said, calculating the time it would take her to reach Moscow. "Yes."

27

It was not unusual for customers to travel days on end to come to Borya's establishment—the Fandorin Bar—so that wasn't what impressed him about the man at the table in the back of the room. It was a truly fine place, with a wall of great glass orbs so strong that nothing less than a bullet could shatter them (the one empty space on the wall, like a missing tooth, had in fact come about during an altercation between two visiting Mafiosi). At least half of the star-shaped lamps still worked.

What drew Borya to the man nursing a beer in the corner was something else. Foreign, sure. But sometimes they had that here. No, that wasn't it. Something in Borya's heart went out to that man in the crumpled jacket. Wanted to help. His first thought was of the prostitute who lived on the fourth floor. Not in the first flush of youth, certainly. But on hand. And in Borya's experience of life, both personal and on behalf of his customers, proximity counted among the greatest goods.

He had telephoned Lenka, who emerged from her lair on the hotel's fourth floor, her strawberry-blonde wig askew, and sauntered a bit unsteadily over to the table in the corner. The foreign customer didn't notice her at first. She sat on his lap and he looked at her in surprise. Then he shook his head, handed her a 500-ruble bill, and said something. She stood, tucked the bill into her ample bosom, walked away. In the lobby, she glanced at Borya, and spat.

Next he called Darenka. Maybe he had made a mistake with Lenka. She was too old. She had really gotten seedier as well—Borya hadn't noticed till now. Darenka was young, plump, with smooth skin and a big smile. She was just what the foreign customer needed! Darenka answered the phone, said she was putting her little one to bed. Kostya? Out, what do you think. Borya explained the situation. "Sure, sure," she said. "When the little one falls asleep I'll come by."

But no, he hadn't wanted Darenka either. She took the refusal more graciously than Lenka—no spitting—but she, too, was sent on her way.

There's no accounting for tastes, thought Borya, sweeping a bit behind the bar. There had been a real first-class fight in here the other night, and he was still finding shards of glass. If that maid, Dasha, hadn't left, he would have tried her. Something told him that the man would have liked Dasha. She had something—a past, you could tell. An elegance, even if she was just mopping floors. It was the way she mopped—cultivated. But she disappeared, without a word to anyone, what, three, four weeks ago? Just after the last vodka shipment, it was. Even Ancient Olga didn't know where she had gone.

Well! That was what happened, in a place like this. Nothing lasted. After this reflection, the barman had one of his brainwaves. What does a foreigner like? Other foreigners! That was when he called Heinzchik-the-German, Red River's resident outsider.

*

Max looked around at the Fandorin Bar, took a swig of beer, and sighed. He had felt positively elated when he found that both Bob Dominion and Volkov's map had disappeared. He had gotten that old Rushmorian feeling in his gut—the one that said, 'There's something here.' The one that said, 'Follow.'

So he had packed his things and caught the flight to Novosibirsk. From there he made his way by train and truck to Red River, the city Sonja had circled on the map.

Now he was here. He had refused Lenka and Darenka and

vowed that if the bartender sent him one more, he was going to punch him. Then a slim, pale, young-ish man appeared. His hair was a transparent light red, and his skin was lightly spotted with freckles. The bartender pushed him towards Max.

"He's a foreigner," said the bartender, with a friendly leer. "You're a foreigner!"

"Mueller-Heinz," said the man, in a clipped German accent.

"Rushmore," said Max. He turned to the bartender. "Two beers."

"Apparently, to the estimable Borya, you looked lonely," said the man, after Borya had retreated to the bar. He looked around the room, with its air of abandonment, and sighed. "In fact, I am a bit lonely myself."

"As long as you're not a small-town hooker," said Max. "I'm happy for the company."

Mueller-Heinz looked offended. "I am certainly not a hooker! I am an ecological consultant." He sighed.

"Call me Heinz."

"Isn't that your last name?"

"*Ja*. It's a long story. My parents they were of the '68 generation. My mother she had many lovers. But she promised to her mother on her deathbed, if she had a boy she would marry. My grandmother was very old-fashioned. She shouted, 'No son should be a bastard,' and ridiculous things of this nature. Her next demand was that my mother would name any son after her uncle—her mother's brother—who died in the war. As a matter of fact, he was held in a camp, not so far from here. For many years he survived. On his way home he was rolled over by a log falling off a truck. This is life!

"So none of the lovers wanted to marry. At the time it was not fashionable in those circles. So my mother married her friend, Mr. Heinz. And she named me Heinz. So have I got my name." He sighed again. "It is a burden. I suppose you are here because of the sleeping sickness, Mr. Rushmore?"

"Max," said Max. "What do you mean, sleeping sickness?"

"Ah," said the young man. "So you are not here to write about it? For the last months, everyone in the region has been falling asleep. Walking, or talking, or doing accounts—suddenly, they nod off, cannot be woken for days. From your slovenly manner of dress, I assumed you were a journalist. Forgive the mistake."

"No worries," said Max. "What's with the sleeping sickness?"

"No one knows," said the German, with a deep shrug of his narrow shoulders. "Some say it is nuclear waste from PO Box 23, just a hundred kilometers away. Others believe it is the earth spirits, angered by drilling. I have heard at least one scientist claim that it is a collective hallucination. Shall we have another beer? Actually I should not, as I have a proclivity to melancholy that is exacerbated by the drinking of alcohol. But as they say in America, 'what the heck?'"

"What the heck," said Max, and he called for more beer.

"I am a friend," said Heinz, "who works with brothers."

"Sorry?"

"I am a friend," repeated Heinz, with a slightly disconcerting precision, "who works with brothers. Who are friends with others. Who are looking into the unknown."

Finally Max got it: the BND always had obscure codes. Probably the result of Germany's overly humanistic education system. Everybody thought they should grow up to be Schiller.

"Ok," said Max.

"I believe you are in a position to help me," Heinz said. "One of our operatives has gone on leave due to the birth of his son. How do you call it, 'father-time'? And, annoyingly, this was not reflected in our calendar," he said, while his eyes glowed with brief anger. "And so we are short one man for a small research mission. We put out a call for assistance—have you seen this new app? Quite impressive, though in my opinion, entirely unsafe, data-wise—and your superior listed you as a non-op visiting this region on business. Timber, I believe it was?"

Max nodded. He hadn't told Dunkirk the deal fell through. Why should he? Anyway, it was a good chance—five days to see if he could pick up Sonja Ostranova's trail. If he could, who knew? Maybe they would give him his old job back. Or at least another gig. Heinz was still talking. "I was going to reach out to you, but here you are! And, what is more, I recognize you! From the fete at the American Embassy in Berlin, when your government served its guests so democratically with boxed lunches from Burger King."

Heinz took a moment to chuckle before he continued. "Here, I live in an entirely vegan manner. That party, it was my first furlough. I became absolutely ill from your Burger King! Regardless, I thought perhaps, since you are here and my supervisor has said he would not object, you could fill in. I"—here Heinz looked around the bar sadly—"am far too well known a figure to play any other roles, even in the next town but one."

"Guess we owe you one," said Max. "After the Burger King."

*

"Tails, Max," said Heinz, when they met the next night to debrief. In the interim, Max had gotten an electronic DGF ('Deniable Government Fungibility,' colloquially known as 'Don't give a fuck') go ahead from Dunkirk.

Now, Heinz swung his backpack over one shoulder as they walked away from town. The road was covered in a thin layer of dirt and ice. Overhead, the moon was flat and cold.

"Tell me," said Heinz. "What do you know?"

"Let's see," said Max. "After you run a fuel rod through a power station, there's always a waste product—a 'tail.' The tails contain spent uranium, and they're toxic. The dirty little secret of the nuclear era is that nobody knows what to do with this waste. In the US, we've got them lying around in fields, cooped up in metal drums. The problem is that the metal's rusting, and any

142

shifting runs the risk of releasing radioactive poisons into the air. Not to mention what would happen if an airplane crashed there. It's not ideal."

"Precisely," agreed Heinz, loping off ahead. Max shook his head and followed his German colleague.

"Western Europe is not better," Heinz was saying. "Germany made a couple of attempts to store waste on their own territory. As a child, I was always missing school in order to protest the storage in Gorleben. You should have seen the naïve artwork that came out of that period! 'No thank you, Nuclear Death,' crayon drawings of flowers and gas masks. My mother saved much of it. Sometimes, I think we should make an exhibit: 'West German Children's Art of the 1980s.' Well, that is neither here nor there. In the end, building storage sites is simply too expensive in Western Europe."

"The French just ship it to Russia, right? Let it stink up some godforsaken stretch in Siberia. Like this one."

"The Germans do this as well," said Heinz. "Or have done. And it is really a scandal. Not far from here there is a parking lot where tons of European waste is just sitting. The Europeans say it is the responsibility of the Russian firm to deal with it. The Russian firm, of course, does not care one bit. So it sits there. Terrible."

Max shook his head.

"In France, they 'treat' their waste in Normandy," Heinz said. "It is an amazing system. The trucks that bring the untreated waste travel along completely normal roads, with only a motorcyclist in front and in back. Traffic is normal. Everything is normal. It would be incredibly easy to attack one of these trucks. Or simply if there is a traffic accident—it is not a nation of drivers. Regardless, the treatment facilities remove a small percent of the uranium and recycle this. Then, they wrap the rest of the waste in concrete and ship it to Africa and Siberia."

"Sounds awful," said Max.

"Yes," said Heinz. "But unfortunately no one cares. There

are other models as well, of course: your country, for example, has come up with an alternate approach. Twenty years ago, the Russians agreed to take your highly enriched uranium—the substance that goes into weapons of mass destruction—and downgrade it for you. The low-grade stuff is sent back to the USA. In fact, it is this low-grade uranium that keeps your country's air conditioners working. Twenty per cent of American power comes from Russian-processed nuclear waste."

Max whistled in the moonlight. "I did not know that."

"Yes, our fates are always more closely intertwined than we realize. But enough of that. In the last decade, Russia has significantly increased their intake of tails. The question is: why?"

"It's not particularly lucrative," said Max. "Unless . . ."

"Exactly," said Heinz. "They lost their major sources of uranium when the USSR broke up."

"So they might be running out," said Max. Heinz nodded. "So the West dumps their old tails, and the Russians scrounge for uranium?"

"Perhaps," Heinz said, nodding. The moon had grown fatter. Now, it seemed to hang directly over them, lighting the softly waving wheat stalks like a giant lantern.

"Dirty," said Max.

"But legal," said Heinz, sadly. "Under international law. However, should we be able to discover that the French," again his eyes darkened, "are helping the Russians use Western tails to process weapons-grade uranium, then we could take action. With proof, we could even send a report to Brussels!"

"That's where I come in?"

"Yes. Red City was built to process weapons grade uranium. But they powered down the processing plant in the '90s. Started making kitchen equipment to keep the town running. Now, the French have struck a deal there. They're building a new high-tech processor for tails, one that will harvest the leftover uranium more efficiently. As long as what they're enriching is for civil use, it's ok, legally. Though to be honest, especially now that my country has decided to shut down its nuclear plants, we don't like it. It's not safe and not healthy. Do you know that to this day in Bavaria you cannot eat the wild boar? Chernobyl rained down radiation particularly badly in that area. And mushrooms, this you can forget about eating! You see what I mean."

Max nodded.

Heinz continued. "Right now, the French are the only ones on the ground everyday. Sure, sure. Your NNSA inspectors come, but they might be treated to a Potemkin village, for all that we know. That's why we decided to—how do you Americans put it? 'Maximize our strengths,' and get our own partnership going. But then my colleague," the anger surfaced again, "he is on father-time. And our meeting is for two days from now. You speak German, yes?"

Max nodded.

"Really, you need do almost nothing. Just make the first contact. We'll have a permanent person come out next time. We just need someone to shake hands. So, we have—how do you say it? 'A deal?'"

"Sure," Max said. "You got a deal."

28

It was only a hundred kilometers from Red River—the real city, the one you could find on any map—to Red City, the first of the secret cities. Traveling these one hundred kilometers, you passed from the world that existed into another zone—or, rather, a series of zones, where different rules applied. Red City was Control Zone B—which meant that you weren't allowed to travel there without special permission, but there was no fence, no checkpoint. If you were Russian, you could get away with it most of the time. If you were a foreigner, you had better have the right papers.

Thanks to Heinz and the BND, Max had the right papers. Atom Town was Control Zone A—which meant that it was surrounded by a guarded wall, or electrified fences, and you had to prove you were allowed in. Then, of course, there was the Forbidden Zone. Here, in the 1950s, one of the Soviet Union's worst nuclear disasters took place.

The little hotel room was narrow like a monk's cell. The flowered wallpaper was peeling, and underneath he could see newspapers that had been used to buffer the glue. Brezhnev's news, suspended not in amber but in glue. Max showered in the shared bath stall in the anteroom. The tiles were disintegrating, as if they were returning to the earth.

In the morning, Max leaned on the desk of the reception area. Behind glass, a woman with purple curls slowly tapped numbers into a large gray phone. When she finished her business, she peered up at him. He handed her the letter Heinz had printed out in an internet café.

"Can you tell me," he said, "how to reach this address?" He spoke broken but adequate Russian, and frequently switched to German. She studied the paper, eyes squinting behind jeweled bronze frames. Powder stuck in the lines of her face. She picked up the phone and dialed, slowly again. When she placed it back on the receiver, she said, "Wait, please. The driver will pick you up in ten minutes."

The driver arrived forty minutes later. The threadbare tires of his Honda let off a smell of burning rubber as he hit the brakes. The radio was on full volume.

The headquarters of Red City Toaster were on the third floor of a building whose crumbling mural had fewer tiles than spots where tiles had once been. The elevator was broken, so Max climbed the stairwell. He knocked and a short, bald man with a nearly perfectly round figure looked up. He was wearing a brown suit with wide lapels; a small, square, golden pin glinted from the left one. On closer inspection, Max saw that the gold pin was shaped like a toaster.

"Did you receive my letter?" asked Max. The man shook his head. "That is a shame," said Max. "I was afraid that would happen. No matter. I am Gerd Schroeder, of Schroeder Toasters."

"Victor Girin," said the man. "Here, I am known as 'Mr. Toaster.'"

"A pleasure," said Max. "Let me introduce my firm, please. We are a small, but if I may say so myself, solid producer of toasters, with clients worldwide. Our home base is Guetersloh, a charming place unfortunately largely destroyed in the war. My great-uncle first began building toasters, converting the smithy into a modern electrical goods producer. We want to expand, into the East, but to do so we need a reliable partner. I am traveling across the country and looking for potential partners. So far, I do not mind saying that I have not found the company I am looking for."

Victor had taken a seat behind the only desk in the little room and crossed his hands. He rested his chin on the backs of his surprisingly long fingers and let out a long, sad sigh. Instead of responding, he bent down and rummaged around under the desk. Max heard the clinking of glass. The man placed a bottle and two cloudy shot glasses on the desktop. He poured in silence, then handed Max a glass. "To health," said Victor. His lapel pin caught the light as he lifted his arm.

He refilled the glasses. The light filtered into the room through glass caked in dust, wafted over a miniature jungle of nearly translucent spider plants. "Guetersloh ..." he said, his voice filled with longing and sadness. "If I close my eyes, I can nearly picture it. How I would like to see your factory ..."

"*Ja*," agreed Max. "We modernized much of the process before my father's death, and have not had cause to regret it. We Germans have a long tradition of handcraft, as you know. The land is poor, and we have had to make the most of our resources. Always, you understand."

The head of Red City Toaster nodded. "In Russia," he said, pouring out another round, "We are not blessed with scarcity. Our woods, our soil, our streams—God made them rich and plentiful. To allow us to become a nation of profligates."

Max shrugged, a slight, two-shouldered shrug that expressed the idea that no man can understand God's designs. Then he stood and walked to the splintering lacquered cabinet that took up one wall of the room. "May I?" he asked, and receiving an encouraging nod, he opened the glass doors. He took out first one steel toaster, then the next, taking care to admire each and every knob, lever, and curve of the Red City Toaster's three commercial models. Finally, Max took a seat. "Yes," he said. "Fine."

His interlocutor beamed. "Would you like a tour of the Red City?"

Gerd Schroeder spread out his hands, palms up, in an expression of deep gratitude that was understood, completely, by his host.

*

The Lada put-putted its way across the massive industrial territory, as Mr. Toaster (as Max thought of him) pointed out points of interest among the cavernous warehouses; one with a metal awning twisted as if by a hurricane, another whose broken windows were patched in wood and tinfoil. "There, our French friends have set up shop—those are the Dynacorp silos," said Mr. Toaster. "They laugh at us, of course, with our toasters. They say, this is a nuclear town, why are you making toasters? But I say, demand for nuclear is only as strong as the government that wants it. Whereas a toaster—every housewife in the world wants a toaster. It is, how do you say, eternal?"

"I couldn't agree more," said Max. "War comes and goes. Breakfast remains."

Mr. Toaster clapped him on the back. Then he sighed. "I can only imagine how it looks to you, Mr. Schroeder from Guetersloh!" Max ducked his head once, in acknowledgment. "My family is from the south of Russia, originally," continued Mr. Toaster, over the noise of the engine as the car rattled over the uneven surface. "In the war, it was nothing like in the Soviet history stories. Half the village collaborated with the Germans. My father told me about it as he was dying. He lay in my arms and remembered. The farmers, the Soviets had taken their farms, he said, so they were happy with the Germans. And our family, we had a good house. So one of the German officers was billeted there. And my father remembered scenes, like a movie, as he was dying. Playing cards with the officer. The stakes were the Finnish butter the Germans received as rations. It was sent from Finland in a special package. My father still remembered it exactly, this waxed paper. And he said he realized, later, that the officer was letting him win. In order to give him the butter. '*Ach, du kleine millionaire*,' the officer said. My father remembered that phrase, as he lay dying. '*Ach, du kleine millionaire*.'" They had reached a warehouse that looked as tumbledown as all the rest.

A barrier lifted, and the Lada driver passed through. "Later, they were sent to Ukraine, the whole family. To work on a farm. They were slaves, essentially. But because they were close to the land, they got enough to eat. It's the only reason they survived."

The car stopped, and the two men got out. They approached a glassed-in booth. Mr. Toaster spoke to the woman inside. Without a word, she handed him an aluminum canister about the size of a toothbrush travel case. A string ran from the side, across the top, and was fastened in place by melted wax, stamped. Mr. Toaster twisted the cap off, breaking the wax seal. "An old-fashioned security technology," he said, pulling out a key, "but still effective."

"R&D, production, distribution," said Mr. Toaster as they entered a hall the size of an airplane hangar. The Russian's pin glinted, again, as he gestured at the hall's contents: a mass of pipes and belts and ancient metal presses, wizened, bulky, like a monument to a dead civilization, or the end of the world.

"*Ja*," said Max, with a single nod. He followed Mr. Toaster into the ruins.

"This," said Mr. Toaster, indicating a steel press with a lever for manual operation, "came from Germany. Requisitioned after the war. Still perfectly functional." Max regarded it like a long lost relative he was not particularly anxious to rediscover. He let his eyes travel once again around the room. Metal sarcophagi, big enough for a family, painted forest green. Rickety staircases leading to patched metal tree houses. Everything spoke of the machine age, as operated by hand: wheels for turning, knobs for pulling, levers to make things stop and go. Narrow metal towers reached towards the ceiling, dented and discolored with age. Broad metal conveyors stretched towards the horizon, equally battered. One machine, towards the back of the warehouse, caught his attention. It was slick and white, shiny and, in comparison to its neighbors, looked positively space-aged. 'Dynacorp,' it read, in blue.

"What's that?" Max asked.

"Ah! That! It is our pride and joy," said Mr. Toaster, with a smile that lit up his entire being. "A laser cutter powerful enough for a diamond! We got this machine at a bargain price. So sophisticated that it will cut within one-thousandth of a centimeter of precision or, with the proper technical adjustments performed by my grandson, create a Red Toaster modulator. So that your toast may be dark brown, medium brown, light brown, or just a little bit warmer than before—'touched by the breath of an angel' as my wife says. Magnificent!"

"It cannot really cut a diamond," said Max.

"No, no, that's just an expression we use around here."

"Why? There are no diamonds here."

"Of course not. The diamond mines are all in the north. Well, there is a crater not far from here—on the way to Atom Town. A meteorite struck, eons ago. Those often form diamonds, but nothing really worth digging up. Anyway, it is only the old women from the countryside who say there are diamonds buried in the crater. The same old ones who say they can time travel. You cannot take anything they say seriously, of course. My wife believes all of that. But it is not scientific."

"Of course not," said Max. "Though we must let our women have their little dreams. Regardless, it is a wonderful laser."

"Yes! It's just like I was saying. The curse of abundance, again! They have too much money in Atom Town, because of this French investment. So they buy machines they do not need!"

"Indeed," said Max. "The French are another kind of people entirely. But it is lucky for you."

He grinned. "For us, the timing was absolutely perfect. This machine has taken our little production line from adequate to outstanding. One day, I hope every housewife in Russia will use a Red City Toaster."

Gerd Schroeder admired the machine as if it were a racehorse: with distance, care, and respect for both its delicacy and its power.

"Atom Town," he mused. "That's a closed city."

"Yes," Mr. Toaster said. "I haven't been there myself. Of course the life inside these closed cities, it is always strange. Generations of people living in places that do not officially exist. Such suspicion, such secrecy. There was a sociologist in Atom Town who wanted to study what happens to people when they live like that. Nadezhda Levantal was her name. She did not get permission. Instead she became an environmental activist. Stirring up problems for the most part. Imaginary illness and so on. Make-believe stories. You wouldn't believe what they say! For example, this year, the story is that everyone in Atom Town has been struck by a sleeping sickness. That the entire city has fallen asleep! Next they will be saying that a thorn-bush has grown over the place and only the kiss of a prince can wake them." He grinned. "You see, I know the German fairy tales, Mr. Schroeder. Regardless, that is what it is—a fairytale. Plain and simple."

He shook his head and shrugged again: toasters, not diamonds, were his business. Nothing could compare with a nicely browned slice of bread. Mr. Toaster beheld his new machine, again, with reverence. "For us, it was a miracle. Who knows how the Lord works? In mysterious ways, Herr Schroeder, in mysterious ways."

*

After he left Mr. Toaster, Max used his thumb and forefinger to pop the back off his low-tech phone. He took out the battery and slipped his Chinese SIM card into the slot. He reassembled the phone. Two loud beeps rewarded him. From the backseat of the car, he asked his driver to drop him at the movie theater.

"What do you want to go to the movies for?" asked the driver. "Your hotel, it's luxury. You got TV, twelve channels. The movie theater, all they play is old junk. No action, no nothing."

Gerd Schroeder did not bother to refute this. "Please, to take me there," was all he said, in more broken than usual Russian. "I am, of cultural interest."

152

The driver shrugged. "By the way," he muttered, "when you go home, tell your NATO to stop expanding. Why are you threatening Russian territory? We're a sovereign nation! Warmongers, that's all you are, in the West. But we beat you once. Don't forget that."

Gerd Schroeder inclined his head respectfully, and the driver cooled down.

The road from the industrial area to central Red City was absolutely banal. Stretches of bare land interspersed with anemic forest. The road itself was rutted, and the driver, who had lost interest in politics, had to swerve now and then to avoid the worst potholes. There was no oncoming traffic. To either side, there were signs that this route had once been closely watched: lampposts at odd intervals, tell-tale mounds in the earth. Now, the listening posts looked abandoned. But those looks might be deceiving. Even relatively low-tech Soviet-era technology would be capable of listening in on any conversation they had now. As early as the '40s, captives in one of Stalin's *shurashkas*—prison camps for scientists—had come up with a way to identify voices based on the way a window vibrated.

Red City was upon them, suddenly. Small, neat, faded. Sleepy. Instead of advertisements, there were slogans. 'Trust in Cadres,' read one. 'It will always be October.' Even the inhabitants looked like they had been transported from another time: matrons moved slowly in mauve prints and sensible shoes; men in hats, despite the afternoon's fine weather; children playing on the sidewalk. "Us against Them," said the driver, with a laugh. "That's what we used to play."

They passed a series of squat, tattered office buildings, to a series of nearly identical squat, tattered apartment houses. At the center of the city was a large roundabout from which Lenin himself peered down on the uneventful proceedings below.

In front of the Comet movie theater, the driver stopped. Max paid him extra for the ride and asked him to meet him in two hours, when the movie was finished. The driver shrugged.

The lobby ceiling was hung with shooting stars, most of which had lost part of their tails. Only half the lights worked. The café in the corner was shut up, its chairs stacked. The ticket taker was absorbed in her iPhone. Max had to knock on the glass before she noticed him. He bought his ticket and went inside.

The lights were already down, and it took a few moments for Max's eyes to adjust. He walked to the back row, like the text message instructed. He saw a lone figure there, in seat 4. Scanning the rest of the theater, he saw that there were only two other people there—a pair of elderly women, sitting in the first row, peering up at a huge black-and-white reel of the Potemkin steps. The triumphal soundtrack of 'The Battleship Potemkin' blared. Max sat next to the woman in the back.

A proud military march played. In the dim light, Max observed her. She must be nearly seventy. Portly, in a comfortable way. She held her head aloft: still interested in the world. Observant. Open. Intelligent. She wore a turtleneck. As they sat, Max could feel the fear radiating from her. In waves.

"Should we go somewhere?" he murmured.

She shook her head. "This is best. Those old birds up front, they're completely deaf."

Max waited for the secretary of World of Hope to speak. On screen, the Czar's men were attacking. A solid line of black uniforms. Moving inexorably forward. Bringing death. He kind of liked this movie. Eisenstein, he once learned, had an un-Soviet habit of drawing dirty cartoons. Bulls having sex with men on crucifixes, pregnant cows being penetrated by woodpeckers. Silly stuff. Oddly sweet. Hushed up, of course. The director of the Hermitage had a secret collection in the archives.

"You're completely mad to come here," she said. "You'll probably be arrested."

"Let me worry about that," said Max.

She shook her head, once. Max handed her the photo of Sonja and Gerard.

"Is that Nadezhda Levantal?" he asked.

Slowly, her hands shaking, she took a pair reading glasses from her purse. She placed them on her nose. She held the photograph closer to her face. Her features softened. "No," she said. "They look almost exactly alike. But no." She sighed, deeply. "Nadya has a beauty mark, here, just under her left lip. No," she said again. "That's not Nadya."

She handed Max the photo and he studied it again. No beauty mark. In the front row, the two old ladies gasped. In spite of himself, Max looked up at the screen, where the baby carriage was poised, for a moment, at the top of the steps. As it plunged down, he turned back to his companion. "And him?" he said.

She shook her head. "I don't know him."

"Have you heard of Dynacorp?"

"Of course," she said. "Though we know very little. Dynacorp is storing waste here. Beyond that, I know even less, now. Since Nadya left, we don't know how intently they watch me. So for now, most communication is broken. It's better for our cause."

"Why did you agree to see me?" asked Max.

From the front row, a wail went up. The World of Hope's secretary ignored it. She turned her full attention on Max. "I was there, in Chernobyl. I was part of the clean-up. I saw what happened. I saw how they plied the men with vodka, said it would protect them. How they left barrels of rubbing alcohol outside the work stations, and told them to douse their bodies in it. As if it was enough. It wasn't enough. I saw that, too. Men whose flesh melted right off their bones. Later, after they had been paid and sent home. Men whose organs came up through their mouths, choked them. And the wives. Weeping." The woman's fear had disappeared. Even in the darkness of the theater, Max saw her eyes flash. With both hands, she grasped her turtleneck, pulled it down. A raw red scar zigzagged her throat. "Do you know what that is?" she whispered.

Max caught his breath. "A Chernobyl necklace," he said.

"That's where my thyroid was," she said. "I'm lucky just to have a necklace."

She paused. "For a long time, I thought it was my duty. To be quiet. To be patriotic. Then I met Nadya—Nadezhda Levantal. She grew up in Atom Town. When she learned what had happened, why her father died, her grandmother, she wasn't silent. She fought it. She changed my life."

"She must be a remarkable woman," said Max.

The secretary nodded. "I don't know how much longer I have. But I am going to use the time that is left me to work against this silence. This acceptance."

She stiffened, dropped her hands. Two men had entered the theater. They sat in the middle row. "You'd better go," she said.

"Thank you," said Max. "Thank you for meeting me."

With that, Max stood and left the theater. In the lobby, he blinked. The ticket taker didn't look up, not even when a young man appeared at Max's side. In a low, threatening voice, he said, "Come with me, Mr. Schroeder. Quietly, if you please."

Max didn't feel the gun as much as sense it. Heinz had given him good papers, it was true. But still, this provincial FSB officer could do anything he wanted with him.

*

"Mr. Schroeder," said the FSB officer, once they were comfortably seated in his Hyundai. "Please show me your papers."

Max took them out and handed them over. The kid was about twenty-five, with a snub nose and a not unintelligent look in his eyes. Dark hair, pale skin. Healthy looking. Zealous. He took his time reading through them. He turned the key in the ignition without handing the papers back to Max. As they pulled away from the theater, Max saw the former secretary for World of Hope leaving. The two men were with her, one on either side. She walked between them with a hard-bitten pride. Head up. Turtleneck covering her hard-won necklace. "Don't worry about her," said the FSB man. "She'll be fine. What about you, though, Mr. Schroeder?"

"What about me? I do not understand the meaning of all this. I have filled out the correct forms. Why are you arresting me?"

"I'm not arresting you," said the man. "But what are you doing at the movies?"

"I admire and respect the work of Sergei Eisenstein," said Max. "'The Battleship Potemkin' is a landmark work. It redefined modern cinema."

"Why did you leave in the middle?"

"I felt sleepy," said Max.

They reached the roundabout now. Lenin looked on as they circled once. "What are you talking to that old troublemaker for then?" said the young man, with a sudden, ugly sneer. "All of this so-called radiation sickness—it's just a bunch of freeloaders who want to live off the state. You don't really believe them, do you?"

"I am primarily interested in toasters," said Max, with an intimation of trouble. Behind them, a car started honking. The young man glanced in the mirror, swore, and pulled over. He didn't kill the engine. The other car parked. An older man got out, walked over to them.

"What the hell are you doing?" he said.

The young man looked abashed. "Questioning a suspicious foreigner," he said, turning pale.

"What the hell, Leonid," he said. "Give me his papers."

The young man turned them over. The older man pointed in anger at the signature. "Look," he said. "Who okayed this? You, me, or your grandmother?"

"You," said the young man softly.

"So back off! Mr. Schroeder," he said, ducking his head at the window, "please accept my apologies. And say hello to Mr. Mueller-Heinz. It's always a pleasure doing business with him." Max nodded his head once in acknowledgement. "Leonid here will take you back to Red River. I think you're at the Sunrise Hotel?"

Max assented again. They drove the rest of the way in silence.

★

At the Fandorin Bar, Borya had created a new cocktail: 'Sleeping sickness special'. Three shots of vodka in a water glass. Well, he thought, you've got to keep up with the times.

Heinzchik wasn't interested. Well, who could expect a foreigner to understand. He ordered two bottles of beer.

When the other man showed up, Heinzchik lit up like a fireworks. Well, that's how foreigners were! They just loved to talk to each other. If Borya had to go to some other country (God forbid!), he would probably feel the same way about meeting a fellow Russian. Even if the man was from Moscow.

When Max arrived at the Fandorin, Heinz was waiting. "Your FSB colonel saved my skin," Max said.

"Good," said Heinz. "That was his job. He doesn't like that little upstart any more than we do."

Max shrugged. Then he told Heinz what Mr. Toaster said. Heinz was beside himself with the news.

"Dynacorp—in Atom Town? Are you sure, Max, absolutely sure?"

"That's what the man said," he replied.

"Atom Town! That's absolutely closed, you know. Absolutely!"

Max pulled out his penknife and opened two beers. Gennady's wax still blunted the sheen of the jewel. Max turned it over, thoughtfully. He wondered what Rose was doing right now. She would like a diamond, he bet. When he got his career back on track, that was the first thing he was going to do. Buy Rose a great big diamond.

"Your knife is not, how do you say, politically correct?" said Heinz.

"True," said Max. "Truer than you know."

PART IV

PART IV

29

The airport was basic. Max bypassed the one-room building that constituted the lobby and made his way straight out to the tarmac. Two loaders were arguing. "Let's have a drink first, vodka protects against radiation poisoning."

"Work protects against starving to death."

"Fuck you."

"Fuck you."

"Fuck you, let's have a drink. Then we'll work"

"Ok."

Max strode across the empty strip to the sole aircraft—an army green propeller plane. Groceries were being loaded into it. The pilot was standing to one side, smoking. Taking a chance, Max approached him. He switched to his perfect Russian. "Any chance I can catch a ride?" he said. "I've been abroad. Now I want to visit my grandmother."

The pilot was a gray-haired man with epaulettes on his thick coat. The sun had come out and was shining on a cold, white day. Winter had arrived, along with a dusting of snow. Max did a quick calculation of his remaining cash and offered half of it.

The pilot shrugged, took the money. "You can sit in the back," he said. "On the toilet paper." Then he grinned. "Best seat in the house."

Max climbed into the hold, found the toilet paper. Made himself comfortable. His view consisted of a pyramid of canned seaweed.

The flight lasted four hours. Before they landed, the pilot shouted back to him to hold his horses and wait till he told him to jump. Max agreed. The landing was bumpy behind the toilet paper as the hold was unloaded. When the pilot gave the signal, Max jumped down. The airport here was pitch black. He hitched a ride with the truckers who dropped him off at a roadhouse just outside of town.

The roadhouse was a rough place, part way station, part brothel. Max rented a bed by the hour and took a seat at the bar next to a man slumped against the wall. He ate a tough steak and drank a half-toxic local beer. Nothing had tasted so good in a long time.

On his third beer, the man next to him stirred. His clothes were caked in dirt. He invited Max to buy him a beer. Max complied. The man warmed up. "Do you know," he asked, eyes burning like coals beneath a fringe of black hair, "what time is?"

"Time is a landscape," said Max. "That you can walk back and forth, back and forth, across."

"Thassright," said the man, and went back to sleep.

The next morning Max hitched a ride with a trucker into town. The temperature was minus fifteen. At the clothing store on the main square, he bought a heavy black coat, a nylon cap, gloves and woolen socks. "Bags got stolen," he explained to the clerk. "Back on the train. Middle of the night. Had to fly here without a coat."

"Bad luck," said the clerk. "My mother-in-law, they took her shoes once. Her own fault. You've got to put them under your head when you sleep."

Thus equipped, Max made his way across the square to the Diamond Hotel. In his room, he showered and looked out the squat window. The square, the hotel, the shabby shopping center. It looked like any other city of its kind. But everything here was built on steel supports, giant bars that sunk deep into the earth to keep the buildings from sinking into the mud during the short summers when the tundra defrosted. In the winter, it got so cold that rubber broke like glass. Sure, Diamant was no Mirny—that city was built right on the edge of Earth's third largest hole, so enormous that airplanes couldn't fly overhead without the danger of being sucked down, into the vortex. Diamant's mine was smaller. But the jewels discovered here were of such high quality that over the years, Diamant had drawn Russia's best jewelers. Raw diamonds from other Siberian mines were still sent here to be cut and polished. So the lifeblood of the place hadn't run dry along with the mine.

Overhead, the mid-morning sky darkened with the promise of snow. Downstairs, in the bar, Max bought a pack of cigarettes. He had quit, officially. He walked out to the square. In a corner, he squatted on his haunches. Lit his cigarette, inhaled. The question was, what was he going to do next?

"Brother! Can I shoot a cigarette?"

Max looked up—for a moment he thought he was hallucinating. A young man in a racing hat was balancing on the pedals of a bicycle, which made him seem even taller than he was. Something in Max's startled expression must have encouraged him, because, grinning, he climbed off the bicycle and let it slide over the ice a little. Max offered him the pack. "Take it," he said. "I don't smoke."

"No, no, no!" said the young man, with skin glossy with good health and long athletic limbs. "Me too, I don't smoke! Just this one cigarette, I shoot from you. Thanks."

He took one, lit it, handed Max back the pack, then extended his hand. "You can call me Alosha," he said. He looked out over the square. "I grew up here. This place is dead! I tell you, there is nothing happening. But I can't go home! My girlfriend, last week, she moved to my place. Now she is living in my house!" He grinned and made a motion to grab his head in both his hands. "She is talking all the time to my grandmother! She is driving me crazy!"

Max shrugged in sympathy.

"My girlfriend, she's a programmer, she can work anywhere," he said glumly. Then he brightened. "You married?"

"Yep," said Max, as an image of Rose, smiling as she tied an apron around her waist, bubbled up in his conscious.

"Can't be helped! Sooner or later." Alosha grinned again. "I'm an electrician. At work, I'm the boss! I come when I want to. Ten

163

o'clock, maybe. I tell my workers, 'You do this, you do that!' They come at nine! Afterwards, I ride my bike around. Snow, ice, I don't care. It's a good life. But I thought it would not be so boring. You been in the army?"

Max assented, bemused. Alosha continued.

"I remember, in the army. I had to go, I was eighteen. When we got there, they didn't give us shoes the right size. And they all—" He grabbed his foot and made a motion as if to pull apart the shoes and the soles. "So what do we do? We wait, until the officers are asleep. Then we sneak in at night and steal better shoes. Sometimes, we get away with it. Sometimes, we get punished. Then, we had to cut the lawn. With toenail clippers!" Alosha hung his head. Then he looked up and smiled. "Best two years of my life!"

Max grinned, now, too. Across the square, sheltered in an abandoned shoeshine kiosk, a man started to play guitar.

"You want to know what's going on in this town?" said Alosha.

"Sure," said Max.

"See that guy playing the guitar? He's doing *halturka*—you know *halturka*? Extra job after work to earn small money? Used to be only professors and engineers. Now even the crooks! We got some big crooks in this town I tell you! But here, Diamant, even mafia got to play guitar for money. Why? I tell you why, Max. Because there are no more diamonds in this place! Fifteen years ago, the mine ran out. What do mafia do? They play guitar. 'Stairway to Heaven'. *Halturka*. You want to know a secret, though?"

Max said he did.

"I got two secrets. First one, you and me, let's go into business. I got a good idea. We make something for tourists. Ghosts! Tourists like ghosts. So we gotta get a castle. Maybe in Scotland? I think that's a good spot for tourist-ghosts. So, Max, you buy a castle. I get a sheet. I cut the eyes out, I work for you, ghost!" Alosha the electrician slapped Max on the back. "I don't drink, I quit smoking, you won't be sorry. I already got sheet. You just get castle, you let me know."

"What's the other secret?" asked Max.

"They got more diamonds, down there! That the mafia isn't going to need *halturka* much longer. Nope, only the electricians are going to need to play ghost for tourists. Don't forget, right Max? Don't hire anybody else. I'm the best ghost you're going to find."

"I won't forget," said Max, who was now watching the guitar player with more interest. The man seemed to notice the attention, and smiled. He had a mouth full of gold. A little white spark glinted from the front left tooth. Strange, thought Max. Hadn't the man in the corridor at Samodelkin's had the same smile?

"There is nothing to do here!" said Alosha. "But I can't go home yet. And you're a tourist, you got to make an experience. We got no tourist office. I guess it's up to me. If I do a good job, you're gonna buy that castle, right? I got to get out of here. I already fixed up two rooms for my grandmother. Wallpaper, new cabinet, I built it myself. You got another cigarette for me, brother? Thanks. So, what I'm thinking, I can show you the only site we got here."

"The mine?" said Max, not quite believing his ears. "But, how?"

"Easy," said Alosha. "Of course it is not allowed. Also, not possible. But there's a service elevator. I found it on my bike, one night. For me, it's no problem. I'm a master electrician! I can turn it on. We go down. We see what we find! Oh, why is my girlfriend so boring? She never wants to do anything with me." He shook his head mournfully. "Anyway, it doesn't matter. It's better to do something like this with men! Just men. It's dangerous! Let's go!"

"Ok!" said Max, standing up.

"But first!" Alosha stood, a good head taller than Max, and held out his hand, stop! "We got to see the view." He locked his bike to a railing and walked into the hotel's lobby, Max in tow. "Got to check the electricity!" he shouted at the receptionist, then led the way to the elevator.

The top floor was a kind of makeshift casino, 'The Crystal Palace.' It was a couple of tables with red and blue plastic tablecloths and a plain girl in a flashy mini dress who looked bored.

"This is the tallest point in the whole city," explained Alosha, nodding to the girl in the mini dress, who smiled. "We're friends," he whispered. "Don't tell my girlfriend! She is crazy jealous!" And again he raised his hands to his head, as if squeezing a melon.

Max followed Alosha to the plate glass windows and looked out at—nothing. Or, not exactly nothing. You could follow the lights of the town, as they formed a yellow grid in the darkness. Then, after two or three blocks, they ended abruptly. Beyond was night, or a void, or both. Darkness. Max had seen aerial photos of Diamant, knew the city was set, like a plaything, on the edge of a large conical pit. But here, up close, you couldn't see anything clearly. Like Mont Blanc, he thought, only the imagination could grasp it.

"So!" said Alosha. "Let's go!"

He led the way back outside, unlocked his bike, and strode ahead of Max down the street. It looked like any other Soviet street. Concrete. Serviceable.

"You know VKontakte, Max?" Max assented: everybody knew the 'Russian Facebook'. "You got a VKontakte account?"

"No," said Max.

Alosha stopped in his tracks. "What?" he said. "How do you steal music?" Before Max could answer, Alosha continued. "Here in Russia, we got the best computer guys in the world. So we don't buy nothing! You go on VKontakte, you get everything you want! And you get it fast. I tell you, Max. The Chinese, they're fast. Russians, they are faster. There's a new Hollywood movie. Maybe Bruce Willis, let's say. Ok, first the Chinese have a bootleg. Before that, there's the red carpet. And before that, it's on VKontakte! Before the movie is even done cutting. We have it! We can see it! It's amazing." He turned forward and continued the walk.

They reached the edge of town. In the pictures it looked like the sidewalk fell off into the pit. But of course, thought Max, real life is never like pictures. This was just a regular town. He had thought you would feel something—a weird hollowness, an emptiness, the earth's yaw—but no. There was nothing. Except the knowledge that this huge hole was out there, somewhere just beyond them. And the wind—the wind seemed to howl, like a lonely animal. Though that might have been Max's imagination. Finally, they came to a chain link fence. With his long arms and legs, it was a matter of seconds before Alosha the electrician scaled the fence and landed on the other side. Max followed, far less gracefully.

"Ok!" said Alosha, once they were over. "Max, we got to work on your parkour talent. I take you to my *Kruschovka*. You know *Kruschovki*? It means, a small shitty apartment built under Kruschev. It's pretty good for training. Not too tall. Five stories. Ok, let's go."

Alosha turned on his telephone's flashlight and, following the bobbing light, they picked their way through an inky blackness strewn with abandoned-looking trucks and machinery.

To the right rose a little square building. As they approached, Max saw that it was exactly what it looked like: instead of a building without an elevator lobby, it was an elevator lobby without a building. As they neared he saw that it had even been decorated: the doors were glass, chained shut. Inside, the lobby tiles formed little geometric flower patterns.

Alosha rattled the thick chains that held the doors together. "Aghhhh!" he shouted, like Tarzan. Then he winked, walked around the side of the lobby-without-a-building, and pulled at the metal siding. It came off and the two men stepped into the lobby. Alosha pulled the siding shut after them. Then he pushed the elevator button. Nothing happened. "Aghghgghg!" he shouted again. Then he walked to one side of the lobby and opened a large utility box Max hadn't even noticed. He bent and set to work, with much (Max expected exaggerated) sparking, buzzing, and swearing.

Finally, he stood, walked over to the elevator button (there was only one, for 'down') and pushed. Nothing lit up, but there was a slow mechanical sound. A rumbling deep in the earth was followed by the more immediate rumbling of the elevator doors as they pulled slowly apart.

"Very dangerous business, Max! But unfortunately if you don't accompany me you will certainly die of boredom. Let's go!"

"You got it," said Max. He followed his new friend into the elevator. A mile down, under the earth . . .

"The only thing," Alosha was saying to Max, "you can't do in an elevator like this," he squatted, just a bit, on his haunches, as if to launch himself in the air, "is jump!"

Just then the elevator ground to a halt with a sickening sound of gears stripping. Oh God, thought Max, now it's really broken.

But no, the doors creaked open. Alosha elbowed him in the ribs. They had been traveling downwards for seven minutes, but it felt longer. Stepping outside, Max noticed an absence of smell. A little earth, a little dust. Musty. But mostly, it smelled like nothing.

"Anyway, Max, don't worry, I did a job down here, so I know all about it. The electricity is a mess! What you want to see first? The pit or the old diamond rooms? Now they got modern ones, up above ground. This is where they worked in the old days. My grandmother told me. She was a diamond cutter. Great lady, my grandmother! I tell you what, we look at the pit first. It's closer."

Max's ears were clogged, like in an airplane. He yawned. He felt as if he could sense the weight of the earth pressing down above them. He shivered, shook it off, followed Alosha, who, flashlight in hand, was loping down a dark hallway reinforced with steel beams.

They made their way along the tunnel until they reached a balcony of sorts. "Careful," said Alosha, rattling the metal handrail. "Not so strong!"

They stood there in silence. At first, there seemed to be nothing to see. The balcony jutted out over a great black void. But the void had a kind of attraction. As they stood, in silence, it took on new dimensions. Max began to see different shades of black emerging. Outer space must be something like this, he thought. Now and then, the cold air of the pit hissed.

"Great, right?" said Alosha.

"Pretty great," agreed Max.

Then Alosha yawned. "C'mon, this is boring. Let's go see the diamond rooms."

They walked back the way they had come, then traversed another labyrinth of hallways. Alosha knew his way around here quite well, thought Max. At a pair of great metal doors, Alosha stopped suddenly. "Open sesame!" he commanded, and at that moment, the doors slowly swung inwards. Alosha elbowed Max in the ribs and flashed his light on a lever located on the floor. "Great, right?"

"Great," said Max.

Once inside, Alosha must have stepped on another lever, because the doors swung heavily shut, with a long, slow echo. They seemed to be in a cavernous hall of some kind. "Wait!" said Alosha, and jumped up on a pipe that Max hadn't even noticed. Alosha fiddled with something in the darkness, then jumped back down and flipped a switch. "*Voila!*" he cried, as a single bulb illuminated the hall.

The floors would have been better suited to a dance hall or a sanatorium than an underground mine: broad, marble-colored slabs with long narrow veins. Cracked here and there, but essentially intact. Overhead, the many arms of a giant bronze lamp glinted. The lights clutched in each tentacle were smashed. Along one wall ran a shelf, waist high, covered in dirty red velvet.

Max whistled. "You never brought your girlfriend down here?" he asked.

"No way!" said Alosha. "She would say, 'Aloshka, it's so dirty, Aloshka, when are you going to buy me a Hyundai, Aloshka, Aloshenka?' Women! Agh!" He squeezed his head again. "Max! Next room!"

Alosha jumped up. Just before he unscrewed the light bulb, something caught Max's eye. He bent, and picked up two gritty pebbles. He put them in his pocket as the room went dark. From the other end of the room, Max heard Alosha swearing. He was rattling a door.

"I wanted to show you the old lab, for cutting and polishing!" said Alosha. "This is where my grandmother used to work. But some jerk has locked it. Strange. Another strike against tourism! Oh well, come on." Alosha grabbed Max's arm.

Alosha was truly a master of that underground labyrinth. After an hour in those dark underground hallways, they emerged, via another elevator. "Thanks for the tour," said Max, as they walked back towards the center of the city.

"Yeah," said Alosha. "How about you show me what you've got in your pocket?"

Max took out the two pebbles, handed one to Alosha. "Fifty-fifty," he said.

"Ok," said Alosha, cheerfully. "I'll show it to my grandmother. Could be a diamond!"

A feeling of deep discomfort came over Max as they entered his hotel. He glanced around in the darkness. He saw nothing. The hotel lobby was deserted. They parted, friends. Max pressed the elevator button and glanced idly at Alosha's departing form in the smoky mirror that lined the walls. Suddenly he saw a dark figure emerge on the empty square. He walked towards the unlucky electrician. Max saw a blade flash. As the boy went down, his attacker reached into his pocket. Max turned just in time to see the man smile. A golden smile. With a glint of light.

Max fought his instinct to rush to the boy's side. He was so still, there was no real point. And Max couldn't afford an interview with the authorities. He packed his things quickly. From his room he could see two, then three figures gathered around the fallen man. There was no sense of urgency in their movements. It was time to leave.

30

A day later Max stepped off one of thousands of identical, battered blue train cars that, strung together like so many vertebrae, criss-crossed the land on their vast metal tracks. The platform was gray, slick with ice, and his feet crunched in the layer of snow forming under a brisk, silent sky. A blast of wind tore through the black coat from Diamant, which Max had unzipped in the coal-heat of the train. Max's teeth chattered as he tramped up a set of perforated metal stairs to the station.

Inside, everything was pink marble. Broad floors. Soaring ceilings. Arched windows framed an enormity of potted plants. At a café tucked away in a corner he ordered tea and drank it slowly.

Outside, he approached the cluster of black-jacketed men smoking cigarettes and stamping their feet. One of them nodded, and Max climbed into the front seat of his car. Max gave him an address in the center of the city. Novosibirsk passed by: squat brick buildings whose facades had long disintegrated, metal overhangs dented. Gray flakes began to fall.

They reached a row of low, ornately decorated wooden buildings. Single storied, painted green, peeling. Before the Soviets put up the hulking city, the place was an outpost of sweet gingerbread houses like these.

A sign in front of the door read: Novosibirsk Historical Society. A threadbare but comfortable room with lace curtains. The healthy-looking girl at the desk was playing with her phone. Max told her that he was less interested in the past than in the future. She yawned, stood, and led him to the far corner of the room. She lifted a broad wooden floor panel and pointed to a set of steps leading into darkness.

Downstairs, the fence's den was moldy and damp. Max conducted his business as quickly as possible. When he emerged, the gray sky overhead felt bright in comparison. Max whistled. The dirty little pebble had brought him $10,000.

*

"The Marriott," he said.

The driver nodded. Three Soviet pioneers, three stories high, gave black marble salutes: East, West, North. In Ukraine, they were taking these down, all of them. There were stories of a leftover foot in Kharkiv; an ear, kept as a memento.

"Cold," said Max, catching sight of a digital sign that flashed the time, date and temperature.

"Minus seven's not cold," said the driver. "Minus forty-seven is cold."

The opera, with its round, shallow roof. Like a UFO landing. The director had recently offended the church with his crucifixion of Jesus onstage and subsequently fled the country. Outside, sturdy old women in beige coats and scarves tied over their heads were scalping tickets.

Just across from it was the Marriott. Brand new. Siberia's first five-star hotel. Built by Novosibirsk's richest businessman so his partners would have a decent place to stay when they came to town. The taxi driver told Max a grocery kiosk used to stand there. "Fire," he said. "Very convenient. The hotel got the land."

The lobby was modern, clean. Crystals dripping from the ceiling. An open restaurant. Not tacky. Big men in pastel polo shirts. Small hamburgers on large, asymmetrical plates. Max sat and ordered one. But when it arrived, he found himself thinking of that poor kid. The electrician. Max couldn't eat. Not one bite.

*

The afternoon light dimmed. Max paid his bill and strolled across the street to the opera. It was the children's matinee. Kids everywhere. Little girls with bows in their hair. Waiting patiently. Little boys in sweaters. Fidgeting. 'Swan Lake.' Max glanced around the front lobby, where the huge swinging doors let in regular blasts of freezing air, bought a ticket from a grandmotherly scalper, went inside. The lobby was cavernous, clad in stone: all the colors of old teeth. The children swarmed. Orderly. Like a beehive. Finally Max spotted him. A tall, thin, nervous man in line to check his coat. Max waited. The coat check was amazingly efficient. Racks and racks and racks. As Max watched a small army of women checked a thousand Siberian coats. Then he joined the other man.

"Max," he said.

The man started. He was fair, Max saw, now that his wool cap was off. Pale, thin hair framed a skeletal face.

"Let's go," he said, and opened a service door. Max followed him through a long, dark corridor, to another door, to another corridor, until he had nearly lost his bearings. Now and again they heard voices, but they encountered no one. Finally, the man opened a door that led them into one of the largest rooms Max had ever seen in his life. More impressive, it was stuffed to the ceiling with props and costumes. A fantasia. White plaster swans. Enormous cherry red lollipops. The huge, laughing head of a devil. Embroidered curtains. Tulle skirts. Black feathered wings. Swords and shields. Suits of armor. Hundreds of silk toe shoes. Dangling, like a wall of the condemned.

"Storage room," said the man, who introduced himself as Stas Kovalskiy. He added, with a hint of pride, "Largest in the world."

"Ok," said Max. Two oversized red-velvet thrones were pushed together in a corner, like living room chairs. Max took a seat in one. "Let's talk."

"Evgenia—the secretary from World of Hope—didn't tell you much, I suppose," said Kovalskiy, sitting on the throne across from Max. Max shook his head. "She has every reason to be afraid," said the man, reaching over and picking up a large, shiny crown. He held the crown up, contemplating it in the dim light. "No one knows where the lines are until you've crossed one. Then, the system can be merciless. They don't care if you're ninety years old and gave your whole life to the Motherland, they'll stick you in a hard labor camp." As he said this, a quick spasm passed over his face. He turned to Max. "I used to be a journalist. Russian TV. In the '90s."

Max nodded. The '90s saw a flourishing of the press—TV, newspapers, magazines. Some of it was bought and paid for. A place for oligarchs to slug it out. But some of it was really good. Free press, in the best tradition. Investigative reports. Idealists. All that was finished now. The man was chuckling. He set the crown on his head, where it sat askew, and pulled open his coat. He was carrying a pistol. "I never go anywhere without it," he said. "I'm an accidental activist, you know. All of us are, I suppose. For me, it happened like this."

Just then, the orchestra began tuning their instruments. The pit must have been very close. Or it was a trick of the acoustics. The cacophony gave a Max a headache. Or was it the dust in the room? He struggled against a weird wave of exhaustion as Kovalskiy told his story. He grew up in Moscow, but his mother's family was from the South, an area known as the 'Black Earth' region. Rich and fertile. Famous for its ancient oak forests and the spirits that lived there. Beautiful country. Unfortunately, the Black Earth also holds nickel. The forests are protected, so mining is not allowed. But a private company, backed by the Kremlin, planned to mine anyway. "It would destroy this entire region," said Kovalskiy. "We decided to protest." He and a few friends organized the inhabitants in the largest local environmental protest ever held. Even the Cossacks joined them. In the orchestra pit, the overture began. 'Swan Lake' was commencing.

"Cossacks?" said Max. "I thought they supported the regime?"

"Usually they do," said Kovalskiy, a spasm of what Max took to be fear running across the thin skin of his face. "They are socially conservative. That's where their interests mesh with the regime's. But they are actually quite independent—far more so than the regime thinks. Respect for the land is part of their ideology. They are natural environmental conservationists. They joined us, with their whips. It was quite helpful, when things got violent. At first, at least. They sent thugs after us. One of my co-organizers was beaten into a coma. He'll probably never be the same again."

"Jesus," said Max.

Kovalskiy's face changed. His features froze for a moment, like a stone statue. He shook it off, came back to life. "I left," he said. "I hid out in Moscow. That's when I got my gun. One day there was a TV news segment about me. They filmed a car with a briefcase full of money, said that I had been bribed to create unrest. That's when I knew it was all up for me, in this country. I went home to pack—I was staying with a friend—and the woman at the door told me they were waiting upstairs for me. I turned around and left. I traveled by night, over the Georgian border. With the fighting there, the border can be porous, if you know the right people. Most of us are based in the Baltics, now. Exiles. We do what we can."

"What are you doing here?" said Max. "Isn't it dangerous?"

He lowered his eyes. "It's my mom's birthday," he said. "I—I had to come to come see her. I'll leave again as soon as I have. Sure it's dangerous. But it's life." He shrugged again. "You wanted to know about Atom Town, right?"

Max nodded. Another wave of exhaustion came over him. The orchestra swelled. From the corner of his eye, he thought he saw a black cape rise and fall like a sigh in the half-light. He shook himself.

"It's very hard to say, of course, because we have no hard data. We don't know what the levels of toxicity were after the disaster in the '50s. We don't know what they are now. But we do have some informants on site."

Max raised his eyebrows in surprise.

"Not many, but some. Dynacorp should only be sending one kind of waste—so-called 'treated' waste. But, it seems that there was supposed to be some kind of waste separation on-site, in Atom Town. Which indicates that there are two kinds of waste coming in. Dynacorp funded not one but two storage areas, with two different sets of specifications. The contractor took off with the money for both, so all the waste is going into a pit. A fairly typical story. Probably not even illegal."

"What about the sleeping sickness?" said Max. "Have you heard of it?"

The mad king nodded. "It could indicate that some of this waste is particularly toxic. But with that kind of thing, you never know."

He stood, picked up a long red velvet cape with ermine trim. Draped it around himself, jumped up lightly onto the devil's head. He took a bow, flourishing the cape. "You'll find your own way out," he said, and vanished.

Max stood, felt another wave of dizziness, steadied himself on the gilded arm of the throne. He walked over to the devil's head. Behind it, there was some kind of trap door. He shrugged and picked his way back through the dark corridors through which they had come, alone.

31

The airport was small, glassy. New. You could see all the counters at once. All but one was deserted. The floors were polished to a high, dangerous gloss. The night outside was pitch black.

Max was on edge. He kept thinking about that poor kid. The shine from the floors made him dizzy.

Max had plenty of time before his flight back to Moscow. That rising fear again. A cup of hot black tea. With lots of sugar. That was what he needed to set him to rights. As he strolled towards the shiny new café, he caught a glimpse in the highly reflective display case that sent a chill through his blood. A stocky, muscular man was striding from the men's room, out of the airport lobby, onto the walkway. He held a pack of cigarettes in his gloved hand. Max didn't even need to wait for the gleam of the front left tooth to know exactly who it was. How long did it take to smoke a cigarette? Five minutes. Max had five minutes. Only one counter was working. The last passenger was checking in, the stewardesses were about to close up shop.

Max hurried over, brandishing Pasha the Playwright's passport. The flight was direct to Venice. (Good thing Pasha had gotten his Schengen visa, thought Max, and silently thanked Pasha's demanding wife for insisting on her Corsican vacation). The girl at the desk took pity on him. Took his money. Handed him a ticket. Told him to hurry. Max's heart didn't stop pounding until he had made it through security, sprinted across the small terminal, and taken a seat on the plane. The small airplane doors closed and Max heaved a sigh. He closed his eyes. Venezia. The plane was small and new, and almost as soon as Max settled into his place he fell asleep.

*

The landing woke him up. Max glanced out the window groggily and saw the two iconic fish. Locked, mouth to mouth. In eternal strife, or embrace.

"Landing," barked the captain. The stewardess who had let him on the plane walked by, quickly and efficiently, checking seatbelts, tray tables, seat backs. As she passed Max, she handed him a glossy flier and continued up the aisle, murmuring, "Seatbelts, tray tables, seat backs ..." Max looked at the flier. It was blue and gray. THE FUTURE IS BRIGHT, it read. Under that: WELCOME TO THE INTERNATIONAL NUCLEAR CONFERENCE. He opened the flier and held his breath. Under the headline KEYNOTE SPEAKER was a photo of a familiar-looking gray-haired man. Trim, feline. DYNACORP'S GERARD DUPRES. A round of applause went up as the aircraft touched down smoothly. The address was a former palazzo on the Canal Grande.

32

The water taxi plowed its way from the airport through a narrow lane before it reached open water. The water here was a greenish gray, choppy. Overhead, a seagull circled and swooped. Its cry was lonely.

The taxi dropped Max at a floating platform. Its striated metal floor pitched and heaved until the *vaporetto* arrived to take the waiting passengers to the city. They passed the high red brick walls of the graveyard. Tall Italian cypress: symbol of death. The glimpse inside. A riot of color: pinks and reds, yellow, orange. Plastic flowers.

As they approached the city itself, the sun struck through the clouds. The water turned a pale emerald hue. Terra cotta walls beckoning. Ah, Venezia. He had last been here ... twenty years ago? A night drop, in and out. Mafia—occasionally they had called him in on Mafia because he had spent that year in Bologna (the 'Red City', so named for the color of its architecture, above those long, arched arcades, and its politics). A waitress taught him Italian. "Between the sheets, we'll have a lesson," she would say, and giggle at his expanding vocabulary. Anyway, that was a long time ago, all of it.

As the *vaporetto* chugged its way to the stop, Max jumped out. He glanced at the flier. 'Il Majestico,' it read.

*

Max only got lost twice as he snaked his way through the city. The crowds of tourists grew thicker. The number of Carnival masks for sale grew more numerous. Almost without warning, he found the number. 'Il Majestico' was a faded palazzo that had become an extremely luxurious hotel.

The lobby was dark, gilded, filled with dull men in good suits. Max decided to try a little experiment. He combed his hair with his fingers and approached the reception desk. "Rushmore," he said to the girl. She smiled, checked her computer terminal, smiled again. "Room 213, *Signore*."

Max checked the schedule, showered in a bathroom the size of a coffin, and came back down just in time for the keynote speech. He picked up his badge where it was waiting for him on the table and hung it from his neck—like a noose, he thought. On stage, in what was certainly once a banquet room, Gerard Dupres stood in front of an enormous PowerPoint slide. It announced, in blue and white, with a click: Gerard Dupres. Then another click, another blue and white slide: Senior Vice-President. A click, and the slide stayed where it was. DYNACORP.

*

After the presentation, which he understood just about none of—something about a 'Supér' and Estonia as a model for energy independence—Max shadowed Gerard outside. He was surrounded by colleagues, of course, so Max had to wait for just the right moment. He found it in the men's room. Plush, thought Max, looking around. The man was washing his hands. Max tapped him on the shoulder.

"Gerard Dupres?" he said. "I'd like to talk to you about Sonja Ostranova."

*

Gerard heard the man's voice, but he finished toweling his hands before showing that he registered it. "Pardon?" he said, then. He turned, slowly. Let his presence make up for his diminutive stature. The strange thing was, Gerard had just been thinking about Sonja. Well, indirectly. The other day, in Paris. On the way to dinner he had driven past her—or, rather, a woman who looked so much like her that he gasped. As he watched, the woman bent over, wiped something from a child's face. Sonja has no children, he thought, first. Then he realized: Sonja is dead. Of course it wasn't Sonja. Still, the incident had left him oddly shaken.

"You heard me," said his accoster. "I want to talk to you about Sonja Ostranova. Your girlfriend, ex, whatever."

Gerard felt a chill settle over him. "If you'll accompany me to my room," he said, quietly. "I can give you fifteen minutes."

*

Gerard's room was larger than Max's. A host of angels looked down on them from the ceiling. Probably admiring the thick mattress's luxurious, cream-colored sheets. The carpet was deep, soft and clean. The room had a feeling of peace, of safety, of deep-seated comfort. Max locked the door and turned on the television. He wished for the good old days when you could stick a pencil in the safe's lock and be pretty confident you had neutralized their cameras. What was the next generation going to do? Exist half in the ether, constantly watched, constantly out of reach. Oh well, thought Max, it wouldn't be his problem.

"So," said Max, "Sonja Ostranova. Tell me about her. And you."

"I don't see what business it is of yours," said Gerard.

"Let's just say the United States government takes an interest in its citizens," said Max. "Particularly when they are at work on our security and we suspect foul play."

Gerard started. "Foul play?" he said. "She died of a heart attack.

181

Very sad—although we had already gone our separate ways. I am planning to be married."

"I bet," said Max. "How about you just tell me a little bit about you two."

Gerard sighed. Taking a seat on one of the heavy oak chairs, he splayed his hands up, towards the angels. "It was an *affaire du coeur*, nothing more. Nothing less, of course. A bright flame, alighting on paper. It burns intensely, but not for long. Her death was a surprise. Naturally, a tragedy."

"But not a real blow," said Max.

"No, monsieur," agreed Gerard, shaking his head ever so slightly, one man of the world to the other. "As I say, our time together had ended. From my side, at least. We met in your country's capital, I didn't feel at home there. Sonja—well, she was different. An outsider, like me. And of course, a physically lovely woman."

"How'd you meet?"

"Some sort of work function. Cocktails at the Embassy—a celebration of nuclear peacekeeping, I believe."

"Did she ever tell you about her work?"

"No. To be honest, what interested me about her was not her nuclear expertise, if you know what I mean."

"Was she interested in your nuclear expertise?"

Gerard shrugged. "Women are always interested in a man's work," he said. "They can't help it—*c'est naturelle*. Of course most of my work is quite banal—sales and marketing, essentially. Nothing secret." He paused, as if he was really reflecting, and added, "Perhaps that is one of the things I liked about her. Since we worked in the same industry, I was required to speak about what I do very little."

"She was an inspector in Red River," said Max.

"Was she?" Gerard sounded bored.

"That's not far from Atom Town."

Gerard looked slightly uncomfortable, Max thought. But it passed in a moment.

"Did you have her murdered because she discovered your little waste separation scheme—or were you in it together?"

Max watched Gerard's face, carefully. 'Murder' didn't seem to have much effect. 'Waste separation scheme,' however, struck home. He decided to go for broke. "And Diamant?" he said. "Was it the diamonds she was interested in?"

Gerard's face turned ever so slightly green. The diamond! he thought. How could he have been such a fool? He saw it all before his eyes: the Brazilian restaurant on Columbia Road with the ridiculous name. Yes: The Grill From Ipanema. High summer. Hot, muggy. Could it really have been a year ago? More. 'Humidity you could cut with a fork and knife!' he had said with a laugh, and she had laughed too. Why had she laughed at his jokes? She was so beautiful. He couldn't resist her when she laughed. He kissed her on both cheeks outside the restaurant. Put his hands on her shoulders. Held her away from him so that he could take her all in at once. Long legs, dark hair, luminous eyes, brow, breasts. He had reserved a table. They sat, side by side, on the padded leather bench that ran along the far wall. She wore her pink angora sweater, the one that he liked so much. Still, she was cold, because of the air conditioning. The room itself he remembered vaguely: dark browns and blacks, shadows and tablecloths. She had eyes only for Gerard—'Gerry,' she always called him—he could tell. He had his arm around her.

He ordered champagne ("I know, it is not Brazilian!" he had said, and popped the cork) and after they toasted, he pulled a box from his coat pocket. Small, velvet, royal blue. Sonja gasped, said she had never seen anything so lovely. Embossed with gold on the top. "Open it," he had said. She did. There was the ring. It was perfect, of course. Elegant, simple. The diamond caught what little light there was in the restaurant, reflected it back a thousand times, a rainbow of colors that culminated in a stunning flash of blue. "The clearest in the world," Gerry had said, repeating what Ruslan, the Russian contractor, had told him. Ruslan had said the diamond was a gift to thank him, Gerard, for his business. That Russians like to give gifts, and this was Ruslan's to him. Gerard had found the stone beautiful. He wanted to give it to Sonja. And so he did. "The purest in the world," he repeated. "Like you. Your eyes."

He had caught her hand, bent to kiss it, then looked up into her face and whispered, in a choked voice, "Your—soul." She had liked that. Very much. Even when the stupid waitress sat that American cochon next to them and he complimented her on her ring, it hadn't bothered Gerard. She had laughed and showed it to him. Proudly.

"I don't know what you're talking about," Gerard said, weakly. But the thing was, he had a hunch. Oh yes, for the first time, he had a hunch.

Max stood. He began to pace. He sensed that the Frenchman had realized something, and he wanted to know what. He—black stars began dancing in front of Max's eyes. Followed by bright, blinding bursts. His head felt light. "Attention!" the Frenchman shouted. Max was aware of a thud, a long way off. Then came a wave of fear and nausea, and everything went dark.

33

Max woke to the sound of waves. Gentle waves. Rolling waves. Waves that came in slowly, over a long, shallow sand bar. It was a good sound. A pleasant sound. A sound that almost lulled him back to sleep. Then he realized he was cold. Cold and wet. Cold and wet and sore. Cold, wet, sore, and sleepy. He shifted his body, lay his face in the pillow, sat up choking. He spit out a mouthful of sand. Max looked around. He was lying on the beach. On the Lido.

Overhead, out past the water, a cold, gray day was breaking. As he watched, a gull swooped down. Calling. A flash of white. Max turned his head with some difficulty and scanned the horizon. Ahead, only water: as if he was at the edge of the world. To the left, only sand. To the right, sand, and—a small, dark figure. A mere dot. Moving steadily towards him. With the unmistakable gait of a policeman.

That was the last thing he needed. With a groan, Max hauled himself up, turned his back to the water. Then he checked his pockets. Wallet, yes. Money, even. Key card, pocketknife. Everything there. He moved one foot, picking it up and placing it in the sand. The sand gave, a little. No problem. He tried the next foot. Same deal. Step by step, he progressed.

Back in his little room at Il Majestico, there were no signs of entry. If they had searched it, it had been done professionally. He walked straight to the door, opened it onto the hallway. He lifted the oriental rug that served as a doormat. He ran his fingers along the hallway's plush bronze carpeting that ran beneath it. At the threshold to his room, he pulled up the carpet tacks and breathed a sigh of relief. Finding his own passport still there meant he could get back to Russia right away. Finding Pasha the Playwright's there, still intact, meant that Pasha's wife wouldn't kill him when he got there.

34

With its stained white tablecloths and springy seats, the restaurant car of the Venice-Paris night train had not changed. Max had a table to himself. His place setting was dirty. As the train chugged across the lagoon, Max ordered a carafe of red wine. When it came, he raised a glass to the past.

The address was not far from Pere Lachaise. The morning was overcast. Chilly. He cut through the cemetery for the hell of it. Stone graves, stone paths. Here and there, a bedraggled tree. A miniature version of the city outside. *Je suis belle, ô mortels! comme un rêve de Pierre...* Three teenagers in some sort of school uniform were smoking marijuana in front of Jim Morrison's grave.

The apartment was a fourth-floor walk-up in the back. It smelled strongly of fried foods. Nadezhda Levantal opened on the third ring. She was astonishingly lovely. Her dark hair was pulled back, accentuating her cheekbones. She had laugh lines around her eyes and mouth, and beneath her full lips, on the left side, a dark beauty mark. She smiled and offered her hand. She moved with elegance. Like a swan, thought Max. If Sonja had half her appeal, she must be quite a woman.

"Max Rushmore," he said. "US government."

She smiled again. "Come in." The flat was small, but pretty. Wooden floors, wild flowers in glass jars. From the next room came the sounds of roughhousing. "I hope you'll excuse my boys," she said. "It's very hard to discipline them. My daughter is easier. She is six and goes to school. But they are ten and fourteen. They can't speak French yet. Right now they are home."

"How long have you been in Paris?" asked Max. The sound of breaking glass and a shriek came from the other room.

"I had to leave Russia in January," she said. "When they decided I was a 'foreign agent.' And on television, there were several reports about me. That I am a traitor. The former head of the KGB, who does not give interviews, gave two interviews about me. My lawyer said, 'They will probably arrest you next.' We moved here eight—nine months ago. Now I am applying for asylum here in France."

"I see," said Max. Suddenly, he felt woozy. Unsteady. He took a seat on a tatty plush love seat. It had a flea market look, but only if you looked too hard. Max shifted, crossed a leg over his knee. Nadezhda leaned against the narrow marble mantle of the fireplace. A tall, discolored mirror framed her, though its veined, splotched surface reflected only the vaguest outline of her form. She watched him, and Max thought he saw that she was pleased. The sturdy form that women liked. "So," he said. "I was wondering, if you could you tell me a little more about your NGO?"

Nadezhda smiled. It was a surprising smile, earthy, irrepressible. "Of course," she said. She crossed the tiny living room, moving lightly in a long, flowing skirt. She took a seat on the little velvet couch facing Max. Crossed her legs: even beneath the long skirt, you could see they were beautiful. "Maybe I should start at the beginning," she said. "I grew up in Atom Town. One of our Russian 'closed cities,' as you know. I never knew what my father did for a living. He told me he produced paper wrappers, for candy. My mother was a doctor. From her, I sometimes heard the word 'radiation.' We grew up knowing that ours was a secret town. That we must never say its name. One of my grandmothers lived in Yekaterinburg. When I went to visit, my parents instructed me not to tell anyone where I lived, or the black car will come and take my parents away. I never questioned it. We were young patriots. We thought everyone was spying."

"Ah," said Max.

"Later, in 1983, my father became ill. He was sent to Clinic #6, in Moscow. It was for victims of radiation. After that, he started drinking. He died in 1985, when I was twelve."

Max shook his head. The noise from the car traffic rose, penetrated the drafty windows. Incessant. Irritating. "I'm sorry," he said.

"It was only in 1991 that I learned the truth. That he had come to Atom Town when he was eighteen, one of the clean-up crew. That my mother's mother, who had died of cancer, was also on that crew. She and her children had escaped the bombing in Kiev, in the Second World War, and came to Russia after my grandfather died. My grandmother settled near Atom Town. After the disaster, she cleaned up there, too. We had known nothing of all this. Nothing at all. They said that the accident wasn't very bad. That was when people began to speak up. The government said they were lying.

"I had my first child then. I was—distracted. Later, I began to study sociology. And I thought, so many people can't be lying. I had my next two children. Finally, I learned about civil society, from mothers of drug addicts. And I created World of Hope. I started to study law. And I began to bring cases to court.

"You see, the problem is that no one says anything. For example, if you are a first-generation victim of radiation poisoning, the state provides funds until you are eighteen. At eighteen, what, there is nothing wrong with you? And there is no provision for second and third generation victims. The state says, 'The accident was in 1957.' As if it has nothing to do with what happens today! Utterly ridiculous."

"Yes, of course," said Max.

"In many ways, we have been successful. People in Atom Town are freer than they were. Before, only mothers were allowed to visit without a reason. Once a year. And only for ten days, not for eleven. Now, visits are more free. There is less paperwork. But the intimidation started to become unbearable. They went after us with taxes. They came to our homes. Finally," she sighed, "it was too much."

There was another shriek and another sound of breaking glass. "Excuse me for one moment," she said, with a smile. She stood, stalked over to the door. "Take your brother to the park! Now, now! Not later! No you can't have any money! Then go to the cemetery! Try to learn something! You bad boys!"

Two tousled-haired boys emerged, greeted Max, exited through the front door. The sound of their feet running down the wooden stairs echoed.

Nadezhda sat, crossed her long legs again under the flowing green skirt, resumed. "What I wanted to do, at one point, was a sociology study of these closed towns," she said. "Because I think the mentality, it's very special and must be studied. But of course I couldn't get permission."

"Do you know Sonja Ostranova?" he asked, after a silence.

She looked surprised. "Yes," she said. "She is my cousin."

"I thought she didn't have any relatives?"

"In fact, I didn't know she existed. Our mothers were sisters—twins, in fact. But they had a terrible falling out, I don't know over what. I rather think a man. Regardless, Sonja's mother left when she was sixteen or seventeen. She went to Moscow and broke off all contact. I think she told people she was an orphan. Well, plenty of people were, then. It was only on her deathbed that my mother told me about this sister. And I tried to find what I could about her. It was pure chance that led to me to Sonjetchka. How funny that she works as a nuclear scientist!"

"When did you find her?"

"Last year, just before I was declared a foreign agent. We met, once. She lives in the United States, you know." She smiled again. "I suppose you do know. She works in Russia still. She was on an inspection tour in Red River. She slipped out at night—she didn't want her colleagues to know about her personal life. That I can understand! Imagine—she didn't know anything. Not about our grandmother who cleaned up the disaster, not even that her mother was born in Kiev. Of course, when we met, it was clear we were related. We could be twins!"

"I'm afraid I have bad news," said Max. "She passed away, in Moscow."

The woman's eyes clouded.

"I'm very sorry," he said. "It seems to have been a natural death, but I'm investigating it. And—I was wondering. Did anything strike you, in your meeting with her?"

Nadezhda lifted an elegant hand, wiped her eyes. Thought, for a moment. "There was something strange, actually," she said. "When I was telling her about my work, there was a lawsuit that seemed to upset her. She had no children of her own, she told me. But when I told her about a case of third-generation poisoning that I successfully prosecuted in court, she almost began to weep. At issue was a little baby girl. She was born with three kinds of cancer. Her great-grandmother had been part of the clean-up. Like our grandmother, just the same." She paused, as if she listening for something, out on the landing. "I've been so lucky with my children. Even my bad boys are healthy as can be."

She re-crossed her legs, sending the skirt swishing over the cracked hardwood floors. Automatically, Max shifted in his seat, re-crossed his legs, left over right now. Mirroring. A good sign, thought Max. It meant she was telling him everything. Nadezhda looked at him. Her eyes were a deep green. "In that case, the government disclaimed all responsibility," she said. "As usual. The girl died before she turned one. But we took the case to court, and won. Compensation is nothing, of course, compared to a healthy child. But it sets a precedent. And that's important."

"Yes," said Max. "I see that."

A tear ran down the woman's cheek, and she wiped it away.

"Of course I hardly knew her," she said. "Still, it's a loss. I'm sorry to hear this."

Max was silent. Let her feel his sympathy. She spoke again: "What was also strange is that Sonja didn't know that Dynacorp has moved their operations to Atom Town from Red City. Even though she was the inspector. I suppose they had kept that from her. Well, they keep a lot back. Even things that don't matter at all. It's part of the mentality, as I said. Secrets, patriotism."

From the street came the sounds of brakes screeching. Honking, angry voices. Then it subsided. The constant sound of traffic again.

Max looked at her. With empathy. "Can you continue your work from Paris?"

"I hope so," she said.

35

Max split the gas with a professional clown driving back home to Berlin. The clown had blond hair and flashing blue eyes. His imitations of political figures, alive and dead, had Max laughing so hard his stomach hurt. The clown's main problem with his mother—he told Max—was that she believed that eating an apple was the solution to any problem that might come up in a person's life. "And she's a psychiatrist!" he said, shaking his head. They reached Berlin by midnight, and Max spent the night at a third-rate techno club, known for its lax door policy, bobbing his head over a bottle of beer. Anonymity had its price.

In the morning he took a cab to the Adlon. There, he made his way to the swimming pool, where he showered and shaved. Upstairs, in the lobby, he sat in a corner and ordered a cup of coffee. It was terrible, but it gave him permission to take a quick nap on the overstuffed chair. At ten, he hailed a cab to Charlottenburg.

"Ah! Herr Rushmore!" said the tailor as Max entered, to the ringing of the brass bell over the door. "Everything is in order with your suit, I hope?"

"Great, great, it's really taken a lot of wear and tear," said Max. "I'm in town and I was just thinking, maybe I should order another. Maybe in a heavier wool?"

"I have just the thing for you!" said the tailor. He disappeared behind a heavy velvet curtain. Max heard his steps traversing the backroom. He had a minute, two at most. He picked up the book of receipts the old-fashioned tailor kept by the cash register, flipped to June. He heard a step, nearly dropped the book. The step retreated. Max found his receipt. 'Rushmore, M.' Next to it was what he wanted. 'Dominion, R.'

The tailor's steps grew louder. Max hastily closed the book and returned it to its proper place. The tailor, bent and cheerful, held out a ream of soft dark wool for Max to feel. Max rubbed it between his fingers. "Wonderful," he said. Then he winked. "I've gotta ask my wife. She says yes, I'll be back."

"Happy vife, happy life," said the tailor, in accented English, winking back.

As the brass bell rung behind him, Max had an epiphany. Robert Diamond! Of course. Outside, on the sidewalk, he slapped his forehead with his palm. How could he not have thought of it sooner? Too obvious, maybe. Right in front of his eyes.

A blast of wind shook the chestnuts. A shower of orange leaves. Bob Diamond's biography came back to him from one of the 'person of interest' circulars Rex had them memorize, back in the day. The father—one Michael Dyamant—was a small town Alsatian jeweler. Fled the Nazis. Met his wife in Tel Aviv. She didn't like the weather in Israel, so the family relocated to the United States in the '60s. Texas, where the weather wasn't much better. There, Mike Diamond (his new name was thanks to Ellis Island and his neighbors) traded the jewelry business for the oil industry. He made quite a go of it. He gave the business to his older son when he retired. The older son gambled most of it away.

The younger son, Bob, was a love child: some twenty years younger than his brother. Bob was in his teens when the money ran out. He dropped out of school. Went back to the original family business. His name proved prophetic: he had an uncanny eye for jewels. He worked hard. His rise through the ranks of the international diamond cartel was meteoritic. The diamond cartel was notoriously secretive. But, according to the 'person of interest' circular, Bob Diamond was believed to be in charge of diamond supply and pricing world-wide. The first American to have ever held the post.

Hurrying down Ku'Damm, Max took out his wallet. He rifled through it. Bob Dominion's card was embedded in a couple of receipt stubs—trains, dinners. Bob Dominion was Bob Diamond's pseudonym. Max was sure, now. As Max studied the imaginary Texas Chicken Corporation's logo, the receipts fluttered to the ground. Max wasn't fast enough. Another blast of wind carried them down Ku'Damm. He cursed. He could kiss those expenses goodbye.

36

"I am telling you," said the cabbie, craning his neck to address Max in the rearview mirror, "that 99% of my clientele, they are against this new airport. And why?" Taking his hand off the wheel, he ticked off the reasons with his fingers. "Tegel, it's a twenty-euro taxi ride. The new airport, it's going to be forty, fifty euros. That's too much. Regular people, they don't want to spend that. Then there's time. It takes too long to get out there. Forty, fifty minutes, instead of fifteen, twenty. People don't like that. Then, there are the Brandenburg taxi drivers, we're going to have to compete with them. And the noise! All those people in Zehlendorf, they don't want the new flight path. I live in Wedding. We don't mind the noise! We're used to it. No." He shook his head. "It's an absolute disaster."

Max shook his head in sympathy.

"The new one, it's all shopping! Capitalism gone crazy! Forty, fifty minutes of shopping before you find your airplane," said the cabbie. "Here, it's 'drive to your gate.' Everyone loves that. Me too! I go to Turkey, see my family, I always fly from Tegel. Five minutes, no shopping. It's great."

"Well," said Max, as they drove up into the center of the airport's octagon. "Maybe they'll never open the new one."

"We can hope."

"Hope is all we have," said Max, and asked for a receipt. He stepped out onto the curb, walked the five feet to his gate, admired, as always, the 1970's décor. The architect had designed everything: colors, tiles, signage, right down to the lettering. Triangular gray ceiling tiles. Red bathroom door handles. What a place. The city's calling card. Soon it would be empty. At the gray paneled desk, he checked in. A Russian discount airline.

The flight was unremarkable. As they landed, Max looked out the window. Funny, he thought, the sign read 'Sheremetovo'. He checked his ticket. That was not the airport they were supposed to arrive at. A little shiver of fear ran through Max. On the ground, an hour went by. Two. No announcements were made. Max considered worrying that he was the cause of this. But his better senses told him it had nothing to do with him at all. Still, there was something odd. He couldn't quite put his finger on it. He turned and looked back at the passengers. They were smiling, relaxed. That was what was missing: they had been waiting, for two hours, at the wrong airport, without any information whatsoever. Max registered a strange absence. He realized what it was: In two hours, he had not heard one complaint. He turned in seat, looked back at the rest of airplane. Of course! That's what was strange. There was not a single Western European on this plane.

Three hours later the plane took off again. It took twenty-five minutes—a remarkably long time, Max thought—to fly from one Moscow airport to the other.

Once on the ground, Max queued in the 'all other passports' line. He stood on tiptoes for a moment, then smiled: he had recognized his favorite customs officer by the curve of her neck.

Without noticing what he was doing, Max found himself reaching into his pocket and grasping the pen knife, which he had secreted away, thanks to a sleight of hand trick, during security check. He felt a strange prickling at the back of neck. An animal signal. Danger. Max turned and scanned the line behind him. At the back of the room, an airport mechanic caught his eye. There was something familiar about him. Max stared, hard. Then the man in the blue work suit looked up. Caught his eye. Smiled. His teeth were gold. From the front left tooth flashed a jewel.

Max pushed his way to the head of the line. At the yellow line, he waited until he heard that one-two thud. Then he went straight up to the checkpoint. Without looking up, Yelena Victorovna pushed a brown lock of hair back. Tucked it beneath her blue military cap. "Please wait your turn, sir," she said. "Or I will have to call security."

"Lenochka," he said, desperate. "Lenochka, please, please, if you let me through this one time, I'll marry you."

"Mr. Rushmore," she said. "I happen to know that you are already married."

"Yelena Victorovna," he said, and all the joking had gone out of his voice. "Please."

She looked at him, then. With those arresting cat eyes. She blinked, once. Then she said, "Passport, please." Sweating with relief, Max handed it to her. "Reason for travel?"

"Business," he said.

"Expected length of stay?"

"Three weeks."

With a click and a one-two thud, he was in.

PART V

37

Max strode quickly through the airport lobby. Crowded. Good. He spotted a young woman in high heels, tight jeans and a big fur vest who was trying to keep not one but two small children from escaping into the crowd. Perfect. As he passed, he reached into her large purse so quickly that she was none the wiser. Silently, and not for the first time, he thanked Pedro, in Quito, who had schooled him in the art of the pickpocket.

In the taxi, Max pulled out his spoils: an iPhone ensconced in a rubber casing with large bunny rabbit ears. Max felt like he was falling. He put his hand out on the door handle to steady himself. The dizziness passed. Max flicked the bunny ears with his thumb and forefinger. He Googled 'radiation poisoning'. Symptoms: nausea, weakness, dizziness.

He looked out the window at the long dull highway. A gray rain had just started to fall. Was it here that Ivan the Terrible rode out to hunt hawks? A dirt footpath ran along the side of the highway. In the distance, it led to a large plastic dome. A metro station. Max told the driver to pull over.

Descending to the underground train, Max dropped the phone in a bent, metal trashcan. On the platform, he stole another phone—a lower tech model, this time—and called Dunkirk.

"Jim," he said. "I want a meeting."

"Can't today, sorry," said Dunkirk, whose voice sounded far away, then grew louder. "I'm at the First Annual International War Olympics. Somewhere outside of Moscow. God the weather

is awful—oh, Jesus. Wait—I can't—they're playing Shosta-
kovich's first Tank Ballet. For fucking real. Oh, Christ. There's
four tanks down there. Dancing. I'm getting too old for this job.
What's that? Sure, sure, come down to the *dacha* tomorrow. The
weather's supposed to be better."

*

Max arrived in the city center none the worse for wear. Here,
in the underground, it was warm and stuffy, like an overheated
living room. Comforting. Comfortable. Shuffling through an
underground hall, Max felt strange again. He leaned against a
wall of purple marble. "Are you alright, young man?" asked an
old woman in a leopard-print raincoat, peering at him through
the thick lenses of her glasses. Max thanked her, said he was fine,
just fine. Ahead, the middle escalator was broken, and a bottleneck of people was assembling.

Then Max saw him, like a flickering mirage.

It was the stance Max recognized. Head forward, the salesman's
duck and weave. Belly out. A man unafraid of his appetites. Bob
Diamond, aka Bob Dominion, was at the head of the bottleneck.
He stepped onto the escalator. He was being carried up, up and
away.

Max would never make it through that bottleneck of people.
He did the next best thing—sprinting to the broken escalator, he
began to run up the brown, toothy stairs. He gained on Diamond,
whose head was bent. Max kept running, his breath coming in
gasps. Max felt a pain sear through his lungs. He pushed harder,
the distance closed. The sepia lighting. The incandescent wands.
A wave of nausea. Max pushed it away. A woman on the escalator
smiled at him encouragingly as he passed her. Max's lungs were
beginning to burn. He felt himself slowing. It was his legs that
were the problem. The escalator steps were steep, not meant for
vaulting. He began to slow.

Diamond pulled ahead. The encouraging woman caught up with Max. Then she was borne up, past him, as if on wings. She gave him a sad little smile. Max paused, gasped for air. Max could just make out the station's domed roof.

The man stepped off the escalator. It was over. He was gone.

When Max's breath returned, he trudged, slowly, the rest of the way. Outside, there was some sort of gathering, a slow moving procession. Max fought his way into the mass of people without really seeing them: he was looking for Diamond. But his progress was strangely slow, as if he was caught in a stream. He looked around, into a pair of vacant eyes. He looked around and saw another and another. No one seemed to notice him. In their hands they carried giant placards.

Max craned his neck and saw each one was an enormous, black and white photo. So these were the immortal battalions! The president had recently encouraged citizens to keep their loved ones' memories alive from the Second World War with these parades—"The dead are always the best friends of dictators," an academic had told Max at an artists' party in St. Petersburg—'immortal battalions' or 'Zombie armies,' depending on your political perspective. Max hadn't seen one up close before.

Max struggled as the crowd swept on, with a force of its own. No Diamond. Finally, he made it to the other side of the human masses and emerged, coughing, on the far sidewalk. There was no one there. No one at all. He stumbled into a side street. Church bells were ringing with an urgency, as if there was a fire. But it was just Sunday.

38

Pick pocketing what he promised the phone gods would be his last one of the day, Max slipped in his last Chinese SIM card. Almost immediately, the little black Nokia that had, until recently, been used mostly by its original owner to invite married women to come over for a drink, began to ring.

"Maxka! Finally! I've been ringing you constantly for twenty-four hours! Where the hell are you? Please say Moscow, or I'm a dead man." It was Pasha the Playwright.

"Conveniently, my friend, I am in Moscow," said Max.

"Where the hell else would you be, with my passport? Don't answer that, I don't want to know. Meet me at the gym. Bring the damn passport, or my wife will dispense with my manly parts. Yours too."

The Lermontov Gym was a product of the oil boom, and once inside its sliding doors you would never know that the economy was slipping into free-fall. Here everything was soft, quiet, lush. "Nice," Max agreed, when Pasha had brought him here the first time. "It's really got that first-world feel."

Three girls in the new-new-new Moscow uniform—khaki pants and long blonde ponytails—handed Max three sets of towels on his way into the dressing room. The smell of chlorine hung in the air. He found Pasha in the juice bar, handed him a rolled-up towel with his passport inside. Pasha enveloped Max in a bear hug.

"Carrot juice?" he said.

Max accepted, and the waitress poured heavy cream into the bright orange liquid. Max sipped, felt a little healthier.

"Pasha," he said. "How can I get in touch with this Constantin Fuks? You know, the one who owns Midnight and all those night-clubs—you know."

"The restaurant baron!" said Pasha. "Hm, I think he spends most of his time at a place called Blackout—it was a big money-maker in the mid-aughts. Not so healthy now, I guess. Publicity. That's your best bet. Say you're writing for one those American magazines."

"Pasha," said Max, "you are a genius. A hero for our time."

"Go for a swim," said Pasha. "You look terrible."

39

After he left Pasha, Max staked out a little table on the balcony under the glassed-in arcade ceiling of the GUM department store. There was a steady, oppressive white noise here. A natural buffer between him and electronic eavesdroppers. For good measure, he started by dialing a food industry analyst in London. She regaled him with stories of rampant theft and food poisoning in Soviet restaurants.

"Great, great," he said, cradling the phone in one ear and taking notes by hand. "That's wonderful, thanks."

Next, he tried the PR office for the Bar Vodka Group. Max had looked it up. The President and CEO was, in fact, referred to simply as Constantin. He read their 'about us' section—a broken-English language celebration of typicality: "Constantin grew up with the typical Soviet cuisine. He loved to watch his typical grandmother cook, and she always shooed him out of the small, typical kitchen. After training in the Soviet chef academy, Constantin dreamed of working in a typical hotel kitchen. When the first McDonald's opened in Moscow, Constantin applied and was rejected. Instead, he worked as chef at Planet Holly-wood. Today, thanks to Constantin's tasty adventure, his Group Vodka Bar opened nearly forty exclusive restaurants and bars in Moscow. Now, when the chief of McDonald's comes to eat at five-star restaurant Submarine, Constantin shakes his hand and says, 'Thank you! Thank you for not hiring me!' We at Group Vodka Bar are always dreaming new concepts for you."

Indeed, Bar Vodka Group seemed to own everything: Penthouse, Playboy (both cafés were collaborations with the American publications), Submarine, Bread (a restaurant decorated to look like you had just wandered into the interior of a loaf of bread), Goldplate (where the plates were gold), Sushi (where the waitresses were naked), and Faith (where you ate beef carpaccio with a view of the cathedral).

The phone rang. "Yes!" said a woman's voice on the other end of the line.

"Hi," said Max. "I'm a journalist with 'Gourmeterie Magazine'. I'm writing about restaurants in Moscow, and I was wondering—"

"Wait," said the woman. She said something, in a muffled tone, to someone in the background. "Who are you?"

"Max Rushmore, 'Gourmeterie Magazine'—"

"Ok!" she said.

"I'm in Moscow and I was wondering if I could interview Constantin..."

"Ha, ha!" she said, with a staccato burst of laughter. "That would be nice, wouldn't it!"

"Um, yes," said Max. "That would be great."

"Ha!" shouted the woman again. There was a pause and a strange click-click sound. Then she spoke again. "Call back next week!" She hung up. Max looked down at the phone. Call back next week. Great. Fantastic.

The phone rang again five minutes later. A man, this time. His instructions were fairly bizarre. Max was to arrive tonight, at 10pm precisely. The location was a place called Blackout, 'the hottest spot in Moscow, killing all the competition.'

Max was to announce himself to the woman at the reception as "Max, just Max." She would ask him if he was interested in the tongue appetizer, and he was to say, "Yes, if it's fresh." She would say, "Today it is not, would you prefer the steak tartar? It is the house specialty." To which he must reply, "Absolutely, that is why I came to Moscow." Then, she would lead him to the private room, where Constantin, or an emissary if Constantin himself was delayed for any reason due to un-postpone-able business, would meet him. Most important, however, was that Max wear a red carnation in his buttonhole. "To avoid unpleasant confusion," said the man, and hung up.

Right, thought Max. From his post under GUM's glass ceiling, he watched the sky deepen, turning a moodier, darker evening shade. Finally, Max set out on foot. He found an old lady with a blue plastic bucket with a bunch of flowers, individually wrapped in plastic. The blossoms were red. Carnations. He bought one, snapped the stalk off near the neck and stuck the flower in his buttonhole. The old woman looked at him, then.

"Big night, eh?" she said.

Max winked. "Let's see."

He hailed a car from the Kremlin. A little blue Lada. They crossed the river. In the distance, as they approached, was the statue of Peter the Great, dark and metallic, unwieldy and comic, perched on the deck of a tiny ship. "The artist is a great friend of the former mayor," said the driver, an art history professor, bitterly.

"It's not great," agreed Max.

"The decline of civilization as we know it," said the driver.

The art history professor let him off at the embankment. Max walked along the water. He stopped for a moment. Observed the Peter the Great statue, black against the black sky. Kept walking.

40

Max rang the bell at 10pm on the dot, Anglo-Saxon style. There was no answer. Russian-style, thought Max. He waited, rang again. Finally the door buzzed and he pushed it open. He stepped inside, where a set of blood-red velvet curtains blocked the way. The door shut behind him and the place was in utter darkness.

"Come," said a woman's voice. "Through the curtains." Max did as she said, waiting for his eyes to adjust to the darkness. He felt for the curtains and found them, heavy and soft, smelling of cigarettes and rosewater. He stepped gingerly through them. He was surprised that nothing changed in his visual perception; by now his eyes should have started to adjust. Instead, it was as dark as ever, darker, in fact. A sudden sense of vertigo overwhelmed him, and he had the sensation that he couldn't step forward or he would fall into an abyss.

He heard her move away and was afraid.

"Welcome to Blackout," she said. "Are you Max, just Max?"

"Uh, yes," he said, feeling vaguely as if she had stolen his line.

"Are you interested in the tongue appetizer?"

"Yes," said Max. "If it's fresh."

"Today it is not, would you prefer the steak tartar? It is the house specialty."

"Absolutely," said Max, beginning to be annoyed at the darkness, at the absurdity of the interchange. "That is why I came to Moscow."

"Good," she said, and he felt her take his hand in hers, then guide his fingers towards her. She placed his hand on a warm, firm, vertical surface. For a moment, his fingers lay there, then he began to make out a delicate, uneven ridge protruding slightly from the center of this surface. Max realized, with a start, that he was touching her bare back; that the ridge was the bones of the girl's spine. She must be wearing almost nothing, he concluded, but did not move his hand to explore further. "Follow me," she said. "Stay close."

With a surer step, but still unable to fully shake the sensation that he was taking a step into an abyss, Max moved one foot, then the other, as she led the way. Her flesh was warm. The only sound, in the darkness, was the clicking of her heels.

*

The hostess led Max into an elevator, he assumed, because suddenly they stopped walking and he felt that they were being carried upwards. The floor bumped to a stop, and she said again, "Come." He had never been so grateful for the tactile feeling of human companionship, and he sensed that she knew this. She stopped, so suddenly that he almost stepped on her, and knocked (he could feel the muscular reverberations in her back) authoritatively on a door.

"Come in, my dear," came a voice followed by a strange yipping sound through the door. She opened it, and they walked through. Max felt her turn, lost contact, then felt her hand on his. Running her hand up his arm, she took him by the elbow and helped him into a large, velvet armchair.

"Now you may speak to Constantin," she said, and Max felt a tinge of regret as he heard her heels go click-clacking away. The door shut, and the echo grew fainter.

"Mr. Constantin?" said Max.

"Yes, how do you like our concept?" came the same, deep voice, followed again by that strange, inhuman yipping. "In a place like Moscow, of course, it makes perfect sense! We are so overexposed. In less than a generation of capitalism, we have seen everything. Everything! In the West, you have proceeded much more slowly. Over generations. You can't understand this sudden saturation. What it does to the senses of Homo Sovieticus. You want to know what is the secret of my success?"

"Uh, yes," said Max.

"I will tell you! Here, we have been going in the opposite direction. At Blackout, for example, we think of Oedipus: only when he is blind, can he see. Also, minimal was very chic when we opened. It was all about understatement."

"Yes, very ... classic," said Max.

"Deprivation! It is the last uncharted territory in entertainment. We aren't stopping at Blackout. Tasteless, that's the next. We will bring in the best chefs from Paris—you know most of our functionaries are not allowed to travel to the West anymore, so we are being patriotic when we bring our Michelin star cooks here. The chefs will produce the most wonderful menus, every night. But—! When guests enter the restaurant, they will be obliged to swallow a pill in the cloakroom. This pill paralyzes the taste buds for several hours." He chuckled. "It was that, or cut their tongues out." Again, the growl came. "So they will eat the finest of everything. But they will have no way of knowing what it tastes like."

"I see what you're saying," said Max. "Very interesting."

"I just hope," the deep voice grew suddenly depressed, "that the timing is right. If the economy continues to collapse, then minimalism, deprivation—this will no longer be in vogue."

"Ah," said Max, fumbling with his pen in the dark.

"Thank you," said the voice, heavily. "I can feel your sympathy. You are a man who cares about others. I sense that. I know. Restaurant men, we can read a person immediately—his strengths, his weaknesses, his morals. At least, successful restaurateurs have this ability. And I am—if I may be so bold—the most successful of all! Ah! Your steak tartar has arrived! Note what the darkness does to the taste, to the feel of blood in your mouth. Yes, you are kind, Mr. Rushmore. It is your strength. And it is your weakness. Which is why, naturally, you try to hide it. In the dark, things become clearer. This is always the case."

Max nodded, trying to write as fast as he could. His pen kept running off the page, in the dark. Max heard footsteps retreating and wondered that he hadn't heard the waiter approach. And what was that snuffling? It was as if the darkness was playing tricks on his ears. He felt, blindly, in front of himself for cutlery, located a knife thanks to its blade. Discarded it in favor of a spoon. He scooped up a bite, and put it, gingerly, in his mouth. All he could taste was blood: a cool, metallic tang. His stomach rebelled almost immediately.

"You are playing a dangerous game, Mr. Rushmore," said Constantin, after Max had paused to write a few notes in his notepad.

"Sorry?" said Max.

"Journalism—ha! It's a dangerous hobby. But that's not what I mean. And you know it."

Max was silent.

"Oh yes!" the other man went on, and again that yipping sounded. This time, though, it didn't stop when he spoke, but continued, a low, threatening tone underscoring his words.

"DAMMIT!" yelled the voice, and Max jumped as a fist came down, hard, on the table, followed by a chorus of inhuman groaning. "Don't play games with me, Mr. Max Rushmore. Do you know that a third of the food we produce in the world goes straight into the trash? And that the water we use to grow this wasted food could sustain the entire earth's population for one year? Disgusting! Especially for a country like mine, which has known hunger. Let us not even talk about the cheese burning! And the pork. This is an abomination, propagated by the regime. Don't write that in your article. If my grandmother were alive today ... I cannot stand waste!"

Max lifted a spoonful of bloody tasting meat to his mouth, swallowed it without chewing. There was silence, and then the voice continued, in an entirely different tone, easy and peaceable.

"You have given me a new idea for a hotspot! I think I will call it, simply, 'Dumb'. What do you think? Recently, I heard about a special high-frequency tone, developed in secret by Soviet scientists during the Cold War. This frequency makes it impossible for the human ear to function. We will play it constantly in the restaurant! Everybody orders food and drink using—how do you call it, charade?"

He laughed. "To make love to a woman, you no longer have words at your disposal. Everything must be done with the hands, the eyes. The body. What do you think? It is very good, very good. But honesty is always best. That's my point."

"I see," said Max.

"That's just the point!" howled the voice. "You don't see anything at Blackout. In addition to being kind, my friend, you are dishonest. Maybe not in the big things. But certainly in the little ones. I imagine your wife suffers a good deal because of this. None of this is the point. The point is, just because you don't see, doesn't mean that I cannot. I have a good view, as a matter of fact. I see things you cannot even imagine. I am happy to have made your acquaintance. It gives me a better sense of things."

"Ok," said Max. "Maybe we could talk a little bit about how you got into the restaurant business."

"SILENCE!" bellowed the voice. "You can read all about that on the internet."

"You can't trust everything you read on the internet..."

"The thing is, Mr. Rushmore, that I'm bored. Have you noticed? After all, what is a restaurant-maker? A fantasist? A seer into souls? A businessman, yes. An artist? In a way. Maybe 'craftsman' is more accurate. But we are also makers of theater, my friend. A low-brow theater, a theater of consumption. The actors are amateurs—a new cast every night. It's very frustrating

213

if you have ever had real pretensions to the stage. I did—and still do. Unfortunately I am not very talented. Fortunately, I am very rich. So in a way, Mr. Rushmore, you should consider this evening an audition. Yes, I am watching, waiting, wondering. What role can you play? By the way, Mr. Rushmore. Don't forget that I own every restaurant in this town. If you ever want to eat out again, you'll stop playing with that steak tartar and finish it. Every last morsel."

Before Max had a chance to wonder how it was this man could see that he had been pushing the raw meat back and forth on the plate, lifting empty spoonfuls to his mouth to simulate consumption—for some reason, his stomach was rebelling—the door slammed.

The lights came on. A white blindness replaced the darkness. Max blinked. His eyes teared. Finally he began to see. He looked around, still blinking. A large, shabby room. It had once been grand. The table was rough. Large enough for a banquet. Each and every place was set, and at each setting there was a plate, identical to his but licked clean, except for traces of blood at the edges.

Looking sleepy and sated, a red fox sat in the seat across from him. When Max stood, he growled, baring his teeth. Max backed out, carefully. The fox let him go.

The lights in the marble hall were on now, too, showing a rather dreary, dilapidated place. Max took the stairs and let himself out a back door.

In a dark little alley, he vomited.

41

Bob Diamond made his way pensively through the aisles of Collective Farmer, picking up neatly packaged goods. Freeze-dried Kamchatka fish. Siberian pinecone jelly, tied with a red ribbon. Heavy cream from Tver. Tolstoy Estate honey. He turned each item over in his big hands. Shook his head at the prices. Observed the rough-hewn floors and flea-market furniture. The breakfasting wives. Looked at the prices again. Maybe he was in the wrong business.

Finally, a young woman in a green and white checked apron approached him. "Mr. Diamond?" she said. He nodded, once, a single jerk of the head. "Constantin is waiting. If you'll follow me?"

She led him through a door, down a long, dark hallway, to a storage closet packed nearly full of jars. In the corner, taking up almost no space at all, was a very tall, skeletal man, with a corpse-like pallor and a shock of red hair. The Russian was folded into himself, nestling his chin in his large hand.

As Diamond sidled carefully into the room, Constantin reached out his unnaturally long arm in greeting. "My friend!" he said. Then the two men sat, knees touching, on two rickety chairs. The waitress closed the door, and the tiny closet immediately grew stuffy.

"What do you think?" asked Constantin, his smile showing a row of gray teeth. Before Diamond could respond, he continued. "Collective Farmer is our newest daytime dining endeavor.

Wildly popular. It's a grocery-slash-restaurant. Very American, no? You people are so inspiring. At Collective Farmer, everything is 'local'. Russian cows, Russian streams, Russian trees. And you don't even have to buy furniture! This whole restaurant used to be our storage space. It's a terrific business plan. Here, try a Siberian pinecone *gelée*—" Before Diamond could demur, Constantin was holding the spoon to his mouth. In an automatic response, he opened his lips. The pinecone was small, the size of a ruble coin. Soft. Sweet.

"It tastes like … the forest," said Diamond, thoughtfully.

"Exactly," said Constantin. "I'm very glad you contacted me, by the way. I've made a lot of progress on the case. It's a very, very interesting situation. One that, without you, might never have come to my attention."

Bob Diamond demurred again. He was growing very uncomfortable in this small space. "I hardly need to explain how potentially disastrous a glut of black market Siberian jewels is for my industry," he said.

"No," said Constantin, with a wink, like a magician. "It's a good thing you spotted that ring on—what was her name? The scientist?"

"Sonja Ostranova," said Diamond. "It was just luck that I happened to sit next to her at that restaurant. It was the first hint of a trail."

Constantin shook his head. "But to think, that people can be so corrupt. Use their access to exploit the natural resources of their native country."

Diamond shrugged.

"You were right to come to me," Constantin repeated. "I am a simple restaurant owner, of course. But friendship, like love, often goes through the stomach. And I have many friends in this country. Perhaps it is enough to say I believe you'll see prices stabilizing soon."

"So you've made progress, in spite of her death," said Diamond.

Constantin nodded.

Diamond stood, and Constantin followed. Diamond handed the restaurant man a soft leather suitcase. Constantin opened it. Under the single, bare bulb, the contents shone. All the colors of the rainbow, with a mysterious blue light.

"*Mazal und Bracha*," said Diamond. "I trust you will not put these back on the market, as per our agreement."

"*Mazal und Bracha*," said Constantin. "Of course I will not."

After Diamond left, Constantin peered into the leather case again. He rubbed his hands together. He had made progress. Oh yes, he certainly had.

42

In the morning, Max woke up, with a headache, to the sound of laps being swum. He groaned, rolled over on his not-entirely comfortable plastic lounge chair, pulled his bathrobe over his head. He heard a neighbor groan, in similar fashion: the indoor pool at the Lermontov Gym was known as a place for disgraced husbands and other wealthy, temporarily homeless men to spend the night. Max felt for the entry pass card he had stolen on his way out yesterday. Still there, deep in the fuzzy pocket. He stood. A quick session in the steam room reconciled him to the day. A red fox. A red fox? What a maniac.

He dressed while the janitor vacuumed the men's room.

Then he set out for the day. The weather, like Dunkirk said, was much improved: sunny, a hint of warmth. A respite, however temporary.

*

Max had always found the American Embassy *dacha* profoundly depressing. From the metro, he caught a creaky electric bus and watched as they passed a strange, half-empty landscape. Communist high rises, construction sites where buildings identical to the Communist high rises were half complete. Flashy, cheap one-story storefronts. Fast food restaurants whose mediocre menus would cost the average Muscovite two-thirds of a month's wages. Japanese, Italian. 'Democratic dining' was what they were calling

fast food, though Max wasn't sure which part was democratic—
that the food was so overpriced, or that it was so disappointing.

The bus turned off the highway and into a residential area.
Here, the A-line and Italianate roofs of mansions peeked out from
behind the two-story walls that blocked them from the street. In
the last decade, this area had become a boomtown for oligarchs
who built luxurious '*dachas*' and commuted, by Mercedes, to the
city center to work.

At the last stop, Max descended from the bus. He walked across
the grassy area that marked the bus route's end, where several very
proletarian-looking families had gathered, holding picnic baskets on
their way to the open beach, and made his way to the residential street.

The *dacha* was the third house on the street, set back on the lot.
The front part of the lot had been ignored by the architect, so Max
picked his way across a bed of rotting pine needles. As he neared
the low-slung building, he could see Embassy men and their
wives clustered at a large, hewn-log picnic bench, and several
others gathered by what appeared to be a potluck buffet. You
could see they were American, the women at least, at a glance:
wearing jeans and running shoes, hair aggressively unadorned. A
defiant adherence to the national costume.

The women, thought Max, were no dowdier than the *dacha*
itself. Part lodge for a Midwestern family camp, part plastic
Lincoln Logs set. Max sidled around to the front of the building,
which faced away from the street, down a derelict lawn towards a
tennis court that had seen better days. He smiled in return at a few
of the wives, who glanced at him invitingly, as if to say, 'Welcome,
who are you?' He looked around for Dunkirk but didn't see him.

A wife who appeared to be in charge came over and took him
by the arm. "I'm Joyce Reed," she said. "And...?"

"Max Rushmore," he replied, hurriedly. "I'm looking for Jim
Dunkirk."

"Ooooh!" she cooed enthusiastically. "Jimmy! He's around
here, somewhere. Would you like something to eat? Paper

plates are over there, help yourself, and the drinks are inside."

With that, she left him, and Max climbed the steps to the concrete slab that constituted the front porch, then entered the lodge's long, dark main room. It was as institutional as ever, he reflected, as he looked around. The place was strangely bare of furniture: a couple of young men sat at a long wooden table listening, rapt, to an older fellow who was talking about war zones ("I've covered forty-three wars ..." Max caught) and how much better he liked his newest project, developing shopping malls in the countryside ('We're bringing these people ... life!' he said, as the boys nodded).

Three Russian girlfriends, presumably belonging to the three young men hanging on the born-again developer's words, sat together in the corner on a pair of shabby stuffed chairs. They were in full makeup, hair up, pants tight, like wild birds in captivity.

There were five bedrooms off the main room which, if they hadn't changed, and Max bet they hadn't, had two to four beds each, and that same spartan, family camp quality to them. Dunkirk might well be in one of them, sleeping the first phase of the party off. Max decided to pour himself a drink at the plywood bar before embarking on his search.

He lined up behind a sandy-haired man and a reasonably attractive American girl; the sandy-haired man poured a plastic cup nearly full of vodka, searched for cranberry juice, and turned to the girl. "Haven't we met before?" he said, clumsily striking up a conversation. "If we did, I was probably drunk..." Max pretended not to be listening as the girl looked at her interlocutor. "Excuse me," she said, "but I don't think that's something you say to a lady."

She poured herself a coke and walked off. The sandy-haired man stood for a moment, blinking. Then he shrugged, sipped his drink, and wandered away.

Max took the sandy-haired man's lead and filled a plastic cup with vodka, splashed it with cranberry, and took a long drink. It burned, and Max felt as if he was awake for the first time in days.

"Max!" he heard, and turned.

Standing in the door of one of the bedrooms was, indeed, Jim Dunkirk. Dunkirk came over and clapped Max on the back so hard that half of Max's vodka sloshed over onto his jacket, so hard that Max wasn't sure if the reek of booze was Dunkirk or himself.

"Let's have a drink. How'dya like our little shindig here? Just like the old days, just like the old days. Want to play tennis? I'll get the rackets."

As always, Dunkirk managed to both direct the entire conversation and pour himself and Max a round of drinks. Before Max knew it, he was half drunk, in possession of a tennis racket, and heading down to the little caged court.

"Here we are, Maxyboy," said Dunkirk, lobbing a ball at him across the net. "What did you want to talk about?"

Max returned the lob and said, "There have been some interesting turns in the Ostranova case."

"Ostranova?" Dunkirk's racket made a round, full thwack as it hit the ball. "Never heard of her."

Max's concentration was momentarily on the ball coming at him with speed. As he positioned his feet to return the volley, he heard Dunkirk's voice carried over the net. "And if you know what's good for you, neither have you."

Max looked up, missing the ball. "What?"

Dunkirk reached into his pocket and served the next ball. "You heard me."

Max returned the ball with too much force so that it hit out of bounds. "Over the line," called Dunkirk. "Let's take a break for drinks."

They sat side by side on the bench next to the court, and Dunkirk pulled a vodka bottle and two more plastic cups out of the tennis bag. He poured. "Look, Maxyboy, do I really have to explain this? Was your assignment to find her? No, it was not. That means even if you do find her, which you shouldn't, she stays lost."

"But her eyes are green," said Max.

"Whose eyes?"

"Ostranova's. Death certificate said brown."

"Written up by some drunk in the morgue."

"But—"

"But what, Maxyboy? She's an expert in nuclear waste disposal. What do you think we've got to worry about? That she'll teach the Russians how to dispose of that stuff safely? Don't be a moron."

"What if she's joined a—an eco-terrorist group?"

"Jesus," said Dunkirk. "Then I really don't want to find her. Let the Russians deal with her—that's just their kind of thing. An eco-terrorist! Jesus Max, you really never learned how to play this game."

"It wasn't a real case," said Max, the truth slowly dawning on him. "You just needed somebody to sign off on it."

Dunkirk shrugged. "I tried to tell you. Somebody's got to do the secretarial stuff. And," he added with a glower, "if I hear another word about it, you'll be out of a job quicker than you can say 'boo.'"

"But—"

"Look," said Dunkirk, no longer smiling. "I mean it. We're doing some pretty delicate footwork with the Russians right now, what with the political situation and so forth. We're talking World War Three, nuclear catastrophe, whole hog. I tell you how I spent the whole day in the rain watching tanks do ballet?" He shook his head. "Jesus. Anyway. Anything untoward could go up in flames, like that. So zip it. Sit tight. Collect your paycheck. Then go home."

He downed his vodka and refilled the cup. He held it up, and Max followed, reluctantly. "Cheers." The two men drank in one gulp. Then Dunkirk said, "Now that we're warmed up, let's get out there and play a real game."

Max lost, 30-love. He got a ride back to the city with a couple of American TV journalists whose tennis rackets he and Dunkirk had borrowed. They let him sit in the back of the van, with the equipment. They dropped him off on the New Arbat, and Max felt simultaneously drunk and already hungover. A good metaphor, he thought as he stood on the sidewalk in the gathering twilight, for his entire life.

43

The following morning, Constantin received a very interesting call. This was unusual for a man like Constantin, for whom success had been almost laughably easy—while most men followed success, dogged it, day after day, to little or no avail, material riches had practically sprinted towards him. All Constantin had had to do was open his hands, receive. There was a price, of course: most of his days were almost unbearably dull. True love, the one thing that would have made life interesting, worth living, had evaded him.

Until now. Now, he thought, now he had a second chance. How many men are so lucky?

After the call, he smiled. He checked the time. He dressed. His chauffeur was waiting. He hoisted himself up into the backseat of the shiny black Land Rover. Inside, the pleasing smell of leather. Constantin watched the streets pass. Moscow was a city best seen by car. Behind dark, bulletproof glass, the city looked lovely at night. The curving boulevards with their leafless trees. The apartment buildings with their massive archways and small, twinkling lights. The unexpected vistas.

At the French Embassy, he descended. He was fashionably late. An elaborate mansion. A luxuriant study in nineteenth-century pseudo-Russian kitsch, the hefty, bulbous building overran its budget and drove its architect to suicide. Inside, in a long, drafty blue ballroom with chipped herringbone floors, champagne was being served on trays. Immense chandeliers cast an uneven light. The men wore suits. The women, subdued cocktail dresses.

One woman caught his eye. She looked French. Chic. She wore a narrow white sheath dress over a boyish body. Her skin was tanned. A string of pearls rested on her prominent collarbone. She was not beautiful. But there was a steeliness to her, in her upright posture, in her gray eyes. He would have given her at least the third best table in the house if she appeared at one of his restaurants without a reservation. He would have been afraid not to.

"The trouble with the Russians," Constantin heard one man say to another, as he moved through the room, "is that they only plan six months in advance." "No normal concept of a future" agreed the other. It did not take long for Constantin to find the man he was looking for.

Gerard Dupres was standing in the corner. He looked nervous. Like his stomach was bothering him. If the man wasn't Constantin's rival—enemy—he would have ordered the kitchen to boil him up a chicken soup. No matter. The important thing was that Gerard Dupres was here. In Moscow. Constantin had thought that the notes alone would be enough to scare him into submission. But he wasn't sure. That's why he had wanted that Rushmore to pay Gerard a visit. Let him know what was out in the open. Let him guess at what else could come out. Constantin chuckled. His plan appeared to have worked.

Now, Constantin sidled up to the Frenchman. Handed him his card. Gerard Dupres took it, casually. Arrogantly. But when he turned the card over he blanched. Good, thought Constantin, glancing over at the message he himself had written on the back of the card. He had signed it, as always, '– C.' The Frenchman looked up into Constantin's eyes with fear. Nodded.

"Later," said Constantin, suddenly inspired—this was a deviation from his plan but he couldn't help it, he just had to hint at the surprise he had arranged. "The two of us, we'll go together to the

Fomenko Theater. I have something marvelous planned! I think you'll find it"—from the corner of his eye, Constantin saw that the woman in white had moved closer to them. Within earshot? He didn't think so—"interesting."

After he left Gerard, Constantin made a few rounds through the ballroom—it was important to keep up relations with his French suppliers, after all. Since the sanctions had started, a turf war had broken out over camembert, for instance, and at least three men had lost their lives for it. But he kept Gerard in his sights the whole time.

What did Sonja see in that weasel? Clearly a weak man like that was better suited to his current partner, the steely female in the white dress. No matter. It would all be taken care of soon. As Constantin left—it was a work night, after all, he still had to visit his restaurants, conduct spot checks, surprise inspections, take the temperature of each place—he made sure to pass near the woman in white. She was engaged in conversation with an elderly Russian general. He wore his full uniform, and his chest was covered with ribbons and medals. He was leaning in towards her eagerly. His teeth were bad. She leaned back, cool, aloof.

Then she leaned in, a low flame sparking in her eye. "Certainly I'll come," he overheard her say. "Your weapons collection from the Second World War must be fascinating."

44

Max woke, again, to the sound of laps being swum. His head hurt. He rolled over on the not-very-comfortable plastic lounge chair. His neighbor snored. He was going to have to find a new place to sleep: at Lermontov there was an unspoken three-night limit. Max groaned. He sat up. To his surprise, there was a note on his lounge chair. He picked it up. "My secretary will telephone. – C"

Before Max could puzzle out the meaning of the note, his phone rang. "Max?" said a woman's voice. It sounded familiar, but he couldn't place it. "Max, just Max?" she purred. Max realized where he knew it from: the naked hostess at Blackout.

"Yes," he answered, annoyed. She was probably calling to forbid him to use any quotes without checking with Constantin first.

"Constantin wishes to meet with you again."

"Oh," said Max. "That's nice of him, but I'm not sure I really have time—"

"He would like you to come to—a special performance. An intersection of sorts—he has conceived of it as the particular meeting of time and space."

"Events," said Max, "are a very hard category for a monthly like 'Gourmeterie' to cover. We pretty much stick to evergreen topics—restaurants, recipes. Things our readers could, in theory, experience for themselves."

"It's being held at the new Fomenko Theatre. A once-in-a-lifetime chance," she said. "We call it 'Midnight.'"

Something clicked, then: the Time Machine. Sonja Ostranova. The eyes that said help me. The lips that said, "Midnight." Constantin. "– C."

Max shook his head. That was crazy, all of it.

"Constantin says don't be late."

45

There were thirteen hours until midnight. Max decided to do a little investigation on his own. Blackout, by day, was unimpressive. A run-down brick building on Red October island. Not so long ago, when the wind was right, you could still smell the chocolate that used to be produced here.

Max walked around to the back. Here, two low-slung buildings were abandoned. A third claimed to be a *banya*. A tiny monastery with ancient golden domes rounded out the yard. The monks had planted a small garden out front. This patch of ground looked empty, as if it had yielded the last of the year's vegetables. Max felt that strange tingling at the base of his neck again. Something told him to look behind the monastery. He made his way to the crooked plaster walls, pressed himself flat against them.

Turning the corner, he saw him: the man with the golden teeth. The man's back was to him, but he would have recognized that figure anywhere.

Max had his arm around the man's throat in an instant. He smelled of salmon. The pocket knife was out, aimed at the jugular. "Who the hell are you?" Max muttered between clenched teeth. "Why did you kill that poor kid?"

The man sighed. He seemed not the least disconcerted by the position he found himself in—which disconcerted Max, somewhat. "You Europeans are all alike," he said. "The boy is only dead in this reality. In another one, that's not nearly as far away as you think it is, he's as happy as can be. Trespassing to his heart's content. Poking his nose in places he has no right to be. Now let me ask you a question."

"Shoot," said Max.

"How did you know I was here?" Max was silent. "I'll tell you how," the man continued. "I took the kid's diamond. So I've got one, you've got one. These diamonds, they're linked to one another. What happens to one, happens to another. And if I've got one, and you've got one, we communicate. With our minds."

"Why didn't you know I was coming?"

In an instant, their roles were reversed. Max didn't know how it happened, but Goldtooth's arm was around his neck, the knife cold against his jugular. "I did," said the man. "I figured you'd be more willing to talk if you thought you were in control of the situation."

He let Max go. Max's neck smarted. He rubbed it. Goldtooth threw the knife down on the ground, and Max picked it up. The temperature seemed to be falling rapidly. A wind kicked up. Max's fingers ached. He wondered where the monks were. If they were watching from somewhere inside. What would they do if Goldtooth killed him? Nothing, he guessed.

"Come on," said Goldtooth. "Let's find someplace to sit."

They walked to Gorky Park. Past Iron Felix, the founder of the Cheka. For decades he stood in front of Lubyanka. After the failed *putsch* of '91, he was removed. But not destroyed. Now he stood in a sad garden, surrounded by other discarded Soviet statues. But lately there had been a couple of petitions to put him back in place in front of the infamous prison. Max sighed.

Through the refurbished triumphal gates of the new Gorky Park, they found a bench. On the weekends, this place was always packed, a kind of post-Soviet Disneyland, with old-fashioned ice-cream and wi-fi. Max had a good view of the *petanque* course. No one was playing. In the distance they heard the sounds of tango music. It played a few strains, then shut off. Midday, midweek, between seasons.

"I intercepted the loan shark you sold the other diamond to, in Novosibirsk. Samodelkin's got that diamond now."

"And the loan shark? Is he happy in another dimension?"

Goldtooth shrugged. "What do you care?"

Max shrugged. "What are we talking about?" In the distance, two girls took turns posing for each other.

"This Fuks," said Goldtooth. "Constantin Fuks. He's an old friend of Samodelkin. They've been working together. Me, too. I'm the great-grandson of the most famous chieftain of the Time Travelers. We're an ancient Siberian tribe."

"I've heard," said Max. "'Time is a landscape...'"

Goldtooth gave him a poisonous look. For a moment Max thought he might have had it, that in another split-second he, too, would be living happily in another dimension. The danger passed before Max had time to feel afraid.

Goldtooth nodded, slowly. "A landscape," he said. "Yes. Much of our wisdom has been lost, of course. Stalin nearly destroyed us. My great-grandfather died in a gulag. Building a power station." He was silent for a moment. "I've been working with Samodelkin for some years now. He says we can regain the power to cross the landscape of time at will. But we need the diamonds to complete this phase of experiments."

"Right," said Max.

"Constantin Fuks claims to have gathered the diamonds. He said he will give them to us. But I have my suspicions. I don't trust this Fuks the way Samodelkin does. Samodelkin is a child in many ways. He creates like a child. But he thinks like a child, too."

"Why should this Constantin give you any diamonds?"

"That's what I want to know. That's why I decided to talk to you. Constantin has been giving me orders—he wanted you on that flight to Venice, you know. And two days ago, when you came back to Moscow, he wanted your blood. You got away. And then you found your own way to Constantin. He told me to forget you. Why?"

Max shook his head. "I have no idea."

Goldtooth shook his head as well. "He was supposed to give us the diamonds yesterday. He asked for more time."

"So give him more time," said Max.

Goldtooth balled his hands into fists. "I don't like it," he said. "I don't trust him. If we lose the diamonds, we might never have another chance."

"Where are these diamonds coming from?"

"Atom Town. A building project unearthed a kimberlitic pipe. The contractor took all the building money and used it to dig. The pipe was small but of an incredibly high quality. Samodelkin says that we can skip all kinds of steps if we can get enough of these diamonds."

"What happened to the contractor?"

"He disappeared. Probably into a river."

"And the diamonds?"

"Gone. Most were sold, internationally, before Fuks picked up the trail in Diamant. Down in the old mine, where the lab used to be, someone set up a new lab. Cutting and polishing in secret. Very clever, in fact. There are so many expert jewelers there. It will take quite some time to find out who is involved. It's too late, anyway. The lab is shut down again now."

"I don't know what to tell you," said Max.

"So I'll tell you: you want to find a woman, right?"

"I won't ask how you know that," said Max.

"And I want to find the diamonds. Let's watch Fuks together."

Max agreed. He wasn't sure he had a choice.

46

The rest of the day passed in cramped, cold boredom. He and Goldtooth—who refused to tell him his name—took shifts. Two hours each, while the other one warmed up. Max suspected Goldtooth didn't want to give him time to wander too far away. One interesting thing happened, however: around 8pm, Max was on duty as Gerard Dupres, looking as if he had screwed up his courage, entered Blackout.

At 10pm, the first car arrived. Black, shiny. Gliding. Like a mechanical shark. A woman in red descended. A bulky man. He moved slowly, deliberately. A man with power. The mechanical shark drove off, parked in the corner of the lot. A kind of death's head on wheels took its place. The black car's grill seemed to grin, at least in Max's imagination—his head was swimming a little again. A woman in yellow. A man who could have been the first man's twin. The death's head rolled off, glinting. Parked next to the shark. Soon the courtyard was full. The B-list guests came on foot. A group of expats. Indifferently dressed.

Max slipped into line behind them. The doorman gave him a look. Let him through.

As the expats—Brits, three women and two men, talking about their dinner reservation in the downstairs cafe—checked their coats, Max located the door to the stairway. When the coat-check girl's back was turned, he slipped behind the curtain, tried the door, pushed it open. He was back on the stairway.

He made his way up the stone steps, worn in the middle so that they buckled. The landing was tiled. A sepia light. A potted jade plant needed watering. On the second floor, Max made his way down the hallway. He stopped at each wooden door, listening. Then he heard voices coming up the stairs. One he recognized from the interview of the evening before.

He opened the door in front of him and stepped inside. He switched on the light, looked around. He was in an office. There was a Soviet-style desk, several metal file cabinets. A row of spider plants. One corner had a metal grate. It was locked shut.

Max jumped aside as the door opened behind him. He doubled over in pain. His stomach. A fist. Radiating. Rough hands dragged him to the metal office chair. Tied his hands and feet. Then a red-headed, cadaverous man entered. A red fox followed him on a leash.

"Ah!" he said. "Mr. Rushmore. I'm so glad you could join us. But I am sorry you have lost your way. Or were you trying to avoid paying the cover charge?"

Max would have known the voice, even without the pet. "Hello, Mr. Fuks."

Constantin Fuks nodded. Dismissed the bodyguards. Walked to the other side of the desk, took a seat on the threadbare secretary's chair.

"I sensed you would be here," he said. He tapped the enormous diamond of his pinkie ring. "Samodelkin has been teaching me about the, shall we say, telepathy-enhancing properties of the Siberian diamond. Of course I lack the discipline to meditate and so forth, which he assures me is necessary. Also, I watched you on the closed circuit video. It's an amazing system—the same face recognition technology installed in the Moscow metro system. We live in such interesting times, Mr. Rushmore. I do, anyway. I'm not sure how long your life expectancy is going to be, the way you charge around, not knowing what you are doing or who you are dealing with."

"Do you have her?"

"Sonja?" Constantin leaned back, looked at the ceiling. In this poor light, his skin looked gray. "She came to me, you see. A year—nine months ago. It had been twenty years. More. We knew each other as children, you see. I—I feel I can tell you this, Mr. Rushmore—I loved her. Completely. I've never loved another woman since. She didn't look at me. Not once. That Volkov—he turned her head. He was untrue, of course. Not in the usual way. Immediately. Completely. In the West I think you would say—pathologically. Finally she saw what was under her nose the whole time. She emigrated. I lost track of her for a long time. But you see," Constantin said, leaning forward over the battered desk, "I was building my empire. I had a feeling something like this would happen."

"What?" said Max.

"When she really needed something, she came to me," said Constantin. "I always knew she would, I think. And I can help her. That's what I'm going to do tonight. Of course, she played quite a trick on me, exchanging her papers with the dead woman on the park bench! I really was taken in. Imagine my delight when she appeared, my Sonjetchka, in the flesh. Two weeks ago? Yes, fifteen days. I thought she was a ghost! She explained what happened. And what she found, in her research."

Constantin sighed. "I suppose she didn't trust me, even then. That's why I have kept her here, on site. I don't want to see her flitting off again!"

"So you've kidnapped her?"

Constantin shrugged. "Temporarily, she is my guest. I render my hospitality regardless of what her personal inclinations might be."

"What did she discover?"

"What do people discover when they look into things like that? Irregularities. Corruption. Ineptitude. Immorality. Poison. That Frenchman she thought she loved is a crook. Sonja really has always had terrible taste in men." Constantin shook his head.

"The worse thing about her little investigations is that I believe she has made herself really ill."

He frowned. "Tonight, I will win her. It's too bad you can't be there. I think it will be quite spectacular. Something for your magazine—if it existed."

With that, Constantin stood. He unlocked a metal filing cabinet. Max saw shelves of night vision goggles. Military quality. American. He had trained with Gen II devices, S-25 photo cathodes. They were good, but not great. The pair Constantin was putting on was Gen III. The best. Once he had the night vision goggles strapped on, Constantin reached down. From the bottom shelf he took a large sack. Constantin grunted as he lifted it. From somewhere in the building, a scream sounded. Constantin smiled.

"Wish me luck, Mr. Rushmore," he said. "I'm sorry, again, that you can't enjoy the show."

*

When Constantin left, Max decided to try to undo the cords tying his hands. He made no progress. He stared at the locked grating. It reminded him of something. Then he tried to free his feet. He groaned. On the other side of the door, he thought he heard an answering groan. That was followed by the sound of a man's body slumping to the ground.

Then he saw the doorknob turn. Goldtooth stepped over the lifeless body of a security goon, and into the room. He smiled, showing his golden teeth. He untied Max.

"He's got the diamonds with him," Max said. "Constantin."

A dark shadow passed over Goldtooth's brow. He nodded.

"Wait," said Max. He picked the lock on the metal cabinet and extracted two pairs of night vision goggles. At a doorway, Max paused. Music. A heavy, pounding base. High, poppy notes. He nodded his head.

"You go," said Goldtooth.

Max nodded. Through the door, he found himself in pitch blackness. He strapped on the night vision goggles and saw he was in a long hallway. He made his way down the hall, cautiously, came to a pair of heavy, hanging curtains, and walked through. Here, there were people. Max stayed close to the wall, watching. Beautiful women sat, strangely unconscious of the way they might look, on low, round benches. Men stumbled over to them, sat down. There was something off in the way people moved, in the way they interacted. A heavy man almost sat on a woman, who didn't seem to notice. A couple was copulating, un-cinematically. A girl narrowly avoided stepping into a pool of vomit.

Max saw a waitress coming towards him, with a steady, directed pace, a tray full of drinks. She, too, was wearing the goggles. Ah, Blackout. The bar where you can't see a damn thing.

Luckily, he already knew the way out.

47

11:55. Max was sweating as the taxi dropped him off at the construction site in front of the newly constructed Fomenko Theater. The wind howled up from the river. Max took the shallow white steps leading up to the glass and steel cube two at a time. They were covered in muddy footprints.

Inside, Max paused. He looked up at the slick, white marble lobby. The soaring atrium. A wall of windows looked out over Moscow City. The 'new' Moscow neighborhood. Conceived of as a modern center of finance. The rising skyscrapers were nearly all built. Bent and twisted in the modern style. But most stood empty. The crash had obviated the need for a modern finance center. Youth hostels and the odd pornography company occupied the offices, now.

Max made his way downstairs. The lobby was stepped, like a white marble amphitheater. Two men in black turtlenecks passed him, heads together in conversation, on their way out the door. "Me and the other directors, we see this, and dream of Greek tragedies," said one. The other nodded. Then he saw Max. "You here for the special show?" he asked. Max nodded. "You'd better hurry," he said. He pointed to a door at foot of the amphitheater. "They're in the black box." Max thanked him.

He opened the door and understood why this was called the black box. As his eyes adjusted, he saw that he was in a room that was shaped like a box. Every surface was black. An usher, also in black, appeared at his elbow. "You're very late, sir," he said, and helped Max to a fold-out chair by the wall.

Max took a seat and tried to get a look at the audience. There were some two dozen of them, it looked like. All seated in fold-out chairs. More women than men. The men were hulking. The women were overdressed. Here and there something glinted: a gaudy necklace, an oversized bracelet.

A spotlight switched on. Its round light framed a hunting rifle, lying on the black floor of the stage. Someone murmured "Chekov..." The woman sitting next to Max sighed, heavily.

Slowly, the black wall facing the audience began to roll up. Revealing a wall of glass. The view was spectacular. Framed in the window was the river with Moscow City glinting, harsh and empty, behind it. The figures that emerged onstage, cloaked in gloom, failed to draw much attention. Then the klieg lights came on. Bathed them in harsh light.

A man—a lithe European, gray haired, in a nice suit—sat at a table. He was perfectly still. Across from him was a dark-haired woman. She looked scared. Gerard Dupres and Sonja Ostranova. Max tensed. On the table between them stood a skull.

A *tap-tap-tap* sounded. Dressed in tails, carrying a walking stick, Constantin slowly made his way center stage.

"Good evening, cherished guests," he said. He paused, took them in. When his eyes came to rest on Max, he looked startled. But only for a moment. He resumed his speech.

"You are bored. No!" He held up a hand, as if to quiet any protests. "I understand you, perfectly. Better than you know yourselves, perhaps. And I tell you: you are bored." He paused. "But why, after all, should you be? This life is so full of interesting things. Theater, for example. Food. Dance. Love. And yet—sometimes the lust for it all, the desire, the appetite vanishes. Why? Who can tell. But I care about you. As if you were my own selves. And so I have been thinking. What is the ultimate barrier that must be crossed if life is to be tasted, to the last drop? So that the sweetness is a pure delight, the bitter a welcome relief? So that salt tears only add to our enjoyment? Yes, my friends, this is the question I have posed myself, of late. And of course there is only one answer. Death."

A round of applause sounded. Heartfelt, this time. "We must grapple with death to know life. But not a theater death. Not an anonymous death. No. Welcome, my friends! This is the new Midnight. What you see onstage is real. Real emotions. Real life. Real—death."

Loud applause. Behind the skeletally thin, red-headed man, Moscow City's lights pulsed. Like a nearby galaxy. Bright. Cold. Indifferent.

Gerard Dupres had still not moved a muscle. It was very odd, thought Max. Constantin walked over to Dupres. Pointed at him. "This man!" he shouted. "Has been poisoning Mother Russia. So tonight, I have poisoned him. Right now, he is paralyzed, but alive. His brain is fully functioning. He knows exactly what is happening. Here!" Constantin signaled, and two stagehands turned Gerard's chair to face the audience. His eyes spoke volumes. Their language was terror. A frisson went through the crowd.

"And here!" he said, placing his hand on Sonja's head. "Here is the romance. I present you a woman who has uncovered his French duplicity. She is the woman, I should add, who makes my life sweet. If she will not have me, then I"—he held up a white pill—"will take this sweet death myself. For you, tonight, onstage."

Clapping again. Sonja was thinner—much too thin—and had dark rings beneath her eyes. "Kostya," she said, looking up at him with fear in her eyes. "What are you doing?"

He ignored her question. Instead, he snapped his fingers, and a stagehand appeared carrying a large, bulky sack. He placed it on the table. He stuck his hand into it. He lifted up a glittering handful of stones. Held it above the wide mouth of the sack. They rained down, through his fingers, a spectacular waterfall. All the colors of the rainbow, with an eerie blue light.

239

"And this," said Constantin. "Is riches. Now we have all the elements we need."

The audience clapped. Sonja looked up at them, then at Constantin. "What does this mean?"

"This man is on trial," answered Constantin. "We are his judges. And the audience"—he gestured magnificently at the people watching—"are going to decide whether or not we kill him."

"Now," said Constantin. "You are poisoning our land with your experimental French waste. A special storage container was not built. Why? Because in the meteorite crater where your Russian contractors proposed to dig, they found diamonds. Wonderful diamonds. In fact, you have seen one of them. Your Russian contact gave it to you. A 'thank you' for doing business. You gave it to Sonjetchka here, one night, in a Brazilian restaurant. Bob Diamond—a personal friend of mine—one of the heads of the international diamond cartel, was sitting next to you. He saw Sonja wearing the ring. It was his first clue in solving the mystery of the sudden glut of black market Siberian diamonds. He followed her," he pointed to Sonja, "until she faked her own death. Then he followed my friend, Mr. Rushmore."

Max shrank a little in his seat.

"As you know," Constantin turned again to address the audience, "I have a wide range of contacts. Thanks to my business, I have many friends. I hear much. I repeat little." A smattering of applause. "But now, I think, it is time to speak up. And to act. We could send this Frenchman to the international courts. What would happen? Nothing. They would rule that his company is not responsible for what happens to the waste they send here once it crosses the border. I think in this situation it is time for a little vigilante law."

"You knew," said Sonja, looking at Gerard. "The moment I saw those plans of yours, to move the storage site from Red City to Atom Town, I knew there was something wrong. My request to inspect Atom Town was turned down. Then I met my cousin and she told me about our grandmother, and then I understood. Why my baby died. I had to do something! I came to Moscow. I called Constantin. Then I went to see it for myself. The waste, with plutonium levels I've never seen before. Lying in an open pit next to a half-finished storage container."

She looked into his eyes. He seemed to be speaking though them. And she seemed to understand, perfectly, what he was saying.

"You didn't know!" she said. "But that's just the point. You should have. You didn't want to know. You didn't care."

Again, he spoke to her with his eyes. Pleading. Begging.

"You deserve to die, Gerry," said Sonja, quietly. "I won't stand in the way."

With a clatter, a very young, black-haired girl made a dive for the rifle. Giggling, she held it up to her shoulder, pointed it at Gerard.

"Natasha!" said Constantin. "Put that down! It's not loaded, and you're ruining the show." She pouted, but didn't move. "Natasha! I will cut off your allowance." He whispered in Sonja's ear. "My wife. An utterly amoral creature. I'll get rid of her when you are mine."

Sonja shuddered.

Constantin turned back to the audience. "Now!" he said, taking the skull on the table and holding it up, as if to carry on a conversation with it. In his other hand, he brandished a small white pill. "For the decision. Should I take this bitter pill, or should Gerard Dupres? We will take a vote, and it will be done!"

A woman's voice rang out from the wings. "Let him go!"

All eyes turned towards the door where a thin woman with a boyish figure stood, perfectly erect, in a white cocktail dress. She had a pistol trained on Sonja. An old-fashioned pistol. A Luger, thought Max. A World War Two original, from the looks of it. "I will kill her," she said to Constantin, "if you do not do as I say."

Constantin looked at her in admiration. "Welcome Madame!" he said. "What a surprise! But please, even if you knew how to shoot, that gun is not a weapon, it is a museum piece."

Eloise responded by taking aim at the skull, still upraised, in Constantin's hand. A shot sounded, white fragments of bone were suspended, for a moment, in the air as the bullet hit its target. A moment later, the bullet's trajectory carried it through the wall of glass. It shivered, then shattered. Raining down shards of glass. Deafening. The wind from the river filled the black room. Sodden. Bone-chilling. Gerard was bleeding.

Eloise trained the pistol again on Sonja. She advanced. "My grandfather taught me how to shoot," she said. "Using a pistol just like this one. A war souvenir."

A look of fear crossed Constantin's face.

"I need a man!" shouted the French woman. The lights in the room came on. Constantin looked at Max, then a silent communication passed between them.

Max stood. "I'll carry him," he said, in a low voice, to the French woman. "I know a way out."

Eloise took in Max's strong, sturdy figure. She nodded. Max walked onto the stage, slung Gerard over his shoulder. Eloise gestured with the Luger. Sonja obeyed. She approached the other woman as if she were sleepwalking. The audience was rapt, though their teeth were chattering.

Max led the way out into the white marble lobby. Sonja followed, Eloise behind her, the pistol to her back. In the door of the black box, the Frenchwoman turned back towards the stage. "The diamonds!" she shouted.

"I don't think you should do that," murmured Max. He thought he felt Gerard move a little. Constantin nodded. A stagehand ran to the table, carried the sack to the door. "You take it," Eloise said to Sonja. The stagehand retreated.

Outside, Max stood for a moment in the construction area. He looked up and down the embankment. Yes, he thought, it should be right near here. He set off, the women following. Rounding the construction site, they came upon a fountain. Three Soviet children, in bronze. At play. The fountain had no water in it. Gerard groaned. Max stepped over the lip of the fountain. At the squat pedestal in the center, he pulled open a door. It led to a long, spiraling staircase. "Come on," he said. "Hurry."

"Where are we?" asked Sonja, when they reached the bottom. They were standing in a cavernous space, indifferently tiled. Her voice echoed.

"Moscow's underground tunnels," said Max.

Eloise motioned with the Luger. "Keep going," she said. "He needs a doctor."

They walked. The tunnel was large, with high concrete ceilings, and slanted down. Gerard began to grow heavy. Max was sweating. How long had it been? He set Gerard down for a moment, and, along the wall, spotted the white bones of what was once an animal. A very large dog? He shuddered.

The French woman kept her vigil. Gun poised. Sonja sank to the ground. Next to the bag of diamonds. Max walked ahead, alone. There it was: a metal door. Using his shoulder, he pushed it open. On the other side, he saw a long, white train platform. He returned to the group. Gerard groaned again and stretched a leg out. "Good," said Max. "It looks like the drug is wearing off."

He shouldered Gerard again, and they all filed onto the platform. The station looked more like Dupont Circle than Arbatskaya. Line B. Built, according to rumor, in the late 1960s. To transport top government officials. Line B joined the rest of the parallel metro system, running invisible above the public system. The red digital sign at the mouth of the tunnel counted down from two minutes. A short, perfectly empty train arrived exactly on schedule. The doors opened on a train car, faded but perfectly maintained. Inside, the seats were upholstered in itchy blue wool. As they pulled out of the station, Max had a strange sensation.

As if a shadow had crossed the platform after them. And jumped onto the back of the train.

They exited three stops later. Max took Gerard under the shoulder. He was regaining use of his limbs rapidly, though he still seemed unable to speak. Just as well, thought Max. We don't need any bloodshed.

Together, they hobbled towards the elevator. The women followed. Max thought Eloise would have liked to shoot Sonja. Sonja looked extremely pale.

The elevator was mirrored on all sides so that their group was multiplied infinitely. The doors opened, this time, onto a locked metal grate. Max kicked it down. They filed out into a hut filled with gardening supplies. Ancient leaf blowers. Rakes. Sacks. A canister of oil. The wooden door was locked, but rotten. Max kicked it down as well.

Outside, he looked around. His eyes rested on a sign. It showed three figures. A cat, a man with a walking stick, and a devil. 'Don't talk to strangers.' Ah, thought Max. Patriarch Ponds. They had reached the center.

Sonja stumbled. He led her to a bench. Gerard was walking on his own.

"Give him the bag," said Eloise. Sonja handed it to Max listlessly. Gerard seemed to try to speak. But he couldn't. Sonja shook her head, once. Closed her eyes. Max walked a little way off with the two French. Passed the bag to Gerard. Good riddance, he thought.

"Don't follow us," said Eloise.

"Sure," said Max. The couple turned, arm in arm, hurrying into the night. He went back to Sonja. She was sitting very still. Much too still. Max felt for her pulse. He felt nothing. A shadow seemed to pass in the night. A cold wind scattered a pile of colorless leaves.

*

244

The monastery bells were ringing as the rookie in charge of filing death reports at Moscow's Main Department for Internal Affairs, on Petrovka street, re-read the form in front of him. The young man scratched his head. He picked it up, walked down the hall to Seryozha, his uncle and mentor. Seryozha had been on the force all his life.

"Odd, isn't it?" said the rookie.

Seryozha's office was large with a long desk—actually, three tables pushed together in the shape of a 'T'. The walls were brown and green, the floor was brown and green. The lamp overhead flickered. Seryozha looked up at his nephew.

"What the hell are you talking about, young man?" he said.

"Look," said the rookie, pushing the paper across the desk. "This woman—this Daria Kedrova—she died of a heart attack. Just like that other woman—the American."

Seryozha scratched his head. After twenty years, you couldn't possibly remember every corpse you came across. "What was her name. Ostrovskaya?"

"Ostranova!" said his nephew, seeing he had his uncle's attention. "Look, they have all the same features—height, weight, coloring—eyes are different. And it happened the same way—heart attack—on, get this, exactly the same bench! You know the one, by Patriarch Ponds."

His uncle's interest suddenly flagged. "Oh!" said the older man, throwing up his hands. "That explains it. That's a weird corner of the city. Forget about it—strange things are always happening, there."

Epilogue

Rose wasn't at the gate when Max arrived in Dulles. She was probably late. He walked down a broken people mover, found a seat near the parking lot exit. From the plane, he had seen that it was a clear, sunny day. Down here, of course, it was always the same. Beige, smelling of stale freezer (he had a prime view of a 7-Eleven shop).

He sighed, glanced at his watch, checked his phone. No messages. Not yet. When she finally parked, she would call him, semi-hysterical, apologizing. He would tell her it was all right, he didn't mind waiting, especially not for such a beautiful woman.

Max noticed that there was old pizza rubbed into the place where the beige plastic met the chair's metal frame. He considered moving. Then he saw that one kind of fast food or another was embedded into the seat joints all along the row. Somehow it made him angry.

He had turned in the papers a week ago. Everything in order, checked and signed off. Sonja Ostranova, American citizen, had died in January of a heart attack. Dunkirk clapped him on the back and sent him home.

He said, "Who knows, Maxyboy, maybe we'll need you back here sooner than you think." As Max left, he added, "Don't forget those receipts. Wouldn't want you to starve to death."

Before he left the Russian capital, Max saw that the French Embassy had issued a travel warning. Two French citizens had been knifed to death in central Moscow in the wee hours. The travel warning urged tourists not to wander Moscow's streets at night with valuables on their persons.

In Paris, he had an eight-hour layover. From Charles de Gaulle, he called Rose. "Ah!" she said. "It's you."

"Who did you think it would be?" said Max.

She was silent for a moment. "Jim's been calling me lately."

"Dunkirk?" said Max, the old fear rising with the new one: he still hadn't told her about losing his job.

"Jim Dunkirk, yeah," she said, with a tight voice. Max felt his stomach clench.

"What did he tell you?"

Rose's voice was breezy again. "Just wanted to talk, he said. He said he feels comfortable with me."

"Great," said Max.

"I'm just kidding," said Rose, with her tinkling laugh. "Glad you're still capable of being jealous."

"Fucking great," said Max. "That's just great."

"Oh, come on, Maxy," said Rose, her voice light now, but serious. "You don't need to worry. You know what Rex told me?"

"Are we fighting already?"

"No," came Rose's voice, transported, instantaneously, completely, wholly, with all its emotions intact, its tones of love and dissatisfaction, as if there wasn't an ocean separating them. "Just before he died—it was one of your awful work things—Rex said to me, 'Jim Dunkirk is a winner. And Max is a loser. Stick with Max. He'll let you be yourself, even if he doesn't understand you.'"

"That's fucking great," said Max. He could almost hear her roll her eyes. He missed her.

"I'll pick you up from Dulles," she said.

*

Now, in the bowels of the airport of his nation's capital, Max tried not to look at the pizza remnants in the joints of the chairs as he waited for the woman he loved to arrive. Instead, he imagined the look on Rose's face when he presented her with his surprise. At a jeweler's at Charles de Gaulle he had had the diamond taken out of the penknife and set in a plain gold band. Simple, beautiful. Rose was going to love it.

Something at the 7-Eleven stand was burning. A hotdog, maybe. It filled the waiting area with an acrid smoke. Max reached into his pocket. He took out the little burgundy velvet case they had put the ring in. It opened with a soft clicking sound.

Max's heart skipped a beat as he admired the stone. All the colors of the rainbow, then that eerie blue light. Maybe it would redeem him, at least a little bit, in her eyes—or in his own. An alarm startled Max out of his reverie. Water sprayed down from the ceiling. A man ran out of the 7-Eleven shouting, "No fire! No fire! Everything ok! Everything ok!"

Water dripping down his collar, Max was about to snap the jewelry case shut. He looked down, and froze. The ring was gone. The alarm was still sounding. The man from the 7-Eleven was trying to disperse the smoke from the charred hotdog with his T-shirt, waving it like a white flag. Max got down on his hands and knees. He searched under the chairs, in the folds of his bag. Nothing. There was nothing. The sprinklers overhead turned off. Max's heart was racing. Where was the ring?

Just then his phone buzzed. He had a message. Sure to be Rose. How long did he still have to find it? How could this have happened?

He didn't recognize the sender. He opened the message, which was postdated. Five years in the future. Some technical glitch. Where was the ring? Where had it gone? Max scanned the message. Quickly, at first, then with more attention.

"Dear Max," it read. "I am actually sending this note from the future. Isn't that wonderful? I am so sorry about your diamond. The thing is, we had to have it! We have gotten many excellent samples. This has already advanced our research by leaps and bounds! But we couldn't do without yours, too. Don't worry: Rose won't mind. In fact she never wears jewelry—I asked her, at the cocktail party where we'll meet, next year.

"Wishing you all the best for your past, present and future.

"Anton Samodelkin."